the
Italian
Island

BOOKS BY DANIELA SACERDOTI

The Italian Villa
The Lost Village

GLEN AVICH QUARTET
Watch Over Me
Take Me Home
Set Me Free
Don't Be Afraid

SEAL ISLAND SERIES
Keep Me Safe
I Will Find You
Come Back to Me

DANIELA SACERDOTI

the **Italian Island**

Bookouture

Published by Bookouture in 2022

An imprint of Storyfire Ltd.
Carmelite House
50 Victoria Embankment
London EC4Y 0DZ

www.bookouture.com

ISBN: 978-1-80019-550-9
eBook ISBN: 978-1-80019-549-3

This book is for Jessie, my editor, for helping her writers keep the flame of inspiration alive during this crazy year.

The characters of Gavriel Goodman and Julian Kilby are loosely inspired by Kim Philby and the Cambridge Five.

PROLOGUE
FEARS OF THE FATHERS

The sand is dry and prickly under my feet, full of little jagged stones. The water beyond me, instead, looks like pure happiness. Nonna is standing strong and upright on the sea-rock beside me, her black-grey hair blowing in the wind, ready to dive. She straightens the bag she carries across her body when she goes underwater to gather the shells. It's the first time I ask her for an explanation – the first time I don't take for granted that I can't follow her into the sweet, cool waters. 'Why can I not come with you?'

Nonna is taken aback – I can see it in her eyes – but her answer is swift and clear. 'Because the sea will take you.'

I ponder her reply. 'Is that a bad thing?'

Nonna lets go of the bag and looks at me as if she's seeing me for the first time. She comes to sit beside me on the sand. 'Yes, it is a bad thing. Because you'd be gone from us, Mimi.'

That doesn't sound good – I'm confused, that the call of the water might be a dangerous thing, when it feels as natural as breathing. 'I don't want to go away from you.'

'And we don't want to lose you, Mimi. That is why you can't dive.' Nonna's feet, brown and gnarled and powerful, dangle over the rocks. Mine are small and white and soft.

'But I want to dive,' I whisper, and I know with all my body and soul that it is true.

Nonna is not looking at me any more; she's searching the waves, and her face is combative, as though she's challenging them. As though she's ready to fight for me. And I feel the change inside me: now, I'm afraid too. The waves don't look as heavenly as they did before. Nonna's fear has ebbed inside me.

I lean my head on her shoulder; she smells like saltwater. I feel her words vibrate from her body into mine. 'The sea will have her last word, Mimi. She always does.'

❧ I ❧

TWO GIRLS

LONDON, ENGLAND

19 OCTOBER 1920

'If you don't stop telling me to push, I *swear* when this is finished, I'll strangle you with my bare hands,' Violet Goodman hissed with a force that belied the hours spent trying to give birth to a stubborn, stubborn baby, who quite simply refused to come out.

Violet wanted it over and done with. They already had one child, and a boy: what was the need for another one? But her husband would not see reason. Avram Goodman wanted an heir and a spare to inherit the family diamond business, and Violet, already dreading the morning sickness, the ruining of her figure and having to cancel more social engagements than she could count, had been forced to agree. Labour was the last hurdle. Then, the nannies would do their part and she could forget all about it.

But the baby seemed determined to make her suffer – and suffer she did until the end, when, with a wail of pure rage, Violet pushed her second child out and into the world.

'It's a girl,' the midwife said, and the baby screamed as if she knew already how unwelcome she was.

'Make her stop fussing, for heaven's sake!' Violet shouted over the din. 'Help me wash and change and do my hair. Someone go tell my husband he has a girl.'

Avram wasn't let in until Violet had had a bed bath and her hair done and put some rouge on her cheeks. He couldn't hide his disappointment – but to his credit, he tried.

'Well done, Violet,' he said, endeavouring to show some enthusiasm.

The midwife wore a determined smile. 'What will you call her?'

The new parents looked at each other – they had no idea. They hadn't planned on it being a girl, of course. Violet's eye fell on the magazine she'd attempted to read during the long, tedious first stage of her labour, when the pain was enough to control her body but not enough to occupy her mind. A glamorous-looking actress, eyes lengthened like an Egyptian princess and a feathery band around her forehead, beckoned from the page: Mira Laurent, moving picture sensation.

'Mira,' Violet said distractedly, wondering how long it would be before she could fit back into her evening dresses and look as dazzling as the Laurent woman.

'Fine by me. Well, my dear, rest now. Mrs Watson will take care of the baby. Congratulations again,' Avram said incongruously, as if he were talking to somebody else's wife.

And so, Mira's life began. The pattern of disappointing everyone's expectations continued as she grew to be defiant when she should have been compliant, and sickly when she should have been strong – not a very inviting prospect as a wife for another rich family's heir – but most of all, she bore the primal fault that had thwarted so many lives, in so many places, in so many ages and times since the very beginning of human history: she was a girl, when she should have been a boy.

୧୬୫

GALATEA ISLAND

'It's a girl!' Nonna announced to the family inside the birthing room and to the sea outside – still the brightest blue, even in October – and praying in that intricate dialect of hers, the ancient, long-forgotten language of the people who'd lived on that tiny island off the coast of Sicily for thousands of years. Carmela laughed joyfully, tears and sweat mixing on her face after her long labour. She had a daughter! The family had a girl, a granddaughter to pass their tradition on to. Another daughter of the sea.

The pregnancy had been hard and full of scares, and many times they thought the baby would just flow away with the tide. But finally, the little one they'd all dreamt of had arrived. She was early – tiny and bright red like a shrimp – but she was healthy and her breaths, albeit short and as minuscule as her lungs, were tenacious. Life flew unhindered inside her.

Carmela held the baby in her arms, skin to skin, while Nonna watched on, her eyes dry. She hadn't cried even when her husband, the love of her life, had been swept out to sea. She was as hardy as the broom that grew along the cliffs and shorelines of her home country. But her heart overflowed.

'Let me come in and see my daughter!' Saverio, the father, called from beyond the door. No man would be allowed in a birthing room – but now, the women were ready to let him in.

Nonna opened the door, and Saverio embraced her long enough for her to smell the fear on his skin. But there was no need to fear any more, now. He strode to Carmela's bedside and contemplated the quiet little baby in her arms. Saverio touched his daughter's cheek and dried his tears with his other hand – he didn't have Nonna's restraint – and then placed a kiss on Carmela's forehead.

'*Miracolo*,' he said. And indeed, it seemed like a miracle that this girl was now there.

'*Miracolo*,' Carmela repeated in a whisper, against the baby's tender skin.

'Miracolo Ayala will be her name, another daughter of the sea,' Nonna proclaimed and turned towards the window to declare it three more times to the sea, the ruler of all their lives. An incantation, another blessing for a new life already blessed.

❧ 2 ❧

A WORLD UNCHARTED

AUGUST 2018

ANNIE

The world seems so small when you scroll through Instagram or Facebook and everything is laid out for you to see, without having to go anywhere. Not so small when you travel to places that even now, in the twenty-first century, are still remote.

Here I was, one hand around a trolley's handle – note to self, trolleys are practical in airports, not so much on stony beaches – and my iPhone in the other, having wrestled with two planes, two trains and a taxi to take me from New York to Sicily, and about to step onto a boat that swayed and danced on the azure waters of the Mediterranean. I was about to put my life in the hands of two fishermen who would row all the way from the town of Coliandra, on the west side of Sicily, to Galatea, the little island where maybe, with some luck – a whole lot of luck, actually – I would discover my family's secret history.

'*Tutto bene, signorina?*' the older fisherman, who'd introduced himself as Ciro, asked while offering his hand to help me step onto the boat. He had an ancient face, I thought. No, not ancient:

ageless. The face of a man who lived outside, in the elements, and whose skin had been moulded by the sun and the sea. The younger fisherman, Salvo – an athletic, dark-haired man about my age – hadn't said a word yet. Both were barefoot and seemed to have been born on the water: every gesture they made, from untying the boat to balancing on it, taking hold of the paddles, was confident. Thank goodness, because I could barely swim and I was petrified of the water, in spite of having been born and raised in a town by the ocean. The irony: a water-phobic girl about to board a little boat on the way to a tiny island in the middle of the sea. Talk about facing your fears.

'*Bene, bene, grazie!*' I replied, showing off two of only ten words of Italian I knew, having learned them hastily on the plane. Thank goodness for Google Translate, which I prayed would not abandon me as we left the mainland and sailed on towards potentially wifi-less lands.

With a shaky breath, I sat on a shelf by the bow, wondering why-oh-why I'd always refused to go sailing back in New York as I tried to hold on to my phone, my trolley and my hat as we left the dock with a swoosh that was almost like a whisper. But after a few tense minutes, I relaxed a little – not too much – and basked in the sunlight. I skimmed the water with my fingers; it was warm and shone iridescent, in a million shades of blue. This was another world from the one I knew – it was vivid, bright, with its shiny blue sky reflected in a blue sea, so different from the Atlantic Ocean, back home.

As the boat swayed on the calm, calm water, my thoughts returned to the unlikely circumstances that had led me here. My mind took me to a slate-coloured afternoon, when the sky was full of pewter clouds almost ready to unburden themselves. They'd gathered slowly throughout the day, swelling grey with rain until they were almost at the tipping point, almost too full to stand it. Just like my heart, too full of tears to keep them inside. I was in my parents' house overlooking the ocean; my father had passed away two days before. I'd chosen to be there with him all the way, nursing him day and night instead of going to college – and I did not regret a single moment I'd spent with him. I'd gone from high school to being my father's carer – and I'd done it for love.

Now that he was gone, some would have said my life was finally about to begin – but to me, the world had fallen apart, and nothing seemed worthwhile. My father had been my compass; there was nowhere I wanted to go, nothing I wanted to do.

I'd stood in my black woollen dress, my hair in a French braid tied with a black ribbon, trying to remain composed during the wake. I'd strategically placed myself beside the bow windows, so that every time I felt like I was suffocating, or that unbridled tears were about to spill, I could look outside and calm myself a little. It was a coping strategy that had always worked for me, ever since I was a child. In emotionally charged situations – which, living with my mother, were a common occurrence – I stood or sat beside a window and looked out to the sky and to the sea. But this time, nothing could take the edge off my claustrophobia, and not even the open spaces a few inches from me, just beyond the window, could make me feel free. And yet, now I *was* free – I could do whatever I wanted, go wherever I wanted, instead of being tied to the house where my father was dying.

I didn't know what to do with that freedom. My world was shattered, and even if my mother was there, even if our house was full of friends and family, my heart was alone.

But I had to keep it together, just like my mother was doing. She'd taken my father's death with composure, and just the right, decent amount of pain – neither indifference nor despair. A well-mannered, composed kind of grief.

I had to do the same; I couldn't give anyone a glimpse of the black hole I felt inside me. In our circle, wild emotions weren't tolerated – rapture or despair would be obnoxious.

And so, I stood in my middle-aged-at-twenty braid and woollen dress, like a clone of my mother. I forgot to mention the pearls: we both wore them, and I played with them to calm my nerves.

People came to me offering words of consolation: your father had been ill for a long time, it was his time to go, it must be such a comfort that you and your mother have each other... They meant well, and most of them had genuinely liked, or even loved, my father, and they cared about us. But their words were no solace for me. Dad had been my only source of love when I was growing up, my lighthouse in every storm. Yes, I'd already lost him long before, when his mind had begun to ebb away – but he was still there, in a way, and I could speak to him, even when he was slowly retreating from reality as illness advanced.

Now, he truly was gone. There would be no more sitting and telling him all that was in my heart: just the two of us in his study, pervaded by the scent of wood and old books and whisky, and sound-tracked by the waves of the sea. I'd almost always felt like a stranger in my own life – but not when I was with him.

His study – I could have called it a burrow – was our refuge. There, his telescope was set up pointing out to sea; his charts, his posters and framed prints of sea life and ships and explorations covered the walls; the shelves overflowed with books. Everything spoke of him and of the love he'd given me since I was born. In that room, we'd shared milk and cookies – sometimes whisky for him – and talked about the world, the universe, the sea... and school and boys and all that would be on a girl's mind, because everything that was part of my life was of interest to him. It was a place for free minds and souls, so different from my mother's office at the opposite end of the house, where everything was steely and stern.

All that was gone now. The realisation of this hit me with every beat of my heart, deeper and deeper. And still, under all those watching eyes, I did not allow myself to cry. I looked over to my mom, standing in the centre of the room with her shoulders straight and not a hair out of place. Had I burst into tears, she would have been mortified. I still tried to please her even though I knew that she disapproved of me. It was an all-encompassing, sweeping disapproval, which stemmed from my lukewarm grades in high school, to my choice not to go to college and look after my father instead, to my steady refusal of every possible boyfriend she'd chosen for me among the sons of her like-minded friends, from her circle of equally wealthy, equally status-driven women. I'd been a disappointment in every way. No wonder that when her friends talked about their daughters at Yale, on some study programme in France or engaged to a law firm's partner, my mother changed the subject.

One thing I knew: nobody would ever love me or understand me as my father had done. He'd left me alone in a world I did not belong to.

From across the room, my mother's eyes met mine. She opened her lips to say something – but she changed her mind and turned away.

The night before I'd slept on the leather couch in my father's study, wrapped in a sleeping bag and with one of his checked shirts he always wore under my pillow. It was cold, but I left the window open anyway; the sound of the waves made me feel closer to him. After the many sleepless nights I'd had as he was nearing his death, I passed out quickly and deeply... and I dreamt of him.

In my dream, Dad stood beside the window, his hands down by his sides – those hands that seemed huge and strong when I was a little girl, and I could wrap my own hand around one of his fingers. He wore a sad smile, halfway between sorrow and serenity.

'You're not adrift, Annie-girl,' he'd said. 'I left you a map.'

I was about to call to him and ask him not to abandon me, to please stay – but then the sea came into the room, warm and calm, and I swam in deep waters without fear, lost in blue and surrounded by golden and mother-of-pearl speckles that shone on the seabed and all around me.

I awoke in tears, half comforted, half heartbroken by the beautiful dream and Dad's words of blessing and farewell. The study was in half-light, flooded with moonshine instead of dream-made seawater.

He'd left me a map. I wasn't adrift, then?

Because it certainly felt that way.

When everyone left the funeral, Mom and I sat in silence in the conservatory. I felt as if I was underwater, moving slowly. As if my brain and body had disconnected and my soul had flown some-where far away. The sun was setting behind the clouds and into the restless ocean. White-crested waves broke on the shore beyond our garden.

You're not adrift, Annie-girl. I left you a map.

I couldn't tell Mom about the dream and Dad's message to me. She would call it a fantasy; she had no time for such whims, or any kind of sentimentality. Right now, she was sitting still, in front of her glass of Baileys. This in itself was strange, how still she was; Mom was always on the move, full of nervous energy. Which was why she didn't carry an ounce of fat on her body, sinewy and hard, with narrow hips and thin limbs – the opposite of me. She seemed emptied out, leaning against the back of the wicker chair, tired but immaculate in her black dress with a black cashmere button-up sweater, and her indispensable pearls.

My parents' marriage had been rocky for many years, back and forth from arguing almost daily to indifference and disregard, having settled only with my father's illness. As an only child I'd absorbed the tension and frustration, like a human lightning rod. All their unhappiness ran through me and paralysed me into passivity: not paying attention in school, not doing my homework, not leaving home after high school. Staying put to make sure there was someone to watch them, those parents of mine and their chronic conflict. I have no idea why they didn't divorce; maybe they couldn't be apart as much as they couldn't be together.

Well, that was all over now. Dad was gone, and Mom had nobody left to despise. She would throw herself into her work, I predicted – even more than usual.

And me? What would I do? Go back to school? Look for a job?

The silence between us was heavy as the clouds outside. 'I'm moving out,' I blurted, just like that.

Am I?

Where would I go? What would I do?

Mom's hand stopped in mid-air, holding her drink. Then she recovered herself and took a sip of her Baileys. 'Where?'

'I don't know yet. I'll figure it out.'

Will I?

Was I supposed to feel brave, buoyant?

Because I had no plan, and not much confidence. In fact, I hadn't even intended to say those words, I hadn't intended to move out at all. But now I couldn't take it back. No: I didn't *want* to take it back. I may not have felt strong at that time, but I was, after all, my father's daughter – and I would see this through.

'Well, I suppose your father has set you up, Anna,' was Mom's answer. She always called me by my formal name. There was a moment of silence, filled only by the sound of crockery and cutlery being gathered – our maid, Nicole, was cleaning up. Soon the house would be restored to order, as though nothing had happened. Life would march on, and my father would be left behind.

I swallowed. I still hadn't had a proper cry – the knot of grief I carried in my chest showed no signs of melting. 'What do you mean, he's set me up?'

Mom rolled her eyes. 'Please, stop playing Miss Innocence. You know that everything he owned was left to you, and not to me as it should have been. You did nothing in your life, Anna, but your father decided you deserved that money more than me. No surprise, there, I suppose.'

'What money? What are you talking about?'

'Come on, Anna! I'll never believe this is news to you. Your father's family inheritance is, shall we say... substantial. To say the least.'

Whether she believed it or not, it *was* news to me. 'I had no idea, Mom,' I said calmly. There was no point in trying to convince her – she wouldn't believe me anyway.

My mother shrugged. 'As you like it. But I can always spot someone lying – I've been a lawyer for a long time. It's part of my job.'

If it's part of your job, you're not very good at it. Because I'm not lying. 'Mom—' She raised a hand to stop me. I thought Mom couldn't hurt me any more with her iciness, her distrust of me, but now she was cutting to the quick. I tried, one last time: 'Listen to me, please. I genuinely don't know what you're talking about.'

My mother's eyes widened a little, and she studied my face; for a second, I knew she was contemplating the possibility I might be telling the truth... and then her gaze grew flinty again, and the moment passed. 'No, that's impossible.' She took a breath. 'Now, let's be practical. You might have money, but you have nowhere to go and nothing to do. You can't possibly leave here at this point.'

I was still digesting the news about this mysterious trust fund. I blinked, trying to absorb what my mother was saying. 'Why not?'

'Because you can't stand on your own two feet, Anna.'

I swallowed. She'd managed to pack all her contempt for me into one hurtful statement.

My chair made a scraping sound as I got up. I gazed at my mom for a long moment. I'd just been told I had more money than I knew what to do with – but that revelation was nothing compared to what I'd just realised.

'You have no idea of what I can do,' I said to my mother, and tried to believe it.

I ran upstairs to pack my things – it didn't matter where I'd go, what I'd do, as long as I got away from there. Coat on, bag in hand, I went to say goodbye to my burrow; I went to say goodbye to my father.

I switched the light on and contemplated the sky from the wide windows. Finally, the rain had begun, and the ocean roared outside. If only I could cry, just as the sky was.

Everything was in its place, just like I'd left it the night before – but the sleeping bag was neatly folded and not in a tangle, and the room smelled of disinfectant. Nicole had been there, cleaning every trace of my dad away. She'd also tidied his desk – now, a pile of documents sat in the centre, and on top of it there was a letter – *For Annie-girl*. I laid my fingers on it, my heart beating hard. When did he write it? His handwriting was neat, confident; it must have been before the first signs of his illness began to show, before his hand started to tremble. He must have entrusted my mother with all these documents, and the letter itself; she'd left them out for me, not even bothering to deliver them in person.

I let my bag fall on the floor and sat on the windowsill. I held the envelope to my heart. Some more words from him, when I thought he was gone — when I thought there would be no more! A small comfort, but still a comfort. Inside were a folded piece of paper — the creamy white paper imprinted with his initials that he used as his personal stationery — and yet another envelope, this one thick and soft. I unfolded the letter first.

My dearest Annie-girl,

And there they were at last, the tears that had waited so long to come, flooding my face while I read the rest of the letter through the mist.

You must do this for me: you must be happy.

Because you know I wasn't. I didn't change my life when I could have. I let the flow carry me instead of making choices for myself. Don't make my same mistakes. Follow your passions, follow your heart. You'll find I have left you the means to do so, and I know you'll be wise with them.

I never knew my biological parents. I always felt that trying to learn more about them would be a betrayal of my adoptive parents, who brought me up with all the love a child needs and deserves. But now that my life is coming to an end, I regret not having tried to find out more about my history — your history as well. I believe I made a mistake in that, and I hope you'll make a different choice. I hope that you'll try to discover who my biological parents, your grandparents, were and how their story unfolded — ultimately, I hope you'll try to discover who you are.

All I know about my mother is that her name was Mira Goodman, and that she was born in London; and all I have from her are the objects I'm leaving here for you — a note, her documents and what I believe is a bracelet. These things were found on me when they liberated the concentration camp she was imprisoned in, where she gave birth to me. The orphanage gave them to the American couple who adopted me, my dear mother and father, who took such good care of me. They were told that my mother had died of typhoid just before the camp was liberated.

This would explain how strange the note is... when she wrote it, she must have been delirious already.

I believe that if you go digging into the past, it will affect your present – maybe that is why I never did, because I was afraid of change. If you choose to follow this thread, be ready for the changes that might come. It's your decision – not something I ask you to do for me, even if I hope you will.

But I do have a request, Annie-girl, and there can't be a no for an answer: live life to the full. Promise me.

Promise me you will, and forgive me for not having been a good example for you, for not having fought harder for my happiness. And most of all, forgive your mother, because she can only be herself, she can't be any different – and I know for sure that although she could never properly show it, she loves you.

Always yours, always watching over you,

Dad

Sobs came thick and fast, and echoed in the silence of the house. Some of the pain seemed to flow away with the long-awaited tears, because I felt a little braver, a little stronger. It was as if the tears had washed my eyes at last, and now I could see the path in front of me. Of course, I would answer my father's call and fulfil his wish; I would end what he'd never started.

I would unravel the mystery of his birth and adoption, and yes, I *would* live life to the full... even if it meant changing everything. *Especially* if it meant changing everything.

'You can count on me, Dad,' I whispered to the gathering darkness, sitting there with my coat on, my bag beside me.

It was time to open the other envelope: inside there was a piece of brown fabric, a yellowed, crumpled passport and a note, its paper worn and soft, ripped from a bigger page. I examined the piece of fabric – it was a bracelet, just like my father had thought. It even had a small button, which on closer inspection revealed itself to be a tiny seashell. I fastened it around my wrist. The passport seemed water damaged, its edges curled up and discoloured. It carried a golden coat of arms and an inscription – United Kingdom of Great Britain and Ireland, with a serial number on the top and a handwritten name on the bottom: Mira Goodman. I opened it, but the inside had faded to the point that the details were illegible. All that remained of the photograph was a ghostly imprint of a woman with dark hair, her features almost completely erased by the elements.

The tiny note, scrunched and dirty, simply said: *Tak Me to Galatea.* The handwriting was messy, and it seemed to come from a weakened hand – that, and the spelling mistake, made me think that Mira was already sick when she'd written it.

Tak Me to Galatea... Take me to Galatea.

These objects were my clues, they were the map my father had left me. This was my answer: I knew now where I'd go, and what I'd do.

I'd never stood on my own two feet, that was true. But it was also true that I would prove my mother wrong, and for the first time in my life, I would take charge of myself.

The sky was bright blue, and the sea reflected the light of the sun in endless crystals – but the harsh, almost cruel heat of midday had now passed. A long, warm, sleepy afternoon unfolded as we sailed on.

We passed several islands, and every time I held my breath – *Is this the one?* But we kept going, further and further out to sea, with the two fishermen rowing in perfect synchronicity. There was a beauty to the way they moved that was almost hypnotic.

Finally, Ciro called out: '*Ecco* Galatea, *laggiù!*' I had no idea what two of the three words meant, but I knew that the black mound appearing in the distance was Galatea. It seemed so barren and dark, and there was something rising behind the island – a plume of dark smoke. A fire?

'*Cos'è?* What is it?' I asked, pointing to the smoke.

'The volcano, of course,' Salvo, the younger fisherman, answered. All he'd said to me up to that moment was his name, and even that he'd muttered, looking preoccupied and not keen on chatting at all. It took me a second to realise that he'd spoken in English.

'You speak English?'

'I lived in London for a few years,' he said curtly, his voice barely affected by the exertion of rowing. He made it look easy, his muscles flexing and dancing underneath the skin.

'Oh, I've never been to... Wait. Did you just say there's a volcano on Galatea? An active volcano with smoke coming out of it?' An eruption would be an interesting turn of events.

'Not on Galatea. On Piroi, a few miles away. Nobody lives there. Every once in a while the volcano rumbles, but we don't take it seriously.' He shrugged, as much as was possible while rowing, and looked out to sea.

'You don't take it seriously?'

'It hasn't erupted in years.' He seemed vaguely annoyed by the conversation, and he was still not looking at me. *How welcoming*, I thought, a bit piqued. However, his lack of manners seemed to be balanced out by his looks, which I'm vaguely embarrassed to say I'd noticed since the start. When we'd left Coliandra, the way he'd pushed the boat out and then jumped in had made him look as agile and strong as a cat.

Anyway. This guy was rude. And barefoot. Not to mention his ragged shorts and a t-shirt that begged to be thrown away.

Oh. I was thinking just like my mother! It wasn't fair to judge the way the guy was dressed – after all, what else to wear while manoeuvring a rowboat on a warm June day? White trousers and a captain's hat? I smiled to myself as I realised how clichéd my view of the world was. I was even *dressed* like my mother in a white linen shift dress – twenty going on forty. I looked like someone from a vintage English film, going to Italy on a Grand Tour. I even had court shoes on my feet, navy with a small heel – and I'd begun regretting that choice the second I stepped onto the boat.

The island was coming nearer – how wrong I'd been about it being barren and dark! It was covered in yellow, blue, white and pink, all plants and flowers I couldn't identify, except for the sea of bright yellow broom. From a distance, the island looked like an Impressionist painting, all splashes of bright colours and shades of green; underneath, I could see the black volcanic rock, and it seemed like a miracle that such lush Mediterranean beauty could rise from a soil so dark and seemingly inhospitable. Galatea was like a bouquet of flowers wrapped in black tissue paper.

The closer we got, the better I could make out the architecture of the land – rocky cliffs on my right and a rocky beach on my left, crowned with white houses that climbed all the way to the top of the island, shining bright against the blue sky. The colours were so intense here – the light made everything vivid, resplendent. There was no blurring, no gentle shapes, no misty corners or muted colours, like back home. At any moment now, I thought, I would see mermaids sitting on a rock somewhere, singing and brushing their long, seaweedy hair, or Poseidon rising from the waves...

'*Bella, vero?*' Ciro said, seeing my enraptured expression. *Beautiful, isn't it?* I thought the word *beautiful* was an understatement.

I replied with a heartfelt '*Sì, bellissima!*' and out of the corner of my eye, I saw that there was a smile dancing on the younger guy's lips too.

As we sailed closer, I noticed that the rocky cliffs on the left were ragged and broken, with openings that let the sea in – the side of the island was eaten away by a bigger cave, as if someone had taken a bite out of it. On the beach were a few fishermen's boats, and a bit further up, the houses began. A stony path marked by olive trees on each side led up to the top of the island.

I watched, a hand on the side of the boat to keep me steady, while the men jumped into the shallow water and pushed the boat onto the pebbly beach. Ciro offered his hand – I grabbed it and tried my best to step off with some dignity, but the boat swayed from under me and I would have landed flat on my face, had it not been for Salvo. With one smooth movement he caught me, put me over his shoulder, and then – thank God – pulled me down with an arm under my shoulders and one under my knees.

It all happened in the space of a few moments. I could smell the scent of salt coming off his skin, and feel his strength as he held me up as though I was light as a feather. When he put me

down and held me for just a second more, to make sure I was
steady, I was breathless and a little giddy.

Which, of course, I hid as best I could, murmuring a *grazie*
and straightening my dress and my hair. As for Salvo, he nodded
quickly in Ciro's direction and walked away without a second look
at me; I was left standing there, my heart beating a million times a
minute.

It was then that I noticed I'd lost my hat. It was floating away
on the waves, carried out to sea. Like a piece of the old me.

I took it as a sign.

ANNIE

Still reeling from Salvo's stunt, and dizzy from the swaying boat, I stood still and tried to find my land-legs again. Ciro had taken hold of my trolley. '*Venga, venga, signorina! Villa Onda è lassù,*' he said and pointed upwards.

Villa Onda was my destination. When I'd called the Tourist Office in Coliandra, they'd told me that there were a couple of B&Bs on the island, private homes that opened their doors to the occasional tourist; but a local man was restoring a three-hundred-year-old, stunningly beautiful villa: would I want them to enquire on my behalf? I was intrigued.

The owner sent word that the place was still a work in progress, but they would put me up if I didn't mind that, so the Tourist Office brokered a booking for me. Villa Onda – Villa of the Waves – the name itself was a poem. I'd googled pictures of it, but I only found a couple, and they were too grainy, too out of focus to reveal anything more than a square silhouette surrounded by palm trees. I couldn't wait to see it properly.

I followed Ciro onto the winding path towards the top of the island. My heels were terribly impractical on the stony beach, and the hem of my dress was soaked and caked in dark sand – I was hatless under the scorching sun, limping and wet, but I didn't care... *almost* didn't care. Everything was so peaceful and quiet, and the air was filled with the sound of the lapping sea, the breeze and the cicadas. Motorboats were not allowed on the sea around Galatea, and cars were forbidden on land, hence the silence broken only by the sounds of nature and the pure, unsullied air.

On one side of me was an explosion of plants and flowers in bright colours – I could only recognise the broom I'd seen from the boat and sturdy white heather, the rest of the vegetation being a multicoloured unknown – and on the other side, beyond the gnarled olive trees that bordered the track, was the sea. Out in the distance rose the shores of the last island we'd passed, whose name I hadn't caught, while the plume of the volcano was behind the hill, somewhere on my right and invisible now. The vantage point made me realise how far I was from everything – a few islands like pebbles across a stream, and many, many miles away, the coast of Sicily. Northern Africa was closer than Italy – in the guidebook, I'd read that sometimes the wind blew desert sand from the Sahara into the island sky, and made it turn almost red. What a strange sight that must be.

We crossed paths with an old man and his donkey – apparently, donkeys were a widely used means of transportation – two shirtless children in shorts, running down to the beach with squeals and laughter, and a black-clad old lady with a handkerchief covering her hair. When she saw me, her eyes lit up – I was probably a novelty. '*Che bella signorina!* Signora Paternò,' she said, gesturing to herself. Her face was leathered from the sun, like Ciro's, and her eyes were surrounded by laughter lines, suggesting she'd smiled often in her long life.

'*Piacere*, Signora,' I said, sure that my pronunciation was abysmal.

Signora Paternò's wizened hand felt up my arm as though she was appraising a piece of fruit, and she shook her head. '*No, no... troppo magra!*' With lots of gestures and some laughter, Ciro told me that the lady wanted me over for dinner because I needed fattening up.

'*Cibo, cibo!*' he explained. Food. Well, who was I to argue?

'*Grazie!*' I said, and the more Italian I spoke, even if it was just little words here and there, the more determined I grew to learn.

The sweet elderly lady finally let us go with a promise of going over for dinner, and we made our way into a smattering of white-washed houses, their windowpanes in several shades of blue. The houses were arranged around a tiny central square that followed the lay of the land, resting on a terrace in between the two slopes. It occurred to me what a skill it was, to build on this island and steal land to work, considering that everything was on a gradient. It also meant that the sea seemed to be always in the line of sight, colouring the view blue-green everywhere I looked.

A light gold building caught my eye at once – it had an ornate facade that contrasted with the simplicity of the houses around it. A church, I realised. The golden stone was arranged in waves on both sides of the door, as if the hard material had been melted until it rippled and then dried in place. In the centre of the facade, nestled in a stony alcove above the door, was a statue of the Virgin Mary with a star on her head, looking up, hands joined together in prayer.

'*Stella del mare*,' Ciro said, pointing towards the statue. *Star of the Sea,* I translated in my mind. Of course, in a community that lived and breathed the sea, what else could be the centre of worship? Maybe the star on the Madonna's head represented the Pole Star that guided ships and boats on their way... A glimpse of my father's nautical maps flashed in my mind.

Annie-girl, I left you a map...

We left the hamlet behind and kept climbing. The path was now a small dirt road following the island's outline; the view beyond the olive trees was disquieting, with rocky cliffs falling straight into the sea. I was grateful for the natural barrier made by the trees. I dared myself to look down, holding on to a trunk, and the waves breaking on the dark rocks at the foot of the cliff made my knees buckle. The sea was calm as oil, but this part of the island was so rugged that whenever a wave hit, it broke in a hundred white foam rivulets. The sound of the water here was different – deeper, almost echoing.

Finally, we left the frightening stretch behind and entered a thicket of olive trees and maritime pines. The scent in the air was as perfumed as that of essential oils burning in a closed room – pine and fennel salt and resin, and the undefinable smell of saltwater. Underfoot was a fragrant carpet of pine needles, and above me were canopies of dark branches, interspersed with bright blue shapes. The crackle of pine needles and the song of the cicadas were the only sounds as we walked on – the bark here and there shone with gems of resin, glimmering brown and amber. Finally, the thicket opened – we'd arrived at the peak of the island. In front of us was an archway, cut into the centre of a low wall made of golden stone, and through it I could catch a glimpse of Villa Onda. I followed Ciro inside and found myself in a garden, lush and unkept. The walls around it were covered in ivy, and weeds grew out of every crack and indentation. My heart stopped and my blood ran cold – a figure in the high grass, strange and grey and still, seemed to be staring at me. But after that terrifying instant, I realised that the whole place was dotted with statues of nymphs and ancient gods, crumbly and coated in lichen and ivy, like old inhabitants of the villa now frozen into stone. I walked on, grass and small bushes scratching my calves, holding my breath, as if all those stone creatures might move and speak to me at any moment. The song of the cicadas was loud in my ears, making everything dreamlike.

My feet were on an old path marked with flat stones almost completely hidden by greenery – occasionally the muffled sound of my heels on the ground gave way to clicking on stone, as blue butterflies rose and flew in my wake, and crickets jumped out of the way. And then I was on a stone pavement again, walking down a path lined with palm trees; at the end of the path was Villa Onda.

The golden stone swayed and danced to create a facade that recalled the waves in the villa's name; a stately door opened in the middle, and two rows of wide, tall windows reflected the light of the sun. Over the door and above each window were statues of strange creatures – gargoyles, mermaids, angels, demons, bizarre beasts, some beautiful, some monstrous. It seemed a random selection, yet I felt they were there to tell a story, one I didn't know how to read. Silent eyes watched me – despite the heat, I felt the hair on the back of my neck rise and goosebumps cover my arms. The din of the cicadas, and the heat, and the stone creatures watching in silence overwhelmed me. I was a long way from home.

My mother's words, when I'd called her to say I was flying to Sicily, came back to me. *You? Travelling across the world, alone? You couldn't even get decent grades in school! I tried everything with you. Sports, music courses. Wasted money. I wondered what your natural talent could be, and then I realised that your natural talent was not being good at anything. And now you think you can—*

I didn't hear the rest. I put the phone down.

I steeled myself. The memory half crushed me, half galvanised me: I'd prove her wrong. I'd spent twenty years feeling inadequate – it was time to believe in myself, even just a little. That niggling voice in my head, the one that droned on about how incompetent I was, belonged to my mother; and yes, I *was* a long way from home. And maybe that wasn't a bad thing.

I walked up to the entrance, under the statues' watchful eyes. Ciro touched my back lightly, to guide me in front of the door, and his touch made me jump. I'd thought that one of those gargoyles had landed on me from above! Ciro put his hands up and apologised, and I felt foolish. He ignored the heavy steel ring with a lion's head and paws wrapped around it – what else could it be? Surely a villa like this couldn't have had a bell! – and shouted, startling me again: 'Elvira! *La straniera è qui!*'

The stranger is here? That was an inkling of how often they had tourists on Galatea.

'*Arrivo!*' a voice resounded from somewhere above us; the sound of steps, and the door opened. An elderly lady was there, unsmiling and straight-backed, while a young girl with dark wavy hair, wearing a blue silk dress and heavy eyeshadow, stood behind her. The girl's face peeked out over the lady's shoulder.

'*Benvenuta,*' the lady said – *welcome* – and even if she wasn't smiling, her dark eyes were warm. She looked elegant and polished in a blouse and skirt, a coral necklace around her neck and silvery hair carefully arranged in a bun.

'*Grazie*,' I replied, and wondered how on earth I would communicate with this woman at all given my limited Italian, let alone trying to piece together Mira Goodman's story.

Ciro waved to us as he walked away, and I called a *grazie* after him too, taking hold of my trolley. '*Venga, entri.*' *Come on in.* The lady took a step to the side, allowing me in... and I think I stopped breathing.

This place was like nothing I'd ever seen.

The walls were decorated with brightly painted ceramic tiles in accents of yellow and blue, the ceilings were covered in frescoes, and the floor was made of tiny stones arranged in geometric mosaics. My head almost spun, trying to take in every detail of this Sicilian masterpiece. The result was an explosion of colour, but at the same time everything worked together in harmony with the dark furniture, the gilded mirrors and the wide windows draped in pure white curtains. The very house was a piece of art.

'Elvira,' the lady said, pointing at herself. She was smiling now, seeing my enraptured expression.

'Annie. *Sono* Annie...' I looked around to greet the girl in the blue dress, but she was nowhere to be seen. She must have slipped away.

'*Benvenuta,*' a male voice said from somewhere above me. Behind us was a marble staircase that split in two – and there, leaning on the stone banister on the first floor, was... Salvo? The brusque, abrupt fisherman who—

Oh. The memory of him lifting me up and holding me made me feel warm, but I shook it off as soon as I could and composed myself. He made his way down – gone were the tattered shorts and dirty t-shirt; now he wore clean jeans and a linen shirt with its sleeves rolled up, hair wet from, I guessed, a shower.

He looked like something out of a movie: razor-sharp cheekbones, hazel eyes that contrasted beautifully with his tanned skin, jet-black hair, curly and tousled.

Very striking.

I reminded myself that he was a little rude, and looked away. What was he doing here, anyway?

My first impression was confirmed when he blurted out:

'You met my godmother, Elvira.' Elvira and I nodded towards each other and smiled, which was the most we could do, given her lack of English and my lack of Italian. Without saying any more, he grabbed my trolley and marched back upstairs again. Elvira gently placed a hand on my back, encouraging me to follow, and I did, stopping halfway to get a closer view of the frescoes. Every inch of the ceiling was decorated with blue skies, fluffy clouds and cherubs playing various instruments. I was glad they hadn't carried the monster theme through to the interior, I thought – until I saw that peeking from the edges of the ceiling were some more stuccoed creatures like the ones outside, more monsters and angels and mythical creatures. I'd judged too soon. I hoped they'd given it a miss in my room, at least; I would have preferred not to have those things watching me while I slept.

We walked down a long corridor dotted with antique consoles, side tables and gilded mirrors, and only stopped at the end of it. Salvo opened the door for me, revealing a room with brightly tiled walls and honey-coloured parquet; a wide, bright window domi-nated the room, and on either side sat a mirrored console and a writing desk, made of the same dark wood. The four-poster bed, with its white linen, looked fresh and inviting – *How cool those sheets will be against my skin*, I thought. A carved wardrobe and a chest of drawers with a marble top completed the room – it would be like sleeping in a museum or shifting into a period drama. I looked up and saw that the ceiling was decorated here too – a night sky with planets and constellations, and fat baby angels with curly hair and wings... but no monsters! *Thank goodness*.

'I hope you like it,' Salvo said. He sounded apprehensive.

He sounded *shy*.

'Of course I do. It's beautiful.'

'*Mio Dio*, I'm so glad. You're our first guest, and I want every-thing to be perfect for you. This place... it means a lot to me.'

I wasn't expecting this. I wasn't expecting the rush of scarlet in his cheeks either, a flush that then seemed to spread onto mine. 'It's perfect. Thank you.'

'Then it was worth running up here to make sure everything

was the way it should be and to make myself presentable.' So that was why he'd run away like that, without a word.

'I'm sorry you had to rush like this.'

'I'd asked someone to help Ciro so I could hold the fort here, but he cancelled at the last minute. Elvira and I weren't quite ready to open – there's still work being done – but when the Tourist Office called us... well, it seemed a waste for you to experience Galatea in any other way.' He spoke perfect English, with a lilt that was peculiar to the islanders, I'd noticed; not the cartoon-like accent Italians are portrayed to have, but something different, terse and clipped.

There was a moment of silence, which in spite of the awkward beginning didn't seem that awkward, this time. Maybe Salvo had run out of words for the day, I thought, and a little smile curled my lips. A soft scent of beeswax wafted from the floors, and specks of dust danced in the sunrays. I wanted to close my eyes in the heat and sunshine, take it all in, in my mind and my senses. The place seemed to have been cleaned, waxed and perfumed within an inch of its life. 'It's not just you two doing everything in here, is it? Because it'd be an insane amount of work...'

'Oh, no, no. We have gardeners coming in, for a start... the gardens are huge and have nearly gone wild. Elvira cooks, and we'll have Manuela, a girl from the island. She'll be a sort of chamber-maid, when it's all up and running.'

'Oh, yes! I saw her when I arrived,' I said, thinking of the girl I'd spotted behind Elvira.

Salvo shook his head. 'You couldn't have. She's still at university, on the mainland... we're not supposed to be open yet.'

'Really? Because I'm sure I saw...' I began. 'Never mind. Too much sun, probably!' At that moment, Elvira peeped through the doorway and said something I didn't quite understand – except for the word *cena*, dinner.

'She says that maybe we could eat together on the terrace tonight? Unless you prefer to eat alone? The dining room is still being refurbished, but we can prepare a table, if you want to.'

'I'd love to join you on the terrace,' I said. 'And please don't worry about special preparations, I'm easy!' *And I'm here to learn more about Mira Goodman, so this would be a good chance to ask about her.* On an island so small, surely someone would have heard of her. Given, of course, that I'd followed the right clue, to the right place.

Once again, I recognised how little I knew, and how I was here on a prayer. I wasn't sure whether this thought troubled or excited me.

'*Benissimo.*' Salvo smiled, and he seemed so young – not much older than me. He was a bit of an enigma – silent and abrasive when we first met, and now that smile... almost naive. 'So... There's some lemonade there for you. See you later, then.'

'Yes. Thank you. Thank you, Elvira. See you later,' I said, and in a moment I was alone – but before I could close the door, Salvo's face appeared once again from behind the doorframe.

'You're absolutely sure you're happy with the room, *sì?*' His expression was so apprehensive and boyish, I had to smile.

'Of course! It's perfect.'

Salvo exhaled. '*Meraviglioso. Ciao.*'

'*Ciao!*' I couldn't stop grinning.

A slave to my phone, I tried to check my messages, but there was no signal. I was relieved – that the world out there would have to wait, and I could be in my Galatea bubble a little while longer, and know nothing of what was happening in the world outside. *And not receive scathing words from my mother, to deflate me even before I begin.*

The window creaked and moaned a little when I opened it wider. I took my dress off and stood in my underwear, letting the sea breeze caress my skin, the wooden floor cool under my feet. The sun played on the glass of lemonade and broke into tiny, scattered rainbows. The scent of citrus was so strong, and the taste so sweet and tangy, that I guessed they must have picked the fruit just hours ago, straight from one of the trees outside.

I leaned my head on the window frame, the curtain resting on my bare shoulder, and gazed outside to sea and the ground below. It was only then that I realised my room was almost level with the terrain, even if I was on the second floor. I hadn't noticed that the house itself was built against the slope of the island, its black summit at the back of the second floor. There was no garden there, but black rocks, some of them shining – obsidian, I thought: a volcanic rock. I recognised it because my father had a collection of stones and fossils in his study, one of his many passions.

If only he could see all this now.

How I wished he could see Galatea, and this strange mixture of a harsh landscape, stark black rocks and obsidian with its sharp edges, together with the lush vegetation, its flowers and palms and lemon trees, and beyond all this the calm, calm sea... as if in that cast-away corner of the world, Eden and the apocalypse had mixed up and co-existed still.

I took a leap of faith: I'm here following the lead you gave me.

I stepped into the bathroom and touched the water in the full bathtub Elvira had readied for me. It was flower-scented, and the freshness of it was a dream after all that heat. The bathroom was old-fashioned, with art deco-style tiles, a free-standing enamel bathtub and a wide mirror framed with gilded wood, brown specks all over its surface, betraying its antiquity. I finished the lemonade in one greedy sip, shed the rest of my clothing, and slipped into the bath. I closed my eyes and dozed a little, and in the silence I became aware of a distant, echoey sound – the sound of waves breaking on the shore. But it wasn't coming *from* the shore, or from outside at all. It came from somewhere *below me*. The sea was reaching out from underneath me – I thought that waves would burst out of the floor, and take me away.

I snapped my eyes open with a sharp inhale. It was then that a flash of blue travelled in the mirror over the sink, like an arc of colour making a parabola in the glass, dissolving just as quickly as it had come.

I froze, a hand on my chest. My heart was galloping, my breath fast and shallow. It must have been my imagination. The glass was stained with rust and my eyes must have been deceived by the brown spots – or maybe a bird had flown over the sun, casting a blue shadow.

It was nothing.

Still, I got out of the bathtub at once, and barely wrapped a towel around me as I rushed into my room, my hair dripping.

There was no way that in the flash of blue across the mirror I might have guessed the shape of a girl wearing a blue silk dress, because it had all been a trick of the eye.

❧ 4 ❧
MIRA'S SONG

ANNIE

What possessed me to even own a navy shift dress down to my knees? It made me look double my age. Elvira, who must have been in her sixties, dressed younger than me. I was going to overhaul my wardrobe, I decided. Nothing I owned seemed to truly represent me any more. The only pretty touch in this severe, office-generic outfit, I thought, was Mira's bracelet. I'd been too worried about losing it to wear it during the journey, so I'd only fastened it after my bath, while getting dressed. Delicate in its earthy colour, it hugged my wrist snugly. The little shell gleamed too discreetly to be noticed by anyone but me.

I rushed down, avoiding all the unpacking that needed to be done – there would be time for that later, and I was too eager to begin my adventure.

On my way down I stood on the stairway again, chin up, taking in every detail of the ceiling. The place reminded me of one of those games of hidden objects, because everywhere I looked there was some feature I'd missed. It was now the third time I'd stood in the same spot, and still I hadn't taken them all in, those sculptures that populated the upper part of the walls and watched me silently with stony eyes.

'Hello... *things* up there,' I called. Every time I tried to cata-
logue them, to list them, new creations seemed to fall under my
eye. Dragons, serpents, a winged lion... *was* it a winged lion?
Some sort of chimera... Each person would see something
different in them, I thought. I wondered why the architect or
whoever commissioned the figures had decided to populate the
house with them – were they the guardians of Villa Onda? Benev-
olent to its inhabitants, but watchful against intruders and ill-
wishers?

As I tiptoed to contemplate a merman more closely, Salvo's
voice startled me. 'Dinner's almost ready. Fancy a glass of wine?
We'll make it an informal affair – you don't mind?'

I laughed, making my way down the stairs. 'I'll put up with an
informal dinner just this time! From tomorrow, though, I want
maids in uniform and a butler!'

Salvo's laugh was deep and hearty. 'I know, I know. I'm compli-
cating things, but all this means so much to Elvira and me, and
you're our guinea pig.'

'The first of many, I'm sure. Guests, not guinea pigs, hopefully.
I have a lot of questions for you guys!'

'And we'll answer them. Come, I'll show you the terrace.'

Salvo led me through the house to the western side, towards
the sunset. We passed through a hall that seemed half finished,
with ladders against the frescoed walls and sheets on the floor.
The frescoes, I noticed, were all sea-themed, with expanses of
water filled with fish, sea serpents, boats, ships, various mermaid-
like creatures... it was like a magical aquarium.

'This is going to be the dining room. As you can see, we have
some way to go still,' Salvo said and pointed to the bundle of
sheets. 'In the autumn we'll have some students from a... how do
you say it in English? Scuola di Restauro – restoration course?'

'Oh, yes, I see. For the frescoes.'

'Yes. They'll be using natural pigments, just like the ones they
used to make these three hundred years ago.'

'It's going to be amazing,' I said, from the bottom of my heart.
This place was bizarre, spooky and beautiful at the same time – it
was astonishing to me how Villa Onda balanced itself between

being a sunny Eden and the Mediterranean version of a Gothic castle.

A small door, carved in stone, opened on one side, and I followed Salvo through it. The incandescent light of the afternoon had turned into something gentler, sweeter. There was a touch of lilac and orange in the sky, and Venus rising over the sea. From there I could see the gardens, wild and overgrown. It gave the place an even greater air of mystery.

There was a story woven in our surroundings, like a watermark in a piece of paper held to the light. A story that *longed* to be revealed: I could sense it. The breeze had turned into something stronger, and it seemed to carry forgotten voices, whispering in my ears as it lifted the hair from my shoulders.

The table, set for three people, was covered in a crisp white tablecloth and decorated with seashells. Salvo pulled out a chair for me. 'Wine?'

'Thank you. Though on an empty stomach I'll start giggling. This table is so pretty! Do you mind if I take a pic for my Instagram?'

'Feel free to take pictures, but you can't send them... Did the Tourist Office people not tell you? We don't have internet here at all. And the landline is hit and miss as well,' Salvo said, pouring a deep, dense red wine into each of the glasses.

'Seriously?'

'*Sì.*'

'You don't have wifi?'

'Did you not notice?' he said, gesturing towards my phone.

'I thought it was just in my room. How do you live without the internet?' I took a sip of my wine – I was no connoisseur at all, but it tasted good to me. Fruity and deep... sunny, if that made sense. 'How will you advertise this place?'

'Well, we won't need to do much advertising, for a start. We'll count on word of mouth for our bookings. There are strict tourism regulations on this island, to preserve the landscape and our way of life. Only a set number of visitors are let onto the island, and anyway, with no cars or motorboats allowed, it's not for everybody. We don't even have running water as such – power comes and goes...'

'No running water? But I had a bath.' My stomach tightened a little as I remembered the noise of the waves, the flash in the mirror. Another sip of wine was needed, for sure.

'Rainwater. People here used to drink it, too. Now we import drinking water from the mainland, but every house has a well, just in case.'

'You import drinking water on rowboats?'

'Exactly. I told you, Galatea is not for everybody.'

'True. But how do you keep in touch with friends?' If there was no signal, I wouldn't be able to speak to my friends, but I also wouldn't be able to speak to my mother either. And that wasn't such a bad thing at all.

'Most of my friends are here. The ones I left back in London... well, I left that life behind.' A girl. I was sure he was talking about a girl. 'And anyway, the postal service still exists, you know?' He laughed.

'Do you use seagulls as carrier pigeons?'

He smiled. 'Sorry to disappoint you, but the postman comes once a month.'

'Wow.'

'You're shocked that people can survive without the internet?'

'No, not at all... OK, yes, I am,' I admitted. I wasn't about to tell him that I never parted with my phone, that I was usually connected pretty much twenty-four hours a day, and my friends were just the same. In fact, with my phone sitting there, useless, I already felt brittle with abstinence. What was I going to do with my thumbs now? I didn't have many friends, having dropped out of 'normal' life when I didn't go to college and everyone else in my class did – but the few I'd kept in touch with would think I was dead or something. I wished I could have given them a warning. I was alone in a remote place, and the only link with the outside world was an unreliable land-line? It sounded like the premise for a horror film. One where there's a storm and the phones are out, and there's a maniac on the loose...

'*Pronto!*' Elvira called and made me jump, materialising

suddenly on the terrace with a laden tray. '*Spaghetti ai frutti di mare!*' she said proudly. Salvo stood to help her, and I found myself sitting in front of a steaming bowl of seafood spaghetti. I was about to bring the first forkful to my mouth, when Elvira gasped.

'*Santa Maria! Il braccialetto...*' She was pointing to Mira's bracelet. I could see the wonder in her eyes as she spoke to Salvo quickly, too quickly for me to catch even just one word. And as my gaze moved to my arm, I saw that the sunset rays had caught it in full, and it was glimmering a soft gold, with faint coppery glints. The brown fabric had come to life. I was stunned too, as much as Elvira.

'Wow,' I whispered, lifting up my wrist. Elvira spoke again, while I was staring at the glittering band.

'She'd like to know how you came to own this,' Salvo translated.

'It's a long story. It belonged to my... well, I *think* she was my grandmother. So it seems, anyway. I didn't think... I didn't know it would shine this way.'

Elvira touched the bracelet lightly. '*Bisso,*' she said, and I turned towards Salvo. I had no idea what it meant.

'In English, you say... byssus, I think. It's very precious, and rare. Some call it gold of the sea. The thread is made with a kind of shellfish, and then cured to make it shine.'

'A shellfish?' I touched the bracelet lightly. It was fabric. How could shellfish produce something like that? Elvira must have seen the confusion on my face, because she spoke again, in her tight, quick Italian far too fast for me to decipher.

'The shells are hard to find, and sacred... How to make the byssus is a secret passed down the generations... Only her family, the Ayala, possess the knowledge. More precisely, only the women.' While he spoke, Elvira nodded.

'*Her* family? Are you not related?'

'She's my godmother. I'm not an Ayala. And even if I were, I'm just a man.' He opened his arms and gave me a mischievous smile. 'Men don't know these things.'

'Men... *no!*' Elvira said, looking quite truculent.

A thread from shellfish and a secret knowledge? I studied my bracelet. If I turned it a little to the left, it was brown and opaque. If I turned it to the right, catching the light of the setting sun, it glistened like dark gold. 'And this... *bisso*, is only made here on Galatea?'

Salvo translated for Elvira, and explained her answer: 'In this hue, yes. They do it somewhere else, in Sardinia, but they have a different recipe to cure it.'

'*Chi era tua nonna? Come ha avuto il braccialetto?*' Elvira asked, and I looked at Salvo for a translation.

'Who was your grandmother, and how did *she* get this bracelet?'

'Good question! That's why I'm here. You see, she was deported during the war, right from this island, I believe. She was taken to Germany, and just before passing away she gave birth to my father. He was then adopted and brought to America.'

'Name? *Name?*' Elvira pressed me in uncertain English.

'That's pretty much all I know about her. Her name was Mira Goodman.'

'Mira Goodman?' Elvira cried out.

Salvo's eyes widened, and a smile danced on his lips. He shook his head and looked out to the gardens, and then back to me. 'Incredible.'

'*Ma sei sicura?*' Elvira cried out. This, I understood: *are you sure.* What? Why? What did they know?

'My father had her documents with him, and a note from her that asked to be taken back to Galatea...' I turned my gaze from one to the other.

'This house belonged to her,' Salvo explained. 'She left it to the islanders. Before it became Villa Onda, this was the Goodman House.'

'We moved everything in here,' Salvo said while unlocking the door right across from mine. 'I didn't want to put Mira's things up in the attic – it seemed disrespectful – but we couldn't miss out on using her room. It's the best in the house.'

'Can I see it?'

'You *have* seen it. It's the one we gave to you.'

So she must have slept in the bed where I would sleep, bathed in the same tub, looked out of the same window, to the same vista... The thought was so suggestive, I was breathless. This woman I knew so little about, who seemed so elusive and out of reach, had been closer to me than I could ever imagine.

All this gave a whole new meaning to the word *serendipity*. I followed Salvo inside where a dusty, moth-y smell hit my nostrils. Dusk had bathed the place in gloomy light, and when Salvo switched the lamp on, strange shadowy shapes appeared all around – it took me a moment to realise that they were pieces of furniture covered in white sheets. Not everything was wrapped away, though – a mirrored console reflected the light of the lamp and a tall wardrobe sat uncovered in the corner. In the middle of the room was a four-poster bed, also shrouded in spotless white sheets. A dark brown box, sitting inconspicuously against the wall beside the console, caught my eye. I crossed the room and crouched beside it. My fingers traced Mira's initials, *MG*, engraved in elaborate gold letters.

'Are you sure it's OK with you if I look through her things?' I said in a low voice. I didn't know why I'd whispered, but it seemed as if Mira was there with us – maybe sitting at her console, spraying on perfume from an old-fashioned glass bottle, curling her hair in forties fashion... Looking through her drawers, or having a siesta during the hottest hours of the day, standing at the window with the sun shining through her hair... I blinked – still images of Mira were so real, it was as if I was seeing them, instead of imagining them.

'Of course. She's your *nonna* after all, isn't—' He must have finished the sentence, but I didn't hear any more. From somewhere out of the window – the rocky black hill or the sea beyond – came a sound I couldn't place, somewhere between female voices and dolphins' calls, or maybe whales? High-pitched and strange, not quite of this world. The room swam around me all of a sudden. I felt Salvo's arm around my waist, holding me up, to my shame, before I almost dropped to the floor.

'Annie!'

What had happened to me? The weird noise was gone, as were the images of Mira. There was just me, unsteady on my feet and my head swimming. I caught my breath until I could mutter: 'Sorry! Sorry, I'm *completely* fine! I don't know what came over me.'

I'd swooned like a Victorian lady in a novel, and I was overcome with embarrassment. I willed myself to take a step away from him, to slip free of his warm hands around my waist.

'I think I'll turn in now. So much to take in...' I laughed a little nervous laugh. But Salvo did exactly the right thing: he stepped away from me, and resumed a more formal demeanour.

'I'll let you be. You must be exhausted. And jetlagged.'

'I am. A few hours' sleep will do me the world of good.' With one last look to Mira's belongings, as tantalising as they were, I stepped out and resolved to leave them until the morning.

I couldn't sleep. I tossed and turned, exhausted and yet fully awake, wondering about the story that lay hidden inside Mira's belongings. I lay in bed, my wrist lifted over my face. Would the bracelet shine differently in the moonlight? I asked myself dreamily. Before I knew it, I'd tiptoed out of my room and across the corridor, pulled by an invisible magnet. I stood in a pool of white moonlight, reflected in the smooth waters. Filling the room was the song of the cicadas and the sound of the waves – and yes, the bracelet did shine in the moonlight: not gold like under the sun, but white and silver glimmers, iridescent and ghostly.

The air was thick, and it wasn't just the heat of a Sicilian summer night. It felt like someone was watching me, like I wasn't alone – and every gesture, every noise unfolded under invisible eyes. As silently as I could, I freed the box from the other trunks, lifted it – it was heavy but manageable – and tiptoed back into my — into *Mira's* room, and gently I placed the box on the floor.

I knelt beside it, barefoot. The metal latches required some convincing but as I lifted the lid, what I found inside was a surprise. I would have never guessed...

It was a turntable, an old-fashioned gramophone. On the needle was a brass label: *Soundbox, Telematic – For Decca, The*

Portable. The word *Decca* was also engraved on the inside of the lid. Would this still work? Maybe I'd find some records to play. I knew how to work it; my father had one. I wondered if Mira had sat in this very room, gazing out at the moon and listening to music. I lightly touched the slip-mat with my fingers, and from somewhere a thin, distant tune began to play. I looked left and right – where was the music coming from? Outside the window, or somewhere inside the house? Maybe Salvo or Elvira had the TV on. I couldn't tell, but the crackling music swelled further and further, until it covered the cicadas' song and the sound of the waves, filling the room, filling my ears and my mind.

Something was happening and I wanted it to stop. Fear overwhelmed me and I tried to close the gramophone lid – but before I could, darkness overtook me, though I knew my eyes were open. It was like earlier on, when Salvo was here and my head swam so much I almost fell, but this time the sensation was too strong, impossible to resist – it pulled me like the tide, and there was nobody there to keep me afloat. A moment of terror, and then I was too drowsy to panic, as the music lulled me into a lucid dream. A scene began to take shape in front of me: moving shapes, voices, like a dance of ghosts and spectres. Colours became sharper, shapes became clearer, and I was there among them, watching it unfold from the inside. A girl appeared in front of me, and it was as if I could hear her thoughts; and then, I saw through her eyes...

❖

MIRA

SOMEWHERE ON THE MEDITERRANEAN SEA, 1939

'Oh, Miss Goodman, this sunshine is *splendid*!'

Sally has a high-pitched voice that is simply impossible to ignore, even if I try my best, and I've been trying since we left England. She's a cheerful, plump, no-nonsense girl who, for a generous fee, agreed to accompany me to this godforsaken place. My personal maid refused to leave England in these uncertain times; I can't quite blame her, but I also suspect she doesn't want to be associated with me, and with our family.

The little boat is rocking back and forth, and it's making me dizzy. More than usual. I have to keep my eyes down on my lap. All the while Sally keeps squealing. She seems to be under the impression that this is the greatest adventure of her life. At least Signor Vittorio Lorace, the solicitor who'd brokered the sale of the house and met us in Rome to chaperone us on our journey, is the quiet type. He sits on the bow, tense and frowning, mopping his face with an immaculate handkerchief, as if he were the captain of a war vessel on some all-important mission.

I have a migraine coming on; my legs are shaking and I need my medicine, which Sally was foolish enough to bury somewhere in my luggage on one of the other boats that make up our sorry convoy. I curse every wave, clinging on to the box beside me with all my might. It contains my Decca gramophone; I can't live without it. If I have to be exiled by my family, I can at least have some music.

I've been sent to the Sicilian island of Galatea like a postal parcel. For my health, they said, because 'sunshine works miracles'. And because a change of air would do wonders to help me forget. But mostly, to help *society* forget, and aid my family's reputation into its long, laboured climb back up after I dragged them so low.

The trip was arranged so fast, the reality of it almost hasn't sunk in yet. My father bought a villa in Sicily, with all it contains, for a few hundred pounds. The owner, a Russian aristocrat by the name of Countess Galina Alyova, closed the sale and then disappeared. I was supposed to disappear too, at least for a while: clearly, the villa and I are the perfect match. Winds of war are blowing, but our family's reputation – compromised by yours truly – concerns my parents more than Mussolini does.

Papa has always had the instinct for a good deal, which explains why my grandfather was a Jewish shoemaker from somewhere in darkest Europe, yet two generations later we live in

Belgravia. Marrying Violet, my mother, was also a good deal. She's much younger and decidedly more handsome than Papa. Sadly, we're not as skilled at family relations as we are at rising up in the world. More than a family, we're four people, including my brother, thrown together by little more than chance. The last conversation we had before I left is burnt in my memory.

'Galatea is miles from pretty much everything. She'll probably be safer than we are,' Papa had said. That statement would have sounded better without the 'probably'. 'I'm sure it's for the best all around. The climate will cure her... ailments.'

By the way – while this conversation was happening, I was there, sitting on the ottoman between them, yet Papa kept refer-ring to me in the third person, as though I didn't quite exist.

To be fair, I was indeed pretending I didn't exist too, and gazing out of the window at the drizzly rain falling, falling on our garden and beyond, over the city of London.

Mother took a puff from her cigarette. 'We can put the whole thing behind us, never mention it again. Just obliterate it from our memory.'

I knew I could never forget. The whole ordeal had been written on my body. Nothing could *ever* make me forget. As usual, the mention of my illness was accompanied by a disbelieving grimace.

I didn't let her words sting me. No, I'm lying. They did sting. They always do. I know she doesn't have it in her to love me – but at least, if she didn't despise me so much... But I digress.

This whole design was quite mad, I thought. Really, shipping me to Italy? On a random island as big as a stamp? With all this talk of war everywhere?

'Not to mention all those lessons you took with Professor Ferretti,' Papa pointed out, finally acknowledging that I was sitting there.

'Not to mention them,' I said, speaking for the first time.

Papa was emphatic. 'They'll come to use, at last.'

'I'm *sure* they've come to use to her *quite enough* already,' Mother said, and I ignored the jibe.

Paolo Ferretti, an Italian academic and poet who'd come to

England to take refuge from Mussolini's purges, was my friend. My mother fancied herself the centre of an intellectual and literary circle, maybe to make up for her own lack of academics; my brother introduced her to Ferretti, whom he'd met at Cambridge. He wore mended trousers and broken shoes, and my mother offered to help – ever the patron of the arts. But the professor was too proud to accept and give nothing in return, and so, at my brother's suggestion, he offered me Italian tuition as payment.

Two years later, *I* spoke decent Italian and *he* had new trousers and polished shoes. He was gentle and softly spoken, called me *signorina* and told me tales of Greek mythology and of his childhood in Venice, where there were canals instead of roads and his family kept a boat tied to their front door.

After it all happened, I became too ill to keep taking lessons; but while London's high society was tearing me to pieces, Professor Ferretti sent me a note, written in his meticulous, narrow handwriting: *L'oro non si corrompe mai.* Gold can never be corrupted.

I cried.

Now I was about to put my Italian to the test. It was a strange coincidence – almost a sign – that Countess Alyova's Italian villa had come up for sale. All we knew about her was that she'd moved to Galatea, leaving her aristocratic husband and children behind. She then promptly sold everything before disappearing into thin air. Isn't it funny, that a girl trying to leave a scandal behind should take the place of another woman who vanished and never resurfaced?

'Also, I was thinking,' Mother began. I could feel a jab coming. She was always fencing with me, except she had a foil, a sharp one – and I didn't. I should make myself one, conjure one up from the depths of my soul. 'Maybe this is the time you'll finally learn to swim?'

Blood rushed to my face. The memory of my swimming lessons in our Sussex home came back to me, together with the terror and tears, dismissed as the antics of a hysterical child. I remembered those lessons like a nightmare. I was sure I was going to drown. When it was clear I would never learn to swim, the lessons continued, even if the instructor had lost all hope in me.

'Oh, now, Violet,' Papa began, ineffective as always. He was a shark in business and a puppy with my mother. She never took any notice of him.

I was saved by one of our maids appearing on the doorstep, clutching towels and sheets: seeing us there, she froze like a rabbit in headlights. With Papa always at work, and Mother in Sussex most of the time, servants moved around the house pretty much freely. Looking back, it's probably not surprising that one of the maids was responsible for the scandal coming to light. Abundant freedom within the house and no loyalty to us – which I couldn't blame, given the way my mother treated them – had resulted in our social demise. My mother pulled all the strings she could in order to contain it, but now they'd found a way to kill it at the root: me.

'What are you doing with those, Lucy?' Mother said, and the girl recoiled, as though she wanted to crawl inside herself. There was no need to ask: taking towels and sheets to the garden house could only mean one thing – my brother, Gavriel, was on his way back from Cambridge.

'I'm sorry, Madam, it's Libby, Madam.' My mother knew her name full well, of course. She just liked playing games.

'Lucy, I asked you a question?' Mother said.

'I'm so sorry. I'm preparing the young master's suite.'

'He's here?' Violet's eyes found my father's.

'He telephoned, Madam. He's on his way.'

'And you didn't tell us?'

Libby's face grew even redder. 'He didn't mention I should. I assumed you knew—'

'He didn't want us to know? What is he hiding this time?' Papa interrupted her.

My brother is the living definition of dissolute; but he's a man, so he lives by different rules from the ones I'm expected to adhere to.

'Brace yourselves,' Mother said cheerily. She worships Gavriel.

We all do. 'Well, when you're finished there, Lucy, you can go and take care of my suitcases.'

'I already prepared them, Madam.'

What? She was going to our seaside house? I'd be leaving in three days, and she would not stay to say goodbye? 'Are you going to Sussex, Mother?' I asked, quite needlessly.

'Not any more. I meant, unpack them! I shan't leave while Gavriel is here.'

'Yes, Madam.'

'You may go, Lucy.'

I sighed and closed my eyes for a second. 'Mother. She's been with us for years. It's Libby! Not Lucy, Libby!'

'What's the difference?'

I was more than ready to end the conversation and leave my parents to whatever they needed to discuss. 'Mother, would you send word that I'll be taking my medicines in the garden house, please?'

I rose from the ottoman, too fast – my head spun, and blood pooled in my shins and feet. I took a moment to recover, while my parents looked on for the longest time. Finally, my father came to support me, and I enjoyed the look of guilt on his face. Being ill has its advantages. 'Are you all right?'

'I'm perfectly fine, as you can see,' I hissed. The new Mira said this kind of thing. The new Mira mastered bitterness. An almost twenty-year-old who'd grown weary with life in the space of a year. The year that changed everything.

I steadied myself, let go of my father's arm and followed Libby outside. 'At least Mira will be off our hands,' I heard Mother saying just as I left the room.

If you've received a million little needle pricks, one more won't make a difference.

The scandal would have been enough, but my constant ill health was an insult to her. Apart from drinking alcohol and smoking sickly-sweet cigarettes, Mother treated her body like a racing horse she had to train. The stronger she showed herself to be, the weaker I became: headaches, fainting spells, fatigue and mysterious aches.

My brother's pied-à-terre – two rooms in our Belgravia garden, which he had claimed as his kingdom – was chilly, but warmed up quickly when Libby lit the fire. My plethora of medication arrived via a maid, and I sat dissolving the powders and pouring tonic on a silver spoon while Libby worked. She made the bed and refreshed the bathroom, all the while keeping an eye on me. Making sure I was fine was part of the servants' duties. I worried, sometimes, that if the time ever came when there would be nobody there even just *looking* at me, something terrible would happen. I would die, or just disappear. But I'm digressing again.

Finally, my handsome, carefree, immensely spoiled and yet so beloved brother came through the back door, hair damp from the autumn mist and a vague scent of alcohol seeping from his skin. I tried to inject indifference into my voice as I greeted him, because that was the way it was done in my family, but he *knew*. He knew that whenever he came home it was as if the sun had just come out to warm us all.

'My darling sister, hello,' he said and stooped above me while I sat. He brought my head to his chest, and I was as happy as a five-year-old at Christmas, and desperate to have him to myself for a little while before my parents stole him. He'd just returned from a few weeks in Russia for his university course, and I'd missed him terribly. To be a wealthy young gentleman whose only purpose is enjoying life – and a womaniser to boot – my brother doesn't speak much. He doesn't need to. His charm is not about talking anyone into doing his bidding like a salesman would – it's about charisma. The way he looks at people – women, especially, but men too – makes them pliable to his influence, and whatever he decides needs to be done: jumping off a roof for a dare, as he and his friends did while at Cambridge last year (my brother's luck held, as usual – they didn't break a bone or get expelled), going to bed with him or taking him to endless liquid lunches in the best restaurants – because his own allowance, as generous as it is, is never enough.

His good looks help. I don't know how such a handsome crea-ture could have been produced by my turnip-shaped father and my beautiful but angular mother, and yet here he was, resembling a Roman statue with his straight nose and jet-black hair, and a tint to his skin that was not dark but also not fair, a light honey that looks good in every season, under every light.

Now he was gazing at Libby as though he could look at her forever, and asking about her mother, and we all know that although he's simply not interested in servants – he likes conquests, not power games – Libby was smitten. And then, one more look, a nod – and she knew she'd been dismissed.

'I'll come and see you over there. We'll have fun,' he said, and went to warm his hands beside the fire.

'Fun? There's a war coming, and I'm being sent to the continent. It makes a lot of sense, doesn't it?'

'The sun will sort you. That's why they're shipping you over there, sister dear. The Mediterranean, remember? Blue skies, dry air and a terribly healthy Mira. Yes?'

Never mind about the war, then.

Gavriel wholeheartedly adhered to the *we won't mention what happened to Mira* rule. It's good not to be reminded, and yet it's hard to carry it inside, all by myself. Sometimes – especially in the mornings, in those first few seconds before I'm fully awake – it seems to me that it never happened. That it was all a nightmare.

'No. But I have no choice.'

'You don't,' he said cheerfully – so self-assured, with those tea-coloured eyes that of course I have not inherited. Mine are a dull brown. 'Mother and Father have run out of patience with you.'

I never show my brother anger, because he would just turn around and leave. He's not one for drama or apologies; if a situation displeases him, he just walks away, easily leaving behind whoever is drowning in it, whoever is hurting. So, instead of shouting, *It wasn't my fault!* I was quiet, and studied the dancing flames. He seemed a little repentant, because he added: 'We'll go to the beach and dry our bones in the Italian sun. It'll be good. I mean it.'

I softened. As usual. 'You *mean* it? You *will* come?'

'Oh, yes. What else do I have to do here, after all?'

'Apart from university?' I teased him.

'We all need a holiday, don't we? Mira. You know I would

never leave you alone. Seriously. I will come and visit, I promise you.'

How easy it always is for him to win me over – a hungry heart drinks up a declaration such as *I would never leave you alone*. And yet, did I believe him? Or with my brother as well as my parents, would it be a case of out of sight, out of mind?

I tried to get up, but my head spun once again and my legs decided they would not sustain me – so he sat beside me and cradled me, which was what I hoped for. How I feared he'd forget about me the moment my ship left its dock.

And here I am now, sailing on my way to exile. We're a flotilla of three, one boat carrying us, the others my belongings – everything except my precious Decca, which is sitting at my feet. Having gone safely from pier to boat, thanks to strong fishermen's hands, I'm not too terrified. The water is blue and shining and transparent – less frightening than the choppy, foamy waters of the Channel. Sally punctuates almost every moment with her chatter. 'Oh, Miss Goodman! Let me hold the parasol a little closer there, you don't want to catch too much sun too quickly... However shall we do for English papers, out here? Hopefully Signor Lorace... Oh, Miss Goodman, look at those birds over there!'

I think I don't want to hear the words *Miss Goodman* ever again. On and on she goes, until one of the fishermen, whose face is a web of wrinkles on leathered skin, beams at me. '*Parla, parla, parla,*' he says and laughs. *Talk, talk, talk.*

'What did he say?' Sally enquires.

I can't help but chuckle, and I don't answer; Sally keeps chatting on, undeterred and quite ignored.

Maybe, soon I'll be glad of Sally's fondness for small talk. I think back to what Signor Lorace told me about life on the island – it sounds more boring than I could ever say. Fewer than a hundred people live there; cars are forbidden; locals move around the island on foot or riding donkeys. No restaurants, no theatres, dance halls or even shops. But would solitude and boredom of this lonely island or the deep, vast expanse of the sea where you could sink and never be found again be worse than what happened in London? Would it be worse than being forever punished for something that wasn't my fault? Would it be worse than being sick every day and not being able to get out of bed for months on end?

Sally begins to squeal and point once again; I rub my face with my gloved hand.

'*Tutto bene, signorina?*' the younger fisherman says, and I'm a little startled. It's the first time he's spoken. It's probably not appropriate for these men to address me so informally — my mother would have never stood for it.

But then, my mother is not here.

'*Sì, sì, bene,*' I reply; he looks towards me, never breaking the rhythm of his strokes as he rows, and I can catch a glimpse of his features, the straight nose and full lips, and those black, black eyes. Everything about men speaks to me of threat and fear now, and more so the sight of strong arms and legs that could overcome a woman in a moment. I look away.

'Miss Goodman! *Look!*'

I follow Sally's pointing arm and her gaze, and what I see makes me draw breath sharply. The island has revealed itself — how wrong I've been about it being barren, when it's covered in lush vegetation, flowers and plants, shining under the sun! Deep in my chest, a flower of hope silently blooms.

Sally and Signor Lorace are talking, maybe to each other, maybe to me, but I can't make out the words. The colours of the island, the bright sky, the sunshine, the sea — a wave of emotions overcomes me. Parts of me that have been dead for so long now give the lightest flicker telling me they still exist, somewhere inside me.

The island has unveiled itself, but maybe my eyes have unveiled too?

Out of the corner of my eye, I see the younger fisherman catch my enraptured expression — a small smile dances on his lips, as if he created Galatea himself, and he's proud of it.

A stony beach dotted with resting boats awaits us — a few more vessels, painted in bright colours, are docked at a small pier. A stony path, marked by olive trees on each side, climbs upwards and disappears from view; my eyes can't encompass the whole picture, with the terraces all the way to the top – it's like an optical illusion where everything looks quite compressed together, and yet as high as the Tower of Babel. Everything on this island is on a slope, and from the ground it's hard to make out what's above us.

I hope with all my heart that we'll dock at the beach and not the pier this time, so I won't have to step off the swaying boat and onto land, but simply be pushed in with the boat itself and helped onto the pebbles. But no such luck: I watch, a hand clutching the side of the boat to keep me steady, the other under Sally's arm, my heart beating hard, while the fishermen jump into the shallow waters and tie the rope to the dock.

'Would you take my gramophone, please?' I call out to Signor Lorace, and my anxious tone defies the formality of the question. I really just want to cry out, *Save my gramophone!*

'Don't worry, I'll defend it with my life,' Signor Lorace says quite seriously, and I'm pacified by that at least – because everything else about the situation petrifies me. I don't want to stand up in case I fall into the water. I try to hide how I'm trembling, but Sally can feel it through our linked arms. The two fishermen leap out with ease and set out to help us. My mother would have jumped in the water and made a big show of swimming clothed and making it to the beach herself. It's just the kind of thing she does, and invariably makes me wince inside.

'Don't worry, Miss Goodman, we'll be safe and dry in a moment,' Sally says, but as always when I'm in a panic, her words don't sink in.

And then it all happens so quickly: the young fisherman, in one smooth movement, lifts me up and flips me horizontal, so that he can slip one arm around my shoulders and one under my knees. I'm so taken by surprise I can hardly breathe.

Once we're safe on the pier he holds me for just a second more, to make sure I'm steady. Sally, who's made it up to the dock before me somehow, rushes in to support me. She stands between me and the man protectively, and glares at him, as if he's taken liberties and his intentions were somehow sinister. I'm quite breathless, and stunned from the shock of being touched by a man who isn't my brother, for the first time since— never mind.

Sally fusses around me while Signor Lorace, still holding on to my gramophone, gives instructions, and the men walk away one by one, each carrying a piece of my luggage across the beach and up the winding path. 'Don't worry, everything will be brought up to the house for you. They're good men, trustworthy.'

'Of course.'

He waves in the direction of somewhere across the beach – I follow his gaze and see a small, dark man with a donkey by his side. 'There's our passage!'

'I'm going to have to ride on a donkey?' I'm not against the idea – just surprised. I haven't considered the possibility. But then, how else would I climb up?

'It'd be exhausting for you to walk all the way up on foot, especially in this heat.' Sally gives her tuppence. Which nobody asked for.

'I need a moment,' I say, my words stumbling out together with an intake of breath.

'Of course. Please, come and sit in the shade, *signorina*.' Signor Lorace takes my other arm, and I begin to make my way across the stony beach in my thoroughly impractical heels, with Sally holding the parasol over my head and walking easily in her modern canvas shoes. They help me sit on a low stone wall and Signor Lorace begins to fan me. A woman with a glass of water is summoned from somewhere. I'm dizzy and quite sure I'm about to faint, and desperate for my medicine.

'Miss Goodman, you're white as a sheet!' Sally lays down the parasol and miraculously produces a bottle from her handbag. I take it from her before she can pour the right dose in the cap, and down a glug. With that and the water, I begin to gather strength again. The worst, I'm sure, is now behind me. There's more light here than I've seen in almost twenty years of life in England.

The man with the donkey is waiting patiently to take us up.

'I took the liberty of asking Countess Alyova's staff to remain in your service,' Signor Lorace says, his watchful eyes still on the line of men carrying my luggage. 'They're respectable – and capable. I've been assured that the house is immaculate and that they'll look after you well. They're waiting for us up at Villa Onda.'

'Thank you. I'm ready to make my way up,' I say, and slowly stand.

At that moment, a strange sound arises from somewhere across the beach: high-pitched, somewhere between human and animal.

Sally and I grab each other's arms and look at Signor Lorace for assurance, but he seems stupefied too. I turn my head back and forth to see where it's coming from, this wailing, almost otherworldly... and I see the source. An old woman, dressed all in black, is standing on a rock looking out to sea, singing. Other women are materialising out of nowhere to join in. My hair stands up on the back of my neck. 'What is this? Signor Lorace, what is this?'

'The women of the island are welcoming you, *signorina*. Nothing to worry about,' he says, though he looks ashen himself. He makes a gesture as though patting something down, scrunching up his nose in disapproval. '*Basta, sì, va bene, basta!*' he calls out. The women ignore him and keep wailing.

It's then that I notice a striking girl, younger and slightly set apart from the group – she's tanned and barefoot, her waist-length hair blowing behind her in breeze. She's wearing a simple cotton dress but she has a strong, proud stance, like a young queen of the island. Even the air seems to vibrate to the sound of the song, even the waves.

Finally, it comes to an end. The girl smiles towards us, surveying the company with welcoming eyes – but it feels as if she's smiling at *me* and me only. Then she walks away with the rest of the women.

'What on earth was that?' Sally whispers, and this time it's me who feels *her* trembling.

I have to hide a smile as I consider the absurdity of our little caravan: me on a donkey, Signor Lorace carrying my Decca, sweating profusely now that he can't use his handkerchief, and Sally holding the parasol over my head, having been finally stunned into silence by the uncanny song.

'I think I'm dreaming,' I say under my breath, my voice hidden by the sound of the cicadas. From Belgravia to riding a donkey on an island halfway between Italy and Africa. I'd like to say stranger things have happened, but right now I can't think of any.

Villa Onda – I mean, Goodman House – comes into view. It's a palace. A palace in the middle of the sea, risen from the waves like a lost Atlantis. Slightly sinister, I think, examining the strange statues carved in the facade. I find those horrifying, but the gardens are beautifully kept and the palm trees bordering the path to the house make a warm, welcoming sound, dancing in the sea breeze.

The servants Signor Lorace mentioned are waiting for us on the stone steps by the door. 'Oh, here you are already! You must have climbed up *so* very fast,' Signor Lorace tells them. 'This is Giovanna, and...'

'Mimi,' the young girl says.

'Mimi. They're Countess Alyova's servants. Do you still want to keep them in your employ?' Signor Lorace studies me from under his eyebrows. I recognise them: the elderly woman who was singing on the rock, and the proud-looking girl with the long, long hair. Now I see what Signor Lorace means: *After that creepy welcome song, do you still want them?*

'Of course. Thank you. *Grazie,*' I say towards the women. They'd both looked wild, almost feral, standing barefoot on those rocks and making those ghastly sounds – but now they seem civilised enough. Giovanna has her hair tied back, Mimi looks tidy in her light blue cotton dress, and they're both wearing shoes, which is an improvement. Mimi has tamed her long hair in a braid, though a halo of dark curls escapes. There's something about Mimi... I can't quite put my finger on it, but it's a little unsettling. And then Sally puts it into words, whispering in my ear, 'Miss Goodman, have you noticed? She looks so much like you!'

Sally is right. Mimi and I have the same amber hue in our skin, the same black hair, though mine is cut and fashionably curled and hers is waist-length; the same shape to our eyes, elongated and with long eyelashes, though mine are brown and hers are a striking, deep black. She must have noticed the similarity too, because when our gazes meet, her eyes widen, just a little.

'*Benvenuta*,' she says with a nod of her head – almost regal, as though she's the one employing me.

I feel Sally stiffen beside me. 'She's welcoming you in your own home?' she hisses, but I ignore her. I think it's a sweet thing to say.

'*Grazie*,' I reply, and I see true joy in her eyes. Mimi seems delighted to see us. We're a curiosity. Two overdressed English women coming in from the grey.

My heels click when I step onto the mosaic floors, and I'm dizzy when I look up and see the frescoes on the ceiling, as though I'm falling upwards. The walls are decorated with brightly painted ceramic tiles, in a style I've never seen before – certainly not the gentle Wedgwood, but an almost Arabic style of design and colour, bright in a way that only a sunny country can produce.

'Giovanna, you know this place better than me,' Signor Lorace says in Italian. 'Would you mind showing us around?'

Only then do I realise that he's still carrying my Decca, sweat rolling down the sides of his face. I'm mortified. 'Can I take that from you?'

'No, no, of course not, let me take it to your room! I mean, if you'll allow me into your room. Oh, *santo cielo*, I've been inappropriate. Please forgive me, *signorina...*'

'Don't be silly!' I try to reassure him.

Summoned, Giovanna doesn't smile; she's solemn, almost dour, as she flicks her chin slightly towards Mimi.

'I'll show you everything, Mira!' Mimi bursts out, rising on her toes like a little girl. This declaration is followed by a collective intake of air.

'It's *Miss Goodman*,' Sally and Signor Lorace snap at the same time.

'*Scusate!* Miss Goodman,' Mimi good-naturedly corrects herself, without any sign of embarrassment. I can only imagine what would have happened if she'd made such a mistake with my mother.

'It's all right,' I say, unnecessarily – because Mimi has already taken off. Sally snorts beside me – she's always at my side, perched like a raven on Odin's shoulder. Or a parrot on a pirate's shoulder? Yes, that would describe her better, chattering and wide-chested as she is.

'But you must be exhausted, Miss Goodman. You should rest before touring the house?' The moment she reminds me I must be exhausted, I feel it.

'Oh, yes, of course. How insensitive of me!' Signor Lorace wails, still in the mood for self-flagellation. Mimi is already halfway up the grand stairs, smiling widely. Her dress is a little too small, and her shoes, black and flat, too big. She's not beautiful in the classical sense, but she has a kind of grace that would make people look at her twice, with her round face and enormous, dark eyes.

'Miss Goodman?' Sally whispers.

'Oh, yes. Yes, sorry. I would love to see my room and get settled. Please, Mimi,' I say in Italian. 'I'd like to refresh a little after the journey, before I see the house.'

'*Parla Italiano!*' Mimi exclaims.

'*Sì, un poco.*' I smile, and the connection is made. Sally seems to rearrange her position with imperceptible movements of the head, arms and heels. The dynamics are drawn already; she's jealous of this strange girl. As for me, I'd like to know where Mimi gets her energy from, that joie de vivre in her eyes.

She's like a little light, while my own light has dimmed. Maybe forever.

'Help. Me. With. Those. Those ones, see? The *suitcases*,' Sally shouts at Mimi – I suppose she assumes that if she raises her voice, Mimi will miraculously understand English. Mimi smiles and nods, nonplussed.

'*Venite!*' she calls – and we all follow, with Sally and Mimi carrying a suitcase each, and Signor Lorace still sweating over the Decca. As for Giovanna, who looks a hundred years old, she grabs one of the heaviest trunks and swings it over her shoulder, seemingly without effort. I'm *extremely* impressed. We turn right where the staircase divides into two, and walk down a corridor brightened by one gilded mirror after the other. The mysterious creatures that decorate the outside are on the inside too, peeking from the edges of the ceiling, some animal, some human, some angels and demons of a sort. I loathe them. They are horrifying.

'This was Countess Alyova's room. It's the best bedroom in the house, so we prepared it for you, Miss Mira.'

'You must call me Miss Goodman,' I murmur inconsequentially and make my way towards the window. The curtains are closed, and I'm dying to see the view. I'm about to touch the fabric when the curtains move, making me jump. There's someone there, crouching against the wall, his back to us.

Giovanna takes him by the arm, and the man stands and turns, looking mortified and muttering apologies. 'Lupo, what on earth! Have you finished or not?' she cries and launches into a little tirade, speaking so fast that I can't make out the words. Sally is holding a hand to her chest, dramatically.

It's the young fisherman, the one who carried me out of the boat.

'I'm so sorry!' He looks mortified. 'I wanted to be sure the light worked in here, and I didn't have time to do one last check, you know, with Maria and the baby...'

'Are you finished now?' Signor Lorace asks, as prim as a high society lady.

'*Sì,*' Lupo says, and flicks the switch on the wall. A chandelier lights the room in a dance of shiny crystals. Electricity on Galatea? They don't have running water, but they have electricity? Signor Lorace seems as shocked as me, while Mimi is beaming, as if she'd made the chandelier shine all by herself.

'Countess Alyova had electricity put in,' Lupo explains. 'It's been a bit temperamental recently, but I think I fixed it.'

'You can turn your hand to everything, Lupo Martorana, can't you?' Giovanna says, still frowning and with her arms crossed, but looking at him somewhat fondly.

'*Scusate, signorina.* I didn't think you'd be here so quickly.'

'It's fine. Don't worry. It's just, you appeared out of the

curtains, and...' I try not to show how startled I'd been. Also, with Lupo looking at me, I'm now conscious of my damp dress and the dishevelled hair I caught sight of in the gilded mirrors. I look a state.

'May I say, you speak perfect Italian! Call me if you need me, Signora Giovanna. *Arrivederci*, Mimi. Signor Lorace.' He leaves the room and I steady myself. I hate how shaky and frightened I am around men now. Will the old Mira ever come back?

'I left some lemonade here. If it's not cold enough, I'll go and get some more ice... and I made some *marzapane*,' Giovanna says. It all looks terribly inviting, and the jug of lemonade is enough to make me salivate. I'm so thirsty after the climb under the hot sun. 'We filled the bathtub for you. If it's not warm enough, just call for Mimi.'

I'm touched by their thoughtfulness – they seem to have gone to such trouble to make me feel truly welcome. I'm now ashamed of the disparaging thoughts I had during the voyage.

'We'll leave you to rest,' Signor Lorace says. Ever since he came into my room, he's been on hot coals – he's an old-fashioned gentleman that way. He rounds up Giovanna and Mimi.

'Thank you.'

Mimi lingers on the doorstep under Sally's dark gaze – I see her slipping a small brown parcel, tied with string and tiny wildflowers, out of her pocket. It looks like a present, and I assume she's about to give it to me – but her cheeks turn very pink and she leaves, taking the parcel away with her.

Sally's whirling around, sorting clothes, folding and unfolding sheets and bath towels, making sure that the bed is made to her standards. I take my dress off, damp with sweat and seawater, and gaze at myself in the gilded mirror, in my slip. How can my arms be honey-coloured already, when I've been in the sun for such a short while? My cheeks are rosy when I'm usually sallow. Maybe I'm developing a fever? Still, I'm surprised at how resilient I've been throughout the journey, when back in London there have been times I was so ill I couldn't even get out of bed.

'Miss Goodman, it would be a good idea to have your bath now, the water is cooling fast,' Sally calls from the bathroom.

'Thank you, Sally. I think I'll take my evening medications a bit earlier today.'

'Of course.'

Everything is laid in front of me on a silver tray. A tonic, two pills, powder to be dissolved in water and sugar. I have a whole trunk full of bottles and jars; it'll last me months, and after that, if I'm still here, a courier will travel from London to bring me more. I can't possibly go without, I'm sure I'll die – in fact, just thinking of running out squeezes my heart in a vice.

After taking my medications, I'm in a daze. Sally helps me step into the bath, and I lie in the water in silence. A low sound lulls me – it's coming from beneath me, as if the waves were lapping at the house itself, and Villa Onda was drifting out to sea.

After a night of deep, uninterrupted sleep – when did this happen last? – I awake in the kind of golden light you never see in England, not even on the brightest, sunniest days. Sally is already in my room, laying out my clothes for the day, when Mimi appears at the threshold fresh and smiling. She's carrying a tray laden with food, its fragrance wafting all the way to my bed. '*Buongiorno, Mira!*' she calls, and the words dance out of her mouth as though she truly is grateful for a new day.

'It's *Miss Goodman*,' Sally enunciates, and I can see her nostrils flare. I suffocate a smile. *The battle of the maids*, I can imagine my mother saying, before swapping their names on purpose or making some barbed comment to stir things, just for fun. 'I'll give *Miss Goodman* this, if you please.'

Mimi lets her take the tray, but stays put. 'I'm so sorry! I forgot again!' She bites her lower lip.

I sit up in bed and close my eyes in the warm light, like a cat. My body aches a little, but in a good way. Usually, my mornings start grey and groggy. 'Don't worry. Oh, this smells amazing!' I compliment her.

It's a shame I won't be able to eat it, because eating is so hard for me. I struggle to swallow, a permanent hard knot in my throat.

'I made the bread and Nonna made the lemon jam! We were here at dawn. I drew water from the well, I opened all the windows and began the dusting and cleaning. Please tell me what you'd like done first, and I'll do it at once. The countess had a rota, because there's so much to do here, this villa is so huge…'

Mimi seems enthused about working here. It's a strange feeling, to wake up and see someone so full of cheer and delight. I pour some milk into my tea – goat milk, I assume, as I've been told there are no cows on the island. 'I shall draw a rota too. Thank you, Mimi.'

'*Prego!*' she says and still stands there, her hands behind her back. She doesn't seem to want to take her leave.

'Come in,' I encourage her, just at the same time as Sally blurts out a curt, 'You may go, now.'

'Come in, Mimi,' I repeat, with a warning look to Sally.

'Thank you, Miss Mira.'

'Miss Goodman,' I correct her gently, before Sally jumps in again. 'Mimi, can you take us on a tour of the garden today? If you have time?'

'That would be wonderful!'

Sally's face is a picture. 'The appropriate answer is, "Yes, Miss"!'

'It's fine, Sally.'

'Yes, Miss,' Mimi says solemnly, making me laugh. 'We can go after Mass.'

'Of course,' I answer calmly. I've never been to Mass in my life, but it's better to blend in. Although I studiously ignore the news, or try to, it is impossible to deny that being Jewish during this time is frightening. It wouldn't be the first occasion in history that Jews have had to lie low.

Well, I'll try a bit of this bread and lemon jam. I won't be able to swallow more than one bite anyway…

. . .

Two bread rolls with jam later, we're walking through the gardens, with Mimi telling us the names of the plants and flowers arranged in circular beds, like sculptures. There's fine grit on the ground, and benches covered in colourful tiles are dotted all around, as if the place had been conceived as an al fresco sitting room. Lemon and orange trees spread their scent around, and the leaves from the tall, old palm trees offer shade from the sun. I can *feel* how deeply the previous owner, Countess Alyova, loved this garden – once again, I ask myself why, why did she leave?

Or more exactly, why did she disappear?

'Come, I'll show you a secret passage,' Mimi says, and she leads us to a palm tree big enough to hide a little archway behind its trunk. 'The view is lovely down there, do you think you can make it? Let me take your arm.'

She slips my arm under hers to help me through, and we walk down a few steps onto black, hard terrain that makes a startling contrast with the greenery we left behind. Sally, peeved that it's not her arm I'm holding on to, is walking ahead of us. One moment I can see her blonde head bouncing in front of me – the next, she's gone. We hear her cry before we see her, crumpled on the black rocks.

'I'm fine! Really, I am, Miss Goodman.'

'What is she saying?' Mimi asks and kneels beside poor Sally, now in a chair with her sore foot up on a stool. We're in the parlour at the front of the house. The walls are painted sky-blue, and the gilded furniture is upholstered in silk of the same colour, simple and restful, unlike the bright colours in the rest of the house.

'She's protesting that she's fine. But it's not true, as you can see.' Sally's face is a light hue of green and her hands grip the armrests so hard, her knuckles are white. 'Better call the doctor. There is one on the island, isn't there?'

'Of course.' Mimi disappears from the room while Sally keeps arguing – she could easily guess the meaning of the word *dottore*, and she's adamant she does not need one.

Sally is sipping a sugary lemonade Giovanna has prepared for her, and looking a little calmer when Mimi returns. Lupo is with her, for some reason.

'Must we take her to the doctor by boat?' I enquire.

'I hope not,' Lupo replies. 'Could you remove her stockings? I'll leave the room and come back when you're finished.'

'Remove her stockings? Where's the doctor?'

Lupo looks at me, dumbfounded. 'I'm the doctor.'

'No, you're not! You're a fisherman.'

'That too, when needed. And I do apologise for my appearance,' he says, and opens his arms as if to say sorry, at the same time encompassing his worn-out clothes. 'I was working – working the land, I mean – but Mimi said it was an emergency, so I just washed my hands and face and didn't take the time to change.'

'Mimi?' I must have sounded like my mother – the outraged tone of someone who's saying, *Could this peasant be a real physician?*

'He's the island doctor, yes. I thought you knew.'

I'm mortified.

'Look, I even have a bag!' Lupo doesn't seem to be offended – if anything, he's amused. A suffocated sob comes from Sally, whose face is still a greyish hue, and Lupo's smile fades. 'She needs to be seen to, now. I'll leave the room, if you could—'

Sally is distraught. 'I'm not going to be touched by this man!'

'*This man* is your only option, Sally.'

'But I only need a bit of rest.'

'Not if you have a broken bone.'

'It's not bro— ow!' Sally seems about to faint as Mimi and I gently remove her stocking. We exchange a glance over Sally's ankle – it has swollen almost instantly, and even just brushing it with our fingers makes her cry out.

Both Mimi and I have to hold Sally's hands while Lupo assesses her ankle and her calf – she's in so much pain. 'It's broken, and it's not a clean fracture. She needs her ankle to be set and to be *ingessata*,' he announces.

'*Ingessata?*' It's too difficult a word for my Italian.

'You know, to be wrapped in something hard and steady, so the bones can be kept still,' Lupo explains.

'What is he saying?' Sally is still not convinced by Lupo's credentials at all. I don't blame her, given his attire, but she has to overcome this notion, fast.

'It's broken. You need a cast, Sally,' I explain in English. 'Can you do it?' I ask Lupo.

'I could, if I were sure that the fracture was clean, but I believe it's not. It's better done at the hospital in Coliandra, or the bones might not set properly.'

When Sally hears the word Coliandra, she balks. 'I'm not leaving you here on your own, Miss Goodman!'

'Sally, you'll do what the doctor says. Mimi, please would you help Sally to her room and start packing for her, while I speak to the doctor?'

'Of course, Mira.'

'Miss Goodman,' Sally says feebly, and I don't know whether to laugh or cry. Poor Sally!

I sigh, and let my arms fall by my sides. What a start to our stay. 'Thank you for coming. I'm sorry for—'

'No need to apologise,' he says, taking up his bag. 'Signorina Goodman, may I ask you a question?'

'Of course, doctor...'

'Call me Lupo.'

'*Bene*, Lupo.'

'Are these all yours?' he enquires, eyeing my medications on their silver tray, left on the coffee table by Sally that morning.

'Yes. I need them.' I look down and shrug.

'I hope I'm not speaking out of turn, but... a healthy young woman doesn't need all this.'

'I'm not healthy,' I say, piqued. 'And it's quite irresponsible of you to suggest this. Without my medications, I might die.'

'Far from any desire to put you in danger, but I believe that those are meant to combat ailments of the mind, not the body... and there could be other ways to help.'

A question passes through my mind – *How do you mend a broken heart? A violated body?* And the answer comes just as quick and fleeting: *Not with medicines alone.* But I ignore it, and clam up instead. 'And anyway, you're not my doctor.'

'True. But I'm the only doctor around. And I'm curious to know – how does someone who needs all those medications, and who struggles to stay upright and walk, from what I saw when you arrived... Well, how can someone in such a state of health bear half the weight of an injured person, like you did with Sally?'

'I don't feel so good,' I whisper, and let myself fall onto the sky-blue chaise longue, my head suddenly swimming.

'You don't feel good because you... remembered.'

'I remembered *what?*'

'That you're supposed to be ill.'

'How dare you say I'm making it up! How *dare* you!' My eyes are full of angry tears. He has no idea, no idea of what I've gone through.

'You're not making it up. I'm sure of that. It's not what I meant.'

'What did you mean, then?' I say mutinously. I'm full of rage, but I can't help noticing that his eyes show concern.

Lupo pauses. 'I'm sorry, Signorina Goodman. I overstepped the mark. If you need to talk, I'm here. As a doctor, and as a friend.'

'If I talked to you, Lupo, you wouldn't like what I would say. If I told you what made me this way.'

'My door is always open. And if I'm at sea, just wait and I'll come back. Any time.'

I don't answer. How did this happen? Sally is the injured one. How dare he drag me into this conversation.

'I'll come back for Sally. She'll be fine, I promise,' he says in the loaded silence. 'In the meantime, she can take fifteen drops of your laudanum.' I follow his gaze to the dark glass bottle on its silver tray. 'No more than that. It'll make her sleepy, weak, dizzy... but I'm sure you know what it does.'

He's already turned his back and stepped out of the sky-blue parlour when I finally speak. 'Lupo?'

'Yes, *signorina?*'

'Please, call me Mira.'

. . .

After a dose of laudanum, Sally falls asleep almost at once and it occurs to me that it's no wonder I'm always sleepy and dizzy, taking this concoction twice a day. How come it didn't dawn on me before? By the time she wakes, Mimi and I have finished packing for her. Lupo is back, looking the part now in a clean white shirt and dark trousers, and accompanied by Palmiro. Thankfully, Sally is too dazed to protest as the fisherman lifts her and carries her down the winding road to the pier.

I'm careful not to catch Lupo's eye. I'm ashamed, that he should find me so weak. It's him who approaches me, and looks at me as he speaks, until I'm forced to hold his gaze; and when I do, I see no pity or reproach in his eyes. Only kindness. 'Will you take my arm, Mira?'

And I do. His arm feels strong and steady. And, although the sense of alarm and distrust that grips me around all men hasn't disappeared completely, there's something calming about Lupo. Not enough to ever take him up on his offer, of course. I would never tell him what happened to me, nor let him interfere with the medications I couldn't possibly go without. But for now, I'm content to hold on to his arm. After all, he's a married man and father to a baby, as he mentioned when I arrived, and this reassures me.

The pier is bathed in September sun, and the multicoloured boats dance on the waves in perfect serenity. But poor Sally is crying. 'Whatever will your parents say, when they find out I left you here all alone, Miss!'

As a general rule, they don't seem to worry much about me, I think, but I don't say. 'You can't help it. It's not your fault. I'll be fine.'

'I'll be back soon, I promise. A few days. Hopefully there will be an English doctor there.' Not much chance of that, I'm sure, but she's frightened enough, so I nod in accord.

'I'm sure it won't be long. You'll be perfectly all right in no time.'

The boat is untied from its mooring and I wave Sally goodbye: the last bit of my English life is gone.

Mimi's standing at my side. 'Don't worry, Mira. I'll help you. You won't be on your own,' she says, and this time I don't correct her; I like the way she says my name.

Step by step, I slowly make my way back up the steep hill to Villa Onda. I'm surprised at how well my legs are carrying me. I don't feel strong, of course – I haven't felt strong in a long time – but my knees aren't buckling, and my head isn't spinning. I lean lightly on Lupo's arm, more for reassurance than anything. He has a pleasant smell of pine and resin and saltwater.

'Mimi!'

The man's voice seems to have come out of nowhere. A man working on the terrace above us straightens as we approach. He's a head taller than Lupo, who's not a short man, and he nods towards me. His hands and clothes are covered in dark earth, and this, together with his size, makes him vaguely menacing. Lupo smiles and nods back, but Mimi seems tense, her eyes moving from the man to me and back. 'Miss Mira, this is my fiancé, Fulvio.'

I sense her apprehension, and I wonder why she should be so nervous to see him.

'How do you do,' I greet him, and he nods once again. 'It's nice to meet you. Do come to see us at the villa. You'll be very welcome.'

There is no reply from Fulvio. 'Thank you,' Mimi says quickly, to fill in the silence. Only then does Fulvio mutter a word of thanks, but his eyes deny his words. They're surly – not malevolent, but quietly hostile. I notice that Lupo's smile has disappeared. I can't decipher his expression but there's a story behind this exchange, a story between Fulvio and Mimi, and between Lupo and Fulvio, that I'm not aware of. One thing is sure: Mimi's fiancé doesn't seem to like me much.

'I'd better get you home safe,' Lupo says, and gently leads me on. Mimi stays behind, and I hear her and Fulvio whispering as we walk away. I turn back briefly, and I see Mimi poised to follow me while Fulvio is still holding her hand, as if he doesn't want to let her go.

'So, you'll get married soon?' I ask Mimi. We're in my room, and I'm showing her how to prepare my medicines. She's frowning in concentration and handling them carefully, with her slender, tanned hands. The meeting with Fulvio has left me a little preoccupied. He seems to hold a grudge against me, but I'm not sure why.

'I'm working at Villa Onda now,' is her enigmatic reply. Again, I don't correct her that it's now called Goodman House, because I can't seem to refer to it in any other way than Villa Onda myself.

'You can't do both? It wouldn't be an issue for me if you married. You could still work here, you can be sure of that.'

A moment of silence, her eyebrows joining in a furrow. 'I'd like to see more of the world. It's impossible, I know... I'm engaged. Also, I'm just an island girl. I don't know anything. I can barely read and write. Where would I go?'

I have no answer to that. I want to say she'd have plenty of chances in the big wide world, but what do I know? I've lived a sheltered life in a bubble where money and connections open almost all doors. The truth is that I have no idea how the world would treat Mimi. 'I'm good at Russian.' She shrugs, as though it's nothing.

'As in, the language?' I remember my brother telling me he'd found it hard to learn, but beautiful to speak. He'd dedicated himself to studying it, which surprised me: Gavriel isn't one to dedicate himself to anything, except partying. But Russia seems to fascinate him.

'*Sì.*'

'How did you learn Russian?'

'Countess Alyova taught me,' Mimi answers, and she launches herself into a little story in clear, confident Russian. Or at least I think it is. But she doesn't hesitate, she doesn't falter. My jaw falls agape.

'I have no idea what you said. But you sound so... plausible!'

'Countess Alyova used to say I have a gift. That I can learn very quickly and imitate accents *prekrasno*. Perfectly.' She smiles and then, like an afterthought, she shrugs her shoulders again disparagingly. But I won't let her dismiss such a gift.

'Let's put you to the test, then. Listen to this. And try to repeat.' I open my beloved gramophone box, fish a record out at random, and the Decca begins to play.

> When our garden blooms again.
> My dear, I'll see you then

'When our garden blooms again, my dear, I'll see you then...,' Mimi repeats word by word, her cheeks scarlet, her gaze focused, her hands hovering in mid-air over the silver tray. My lips mouth the words with her.

It's like hearing a recording. She truly has a gift. It's astonishing to think that this girl had never heard English before I arrived. I lift the needle, and the music stops while Mimi is in mid-sentence. '*White roses for you, red roses from the blue—*'

'Oh, Mimi!'

She reverts to Italian. 'Did I say it wrong? I sound stupid, don't I?'

'No, not at all! I was surprised because you sound... you sound perfect. Say the verse for me again?'

As she repeats the verse, her voice begins to modulate the music, and I sing alongside her – we both start giggling and singing at the same time, she offers me her hand and we dance and laugh like two little girls, turning 'When our garden blooms again' into a jaunty tune until I let myself fall on my bed, out of breath. I can't remember when I last danced, or laughed so much.

'You truly have a gift, Mimi. And you must use it,' I tell her, as soon as I can breathe.

She sits on the windowsill and, with the window as a frame and the sea as the background, she looks like a painting. It's quite uncanny how alike we look, like a variation on a theme: her skin is tanned, her hair more abundant and shinier than mine, her hands worn with work. I'm still pale, my hair shoulder-length and not that vibrant, as if it reflects how I've been feeling inside, and my hands are soft and white.

'Just because I can imitate what somebody says, it doesn't make me clever,' she says, and I read on her face that she hopes I'll contradict her.

'Rubbish. Like I said, it's a gift! And you *are* clever. Would you like to learn English? Properly, I mean. I can teach you. And I can help you with reading, and writing too, if you want.'

'I would love that. I would love that *moltissimo*,' she says, and the sun plays with her dark hair, making it shine almost pink. Her smile is my reward.

It's been a long time since I've danced and laughed; but how long has it been since I've had a friend?

Weeks later, life on the island has formed its own shape and rhythm, and I almost feel at home. Sally didn't come back. I sent a local fisherman to Coliandra the day after she'd been taken to hospital, and he came back with a desperate letter from her: she was to stay there for an unspecified period of time, and then my parents would get her back to England. She couldn't work for me a long while, certainly not on the rugged terrain of Galatea. She was distraught, because she'd wanted to come here so badly and she'd taken the responsibility of looking after me very seriously. Poor Sally; my heart goes out to her and her disappointment.

Giovanna's food is so good that it makes me *want* to eat. Meal-times in London used to be an exhausting affair, sitting there by myself, in front of enormous portions that my parents had ordered Cook to make for me. Every morsel stuck in my throat as if I were eating sawdust, and the food would return almost untouched to the kitchen. But vegetable soup with sunshine-fed tomatoes; little bits of fish caught that very morning; bright yellow bread made with spices; coffee with almond biscuits and marzipan: it all goes down a treat. Not to mention the fact that I have someone to talk to. Mimi and I now eat together every day. Mimi's presence, the view over the gardens and the sea, and the beautiful scents and tastes make meals an entirely different experience from the one I had in London.

'There you are, you love these, Miss Mira, don't you?' Giovanna says, placing the coffee tray on the table. 'Mimi, time to give me a hand! Are you sure the girl is not bothering you?' Every time Giovanna speaks, I have to concentrate because she has a thick accent, much more pronounced than Mimi. I don't dare correct Giovanna about the Miss Mira/Miss Goodman debacle, of course. She's too authoritative to invite reproach.

'Not at all! Mimi is keeping me company.'

'Ha! Here I am, serving my own granddaughter! And she's sitting down like a lady!' Giovanna protests, but looks at Mimi fondly. She disappears into the kitchen, carrying dirty plates, and Mimi and I are left with our coffee and sweets. Mimi drinks it quickly and grabs a biscuit.

'I'll go and help Nonna,' she says, but when she's about to slip through the gently flapping sheets, she stops. I tilt my head, waiting for her to talk.

'Miss Mira.' Deep breath. 'I have a gift for you. *Ecco*,' she says, and takes out a tiny bundle from her pocket. It's the parcel I saw her carrying the day I arrived.

'Oh, Mimi. This is so kind of you. But you shouldn't have.' She scrunches up her nose. I've noticed it's a mannerism of hers, something she does when she's happy. I open it carefully, and inside is a crocheted brown bracelet – a cuff, almost.

'I'll help you put it on,' she offers, and slips it onto my wrist. She fastens the tiny button – an iridescent seashell. It's a strange material – not wool and not silk. It reminds me of chainmail, and yet it's impossibly light.

'I've never seen anything like this... did you make it?'

'Yes. Wait, look.' She takes my hand, leads me towards the light and lifts my wrist up in the direction of the sun. The bracelet shines like gold, gleaming as the linen sheets dance on each side of us.

'Oh! Is it a kind of gold?'

'It's shellfish. This thread comes from the sea. It's the soul of the sea. It's sacred. We call it *bisso*. Nonna harvests it, and I weave it and dye it. We make things for people who come to her for help – especially women who want a child... for good fortune and fertility.'

I tense up. 'I see. Maybe I shouldn't wear it, then.'

'Do you not want good fortune?'

'I've lost my good fortune,' I reply, and I don't want to talk about it any more. I take the bracelet off and return it – I don't want it, not even when Mimi looks at me as if I've slapped her.

'What happened to you, Miss Mira?' she asks, holding the bracelet flat in her palms, reverently.

I'm speechless. No servant would ever have asked me this back home. *It's none of your business*, is the answer on my lips. 'I'm very sick,' is what I say.

'Yes, but with what?' Does she *mean* to be insolent? 'There was a woman on the island, when I was little,' she insists. 'Her husband died at sea, and she became ill after that. She couldn't walk any more. A doctor came from the mainland to see her. He said it was a sickness of the heart, not the legs.'

'What are you trying to say?'

She looks down, her confidence shaken by my harsh tone. 'That you have a sickness of the heart.'

'I should let you go for saying this.'

'But it's not too late for you,' I hear Mimi muttering under her breath as she goes.

That night, in my room, I'm alone with the silver tray of medicines. My hands shake as I lift the cap of the cut-glass bottle.

And then I put it back down.

5

THREADS

ANNIE

'Annie?'

It took a few seconds to come back to the surface. The one-word call, my own name, seemed to stretch as if it'd been recorded and then played back in slow motion. What on earth happened? I was on the floor and the window was open, the flimsy curtains blowing in the breeze. Gone were the moon and the purple sky, replaced by a resplendent blue morning and a shiny sea. The gramophone lay open beside me, silent. I must have fallen asleep and into a vivid dream... very vivid. Almost real. Could it have been only a dream?

'Annie?' This time the call was more urgent, almost alarmed. I dragged myself up and went to the door; Salvo was there, wearing a black t-shirt and jeans, his raven hair dishevelled and an anxious expression on his face.

'*Buongiorno*,' I said, and immediately a yawn began in the back of my throat. I felt like I hadn't slept one moment, and instead walked every single step Mira had walked, spoken every word she'd spoken. Wait – was I awake right now? Or was this a continuation of the dream? My eyes returned to Salvo, and I gave a vaguely apologetic smile.

Salvo took one look at me in my crumpled dress, eyes like a sea creature just come to the surface, and over my shoulder, at the gramophone open on the floor. My apologetic smile grew bigger. 'I'm so sorry, I should have let you sleep. Only, I had something planned, so I came to call you, but then you didn't answer and I was a little worried. Are you sure you're OK?'

'Yep! I just had a very... realistic dream.' There was no way I could explain what happened, what it felt like. He'd think I was crazy. Was I? 'Do I look so terrible?'

'No, of course not, just—'

'Yeah, no, I'm awake! Aside from the dream, I had a really good, *perfectly normal* night!'

Salvo seemed taken aback. 'Er, good to know.'

I swept my messy hair back from my face. 'Yeah. So... what's your plan?'

'Well, I have some free time this morning, so I wondered if you wanted to come sightseeing with me?'

'Sure. Sure, I'd love to. I...' I turned around, surveying the mess. 'I just need to get ready.'

'Of course. Take your time.'

It took more than a few minutes to shed the experience. I looked at my hands, my face as I stood in front of the bathroom mirror – I almost couldn't believe I was me and not Mira – and I remembered the flash of blue I'd seen while in the bathtub and the fleeting image of the girl in blue behind Elvira.

Ice filled my veins.

Has she been waiting for me?

I'd come here to learn about my grandmother – but I might be getting more than I'd bargained for.

I joined Salvo outside under a perfect blue sky, the air laden with perfumes. The morning was warm but not hot, and a silky sea breeze swept away the cobwebs from my mind. It was enough to bring me back to the here and now, and dissolve the apparitions of the night.

Almost.

The record player was safely back in the wardrobe, and I didn't want to see it again, whatever it could tell me about my grandmother. It was too frightening, and anyway, nothing of what I saw was true. It was a dream – the combination of an overactive imagination, jetlag and the sweet wine Elvira had served at dinner.

I was dressed in my only pair of jeans and a white linen shirt, and I'd slipped on the first wise clothing choice of the whole journey: trainers. Still, there must have been something wrong with the way I looked, because Salvo stared at me. 'Do I have something on my face? I put on sun cream, maybe... white streaks or something?'

'No, no. Sorry. Right, let's go.' I followed him round the back, along the blonde stone walls and down the hill.

'But why were you staring at me?'

'I don't know. You look different.'

'Different how?'

'Young.'

'I *am* young.' I struggled to keep up with him as he moved fast over ground he knew well; I was guessing my footing on half-hidden stone steps.

'Well, you look it, now.'

I stopped in my tracks, arms folded. 'Er, excuse me? Did I look old before?'

He clearly thought it wise not to answer. 'Come on, let me show you why Galatea is called the jewel of the Mediterranean.'

'Is it?'

'No. But it fits, don't you think?' He took my hand to lead me forward, and I let him. I wasn't the only one who'd changed, it seemed, because after all the formalities of the day before – how and when the dinner would be served, how I was their first guest and they wanted everything to be perfect and all that – now we were simply a boy and a girl on an adventure. And I loved it.

'Where are we going?'

'For a donkey tour of the island. Also, I want to show you a special place. Somewhere not many people know.'

'Yes to the tour and the special place, but... are you asking me to ride a donkey?'

'Of course. Do you not trust me?'

'I'm sorry, what?'

'Our chosen transportation,' Salvo said and smiled. 'Do you not trust me?'

'Would it be rude if I said no?' I grinned.

'It'd be understandable!'

Just after a small bend, we came to a simple stone building, square and whitewashed in the traditional style, with a terracotta-paved terrace that opened to the sea. 'So, this is my childhood home. This is where I grew up, and where I live when I'm not up at Villa Onda. My mamma still lives here – she's in Ericusa to visit her sister today, but she'll love to meet you, I'm sure. She was almost as excited as Elvira and I were about having our first guest! She won't be away long.'

'I'm looking forward to it,' I said. I couldn't wait to meet more island people and get a better flavour of what life was like here. I looked around me. Salvo's family house was built on a gradient, and clung to the cliff like a barnacle on a rock – the flat space had been worked inside the land, with its terrace, the building itself and a small vegetable patch behind. I noticed a dark carved stone right beside the house, with a deep gouge in the middle: it gathered rainwater, I realised. Everything spoke of hard work, of human beings eking out a living on rugged soil, and yet the beauty was breathtaking. 'Must have been amazing to grow up in a place like this.'

'It was. I have many happy memories of this place. My father has passed away, but I have my mother, and a *huge* family. I mean, huge! Almost everyone on the island is my cousin, once or twice removed.' He smiled.

'You're lucky. I'm an only child of two only children. I would have loved to have a big family.' A pang of loneliness made itself felt, which often happened when I thought about my family – or more like, my non-existent one. I would have loved siblings, and aunts and uncles and cousins, and to have grown up within a warm, affectionate tribe. But no such luck. All the love I had to give was buried with my dad. I forced my thoughts to take a different direction.

'Do you think your mamma can tell me more about Mira?'

'Probably. Mamma is like a human archive: she remembers all the family ties, the whole kinship web over the island,' Salvo said, while grabbing a broom that was leaning against the wall and sweeping dirt and leaves off the terrace floor. 'It was windy last night. I don't want Mamma to find a mess. There.'

How thoughtful. Suddenly I wondered if there was a girl in his life. It was the second time I'd asked myself that, and I was mildly annoyed at myself. I had more important things to do than wondering if my host had a girlfriend. 'She must have been delighted that you came back. To live here, I mean.'

'Oh, yes. Although she never put pressure on me to return. There was someone in London, but, well, it didn't work out. Galatea and I are a package, you know. And Tanya – my ex-girl-friend – hated it here.'

Did I actually ask that question, or only think it? Because there was my answer. Not that it made any difference, of course.

'I'm sorry,' I said.

He leaned the broom back against the wall, and turned towards the sea. We stood side by side under the blue sky. 'Better this way. You? Is there someone, back home?' he asked casually. A little too casually, I realised with a certain satisfaction.

I shook my head. Sometimes I'd wondered if there was something wrong with me, because I never seemed to like someone enough to get properly involved with them. My emotions were buried so deep, I could barely feel them. 'No, nobody. I dated a little in high school, but life had other plans. I looked after my dad, he was sick. He passed away too... and here I am.'

Salvo placed a light hand on my back and stroked it, a gesture meant for comfort and consolation, but which gave me an entirely different feeling. I swallowed. Every time this man touched me, my body reacted in weird ways, and I couldn't do anything about it. Now I was stuck somewhere between taking a step away from him and nestling in closer. I'd never felt that way before. I had pretty much zero experience of romance, and fear matched the excitement that was blooming inside me.

Suddenly, I startled and jumped back as a huge, brown-furred creature walked onto the terrace. I gasped – for a second I thought that one of those strange stone figures from the house had come to life, but then I saw it wasn't a giant dog as I'd first feared, but a placid, sweet donkey with the longest eyelashes I'd ever seen. She looked so feminine with those enormous, kind eyes.

Salvo smiled. 'Don't worry, it's just my Bella!' He patted her side. 'I give you my beautiful friend and associate, Bella. You must admit she's gorgeous.'

'Oooooh! She's beautiful indeed. So sweet.' I stroked Bella on her forehead; she closed her eyes and moved towards me to rub her muzzle against my side. 'She's so… affectionate!'

'You should have seen her when she was a baby. She melted me. Donkeys are highly underrated, you know? They're strong, loyal and very… how can I put it… zen-like.' *I should take a leaf out of their book, then.* 'So, you ready to hop on?'

'Mmmm…'

'Are you scared?' he teased me.

'It's not that! I've gone horse riding before, but… will she hold my weight? She seems so small. I won't hurt her, will I?'

'Nope. Not all donkeys like to be ridden, but Bella does. She loves company and being given tasks. She can handle more than double your weight. And she's indefatigable. Not to mention stable, which is a plus when you're always half a metre away from rolling into the sea.'

'I'm going to ignore that last statement. OK, then. You convinced me.'

He offered me his hand. 'May I?' I took it and easily climbed onto Bella – I leaned down to give her a little kiss before we started moving. Her fur was as soft as flannel. 'There,' Salvo said, and handed me a small, scrunched paper bag from his pocket. Inside were a few sugar cubes. 'You can encourage her with these. Special treat!'

'Will do. Do we have a destination, or will Bella be like one of those roofless sightseeing buses?' I smiled at the thought.

'I told you, we're going somewhere secret. Hard to reach,

unless you get in from the beach and swim part of the way. Can you swim?' He cocked his head.

'I can, but I'd rather not. I'm kind of scared of the water.'

'You're in the right place, then!' He laughed. 'I can teach you, if you want. I mean, I can try to take away the fear. Water is your friend, believe me.'

'Mmmm... yeah. Maybe. Go, Bella, go!' I said enthusiastically. She didn't move an inch. Then Salvo patted her and made a hand gesture, pushing her gently forward, and off she went, climbing down the hill on a small grit path.

Bella was indeed a sturdy little thing who held my weight effortlessly. Maybe it was because I kept giving her sugar – I couldn't help it, she was too lovely.

The tiny grit road we were on wound down steeper and steeper, with a ravine on our side, tumbling all the way down to clusters of sea-rock. Water sprawled all around us, and the island seemed to be floating. The more we proceeded, the more Bella seemed to hang on the stony hillside by a miracle, and Salvo had to walk so close he was almost glued to us.

'There's no chance she'll topple over, of course?' I tried to keep my voice light, but I was half in awe of the beauty around me, half terrified that we would tumble to the rocks below.

'No chance at all; she knows the way,' Salvo said and stroked her muzzle. 'Also, I wouldn't kill my first guest.'

'Good to know!'

'I have invested everything I have in Villa Onda. You have no idea how much I missed this place when I was in London.'

'What did you do there?' I asked. Maybe the conversation would distract me from impending death.

'I'm an environmental planner. I help people plan and build the green way. I work with architects, engineers and conservationists to build in a way that is as respectful of the environment as it can be.'

'It sounds like an amazing job.'

'It was. London is full of opportunities, and I loved it... at the beginning. It came to the point where I couldn't stand the noise and the people and the rush any more. That's what happens when you grew up on an island of four hundred people and no cars, I suppose. Also, I missed my family. But the job was fantastic. However, the best way to do it was protecting Galatea, don't you think? The ultimate conservation project.'

'So you came back.'

'*Sì*. This opportunity came up. The *regione* – the local authority, basically – decided to offer Villa Onda to anyone who would restore it and manage it, to help Galatea flourish, but in the right way. The island is protected because of our flora and fauna, both underwater and overland. We've been lucky, up to now. But money buys anything, and some people would rather have Galatea become a new Ibiza than the natural paradise it is.'

'That will never happen.'

'Not while I'm alive, no. My dream is to buy Villa Onda, not to keep it for myself, of course, but to make sure it stays untouched. And Elvira would like to open a byssus museum.'

'It's a fantastic idea.'

'*Sì*. All that stands between us and making it come true is money, so we're applying for every single grant we can find. Wish us luck!'

'Good luck!' His and Elvira's project was so worthy. I was almost jealous that he should have this goal, this singlemindedness in his life. I had no idea what to do with myself yet – there was nothing I wanted desperately, or I believed in with all my heart. I hoped that this trip would uncover more than my family history: I hoped it would uncover... me.

We were quiet for a bit, but he kept glancing at me. 'Are you sure you're well? You seem lost in thought.' I wanted to tell him about my dream, but I fought that impulse.

'Well, there's a lot to take in... Oh, wow!' We stopped as the small road ended at a ravine that led down to the sea. Bella was unfazed, while I felt my hands and feet tingling with the first signs of panic. This island was all about beauty and danger, I thought. If you didn't know where you were going, you'd inevitably end up falling off a cliff whilst staring at the most stunning view you'd ever seen.

'It's all on foot from here,' Salvo said, and gave me a hand to jump down from Bella. 'On foot, or swimming.'

'Will you ask me to roll all the way to the sea now?' I asked, peering down the ravine.

'Silly. I wouldn't take you anywhere dangerous.'

'Mmmm... yeah,' I said, contemplating the small but still frightening abyss. 'Oh... What will happen to Bella?'

'She'll go for a wander and find us eventually. She never gets lost, believe me, it's like she has an in built compass. Come. I won't let you fall,' Salvo said, and offered his hand. I hesitated, and then I took it. Our eyes met just as our fingers touched, and something electric passed between us.

'Are we going down to the beach?' I asked, to defuse the moment.

'Not exactly. You'll see.'

And down we went. The slope was so steep, and the dry, rocky ground so treacherous, that I had to balance against Salvo many times. I stopped for a second to take in the view, even if my legs trembled a little: the perfect sky, cut in two by the smoke ascending from Piroi, and the Mediterranean below us. A deep, rich fragrance of salt and sun-baked vegetation filled the air, beauty expanding in all my senses. And the scent of Salvo: manly, clean and fresh, but with a deeper note that went straight to my head.

He squeezed my hand. 'Almost there. This way,' he said, and gestured not downwards but sideways, along the slope. I couldn't see anything of note, except for the breathtaking landscape.

'What way?'

'Along here... see, put your feet on the steps.'

'There *are* no steps! Unless you're a mountain goat!'

'Those are steps!' Salvo laughed. 'Remember what I said? I won't let you fall. It's a promise.' While keeping his feet firmly planted on some rocks, he turned his body away from the hillside and opened one of his arms, like an invitation to fold myself into him. I took a tentative step, and his body covered mine and protected me from the void.

It also pressed me against the slope, with only his body

between me and falling down to the sea. I felt his breath on my neck, and the weight of him on me – it was thrilling and a bit daunting at the same time. He seemed to have a strange effect on me – there was a kind of draw to him that took me in and brought me to places I was afraid of, and yet I longed to go.

I took a step, still within the protection of Salvo's embrace, and found myself standing right in the middle of a round, black opening. The sudden darkness made me lose my balance, but Salvo reached out for me and caught me just in time.

'See? I told you I wouldn't let you fall,' he whispered, his mouth close to my ear. We were close to each other, in total darkness.

How easy would it be to find his lips now?

How long had it been since someone kissed me? All I knew about love was shallow dates that hadn't meant much to me, nor to the guy involved. Nobody had ever caught my attention and held it long enough for it to become something serious – I'd never fallen for anyone and no one, I believed, had ever fallen for me.

I took a small step back, still holding on to Salvo, and blinked until I could see shapes again. The deep darkness became a symphony of black and greys: I realised we were in a cave, but I couldn't gauge how deep. The air inside was fresh and damp, after the dryness and sunshine outside; goosebumps rose on my skin, and not just for the change in temperature.

'We're in the Mother's cave,' Salvo whispered, and I replied in a whisper too – any noise here seemed like sacrilege, for some reason. I lowered my head instinctively, even if the ceiling was high enough to accommodate Salvo's height, and more.

'Why is it called the Mother's?'

'You'll see. Be careful,' he warned me, and took my hand again to lead me forward. 'The ground is uneven. The further we go, the damper it will be. It's very slippery down there.'

'I'll be careful.' I swallowed, as the light from the entrance grew dimmer and we walked forwards into the darkness. The sound of the sea, however, was still there – even as we advanced, it didn't seem to grow dimmer. It was as if the ground was hollow underneath our feet, and the sea could penetrate places we couldn't see. Just like under my room, now that I thought of it.

Or maybe the island was an illusion, like all I'd seen last night, and I was actually among the waves, dreaming of Galatea? Strange thoughts. The dark was making me light-headed, and it was harder to think clearly. 'How far shall we go?'

'Until we see the Mother,' Salvo answered.

'Oh. Hopefully the Mother is not some sea monster you're going to feed me to. Because you and your family are part of an ancient cult and I'm the sacrificial victim.'

Salvo's laughter sounded muffled and echoed against the rocky walls. 'Of course! What else? You have a crazy imagination, don't you?'

If only you knew.

The entrance was too far away now. It was nearly pitch black, and I was petrified of falling. And yet, I kept going. What was it about Salvo that made me follow him this way, almost blindly?

He took out a tiny torch from his pocket and shone a light onto our feet, and then on the walls all around us. Now I could see the black stones, the thin film of moisture that covered everything. We were in a long tunnel, thankfully not too low – that would have made me panic for sure. *Imagine being stuck here, imagine the ceiling falling on us...* Just then, the tunnel became lower and lower, the perfect recipe for claustrophobia.

As the roof closed in, and when my knees and back couldn't bear to be bent that way any more, I had to kneel on the floor. Salvo did the same, and we both crawled on until, at last, we came to a small room encased in the stone. I stopped, still on my knees, trying to find my bearings. Salvo's torch shone on a tiny alcove. Something was in it – a carved object.

'And she,' he whispered, 'is the Mother.'

It was the statuette of a woman with heavy breasts and a pregnant belly, with tresses on both sides of her head – her eyes were closed, and her chest was decorated with a geometric necklace, or a collar. White lines were painted on her neck, her arms, her belly, and there was a crescent shape – maybe a moon? – on her forehead.

'This is magical,' I whispered.

'She's thousands of years old. Nobody knows for sure how old this place is because nobody with the necessary knowledge has ever studied this site, and nobody ever will, if I have my way. If this place were to be discovered, I know it wouldn't be respected.'

'I understand.' It was to be kept secret. Just like the island was protected, this would be protected from strangers. But I was a stranger too. And he'd shown it to me. 'Why did you bring me here? I'm a tourist, I'm one of the people you want to protect the island from.'

Salvo shrugged. 'I don't know, actually. Ever since you told me about Mira Goodman being your grandmother— no, before then. Ever since I saw you on the boat... I wanted you to know my island. To know the real Galatea.'

A small laugh escaped my lips. 'You didn't utter a word to me on the boat. In fact, I thought you were a little rude.'

'I was nervous.'

'You were good at hiding it.'

'Yeah, I've had practice. Anyway, I thought you looked like a fish out of water. But there was something about you...'

The Mother was witness to everything we said, and I could feel her presence, warm and comforting. And I felt at ease with Salvo, enjoying our conversation even if the setting and circumstances were pretty strange. All of a sudden, however, my attention was caught by a white little bundle beside the statue, slightly hidden behind the stone.

'Salvo, there's something there, look.' I stood and reached out for the bundle, but I couldn't quite get to it, even if my hand was right there. And then it fell on the ground, and I felt for it on the jagged floor.

'What is it? Nobody comes here. Only a few know of this place.'

'Wait, it's a...' I lifted it up, stretching my arms. 'A handkerchief, I think.' There was a small motif embroidered on the side, tiny yellow flowers. I was almost sure that when I first looked at the Mother's statuette, the handkerchief wasn't there – almost. It must have been a trick of the eye. I crawled up to the stony wall and felt the surface – there was an opening there, darker than dark. The cave continued.

'Don't, Annie. It's not safe. The sea comes in from the other side and the rocks aren't stable.'

'The other side? Does this tunnel run under the whole island?'

'I think so. It should be explored properly, I suppose, but—'

'Yes. Keeping the island a secret, I understand.'

'Anyway, someone must have been here. Otherwise, this hand-kerchief—'

'It looks old. And I mean old, not just spoiled by dust and damp. The fabric feels so fine. I'd like to see it in daylight.'

'Sure. Let's go,' Salvo said, and as we turned towards the exit I threw a glance towards the mysterious opening. Yes, it was unsafe. Yes, it would probably fill with seawater.

And yes: I would find a way to explore it.

I kept the handkerchief close to my chest as I bent down to crawl out of the chamber, but before I could, something shifted. More goosebumps rose on my skin, and the cold and dark seemed to weigh further on me. The handkerchief grew warm, too warm, in my hands. In the feeble light, I saw Salvo's lips parting to say something – but I'll never know what he was going to tell me next, because it happened again. The roar of the sea became louder and louder in my ears, just like the phantom music had, and the piece of fabric seemed to twist and swirl against my chest – once more, I was lost to myself.

❦ 6 ❦

FAIRY TALE

MIRA

The saltwater is warm around my feet, and I kick back and forth like a child. Mimi and I are sitting among the rock pools that open in the volcanic ground, and I'm delighting in the shades of blue and green of water and seaweed against the black. I'm no longer worried that the water will spoil my silk dresses. It's been two weeks, but it seems I've been on Galatea forever now. I raise my face to the blue, blue sky, half in shade because of my wide-brimmed hat. 'I bet it's raining in England,' I say dozily. 'Poor Sally.'

'She wanted to come here, yes?' Mimi says. She gets up and stands on the rock beside me, like a mermaid waiting for a ship to come too close to the island. More than a maid, she's now my companion, while I've hired another local woman, Beatrice, to help with the unending physical work needed around the house. The unending physical work needed *everywhere* here. There's a slice of it for us to see just down there, along the shoreline – fishermen fixing the boats, women unknotting nets, mounds of precious catch to be cleaned and salted – everyone on the island, apart from the babies, have hard, calloused hands, reddened by working with salt. A line of old women sit cleaning fish, children who are not much older than toddlers carrying pails. And out on the sea, little boats at the mercy of the waves, gathering up their livelihood. Life on Galatea isn't easy, and I realise every day how comfortable my existence is compared to the islanders'. Let's just say, my parents will never know how much of my allowance I'm spending on ordering goods for local families, and generally trying to make things easier for them.

'Yes. She wanted an adventure.'

'And you, Miss Mira? Did *you* want to come?'

'No. Not at all. I was made to.'

'Why?' Mimi is always candid. So candid, she would be deemed insolent in other circumstances. But her black eyes show nothing but curiosity.

'It's a long story, and not one I want to recall.'

I close my eyes in the sunshine, and Mimi is quiet. And then she does that thing – she bites her bottom lip, and I know she's pondering something.

'And now? Are you happy to be here? Would you leave, if you could?'

I think about it – I consider the last few weeks and how different I feel from the day I arrived.

The times Mimi and I spent listening to the Decca in my room and singing (badly) over each song, gathering shells on the beach – me, who'd been barely able to stand for months and months – chatting with the locals who always insist on giving me something, flowers or a loaf of bread or freshly caught fish...

Empty plates after Giovanna's meals, and almond biscuits on the terrace, and picnics in the garden, while in London I was always starving and simply could not eat.

The mornings and evenings when I forgot that the silver tray, with the medications I used to be sure were saving my life, even existed. And yet, I'm still alive – more alive than I was when I took them. *A healthy young woman doesn't need all this...*

Lupo.

Wait – why should he come to mind now, when I've tried to keep him at arm's length, and indeed succeeded? Even if I could overcome the fear that has gripped me since the scandal, he couldn't be the one who aids me out of the memories: he has a wife, Maria, and a new baby. God help me, with what I've suffered. I've come across him only once, when he turned up at the house of an ailing elderly lady just as Mimi and I were delivering food to her – but I was so icy, he gave up talking to me.

No. He's not one of the reasons why I wouldn't leave Galatea – but I have many, many others.

Finally, I emerge from my thoughts. 'I wouldn't leave Galatea, Mimi, no. Not for now, anyway. Would you?'

'Yes!' She exclaims, as if she's letting out a huge burden, together with a sigh she's held inside for a long time. I'm surprised – she seems so happy and settled. I suppose you never know what goes on in people's hearts and minds, even those close to us. 'Yes, I would. I... You know that I'm not allowed to swim, Miss Mira?'

'Really?' Another surprise. When I arrived and she was among the women singing, she seemed to have such an affinity for the sea – standing on that sea-rock with her hair blowing in the wind. The girls on the island swim routinely, diving for shellfish or just for recreation.

She nods. 'Something happened when I was a little girl,' she begins. In her hands, a small shell that she twists and turns between her fingers. 'The sea tried to take me. Since then, I'm stuck on dry land...'

'The sea tried to take you? How?'

'I don't remember much of that day. Mostly, what happened has been recounted to me like a bedtime story, one of those with a warning inside, you know, to teach children not to do something. You see, the Ayala women are the best swimmers on the island. We have no fear. But one evening – I must have been around three – we were dipping into the warm water, and I slipped out of Nonna's hand. A freak undertow swept me away. There are no currents in the sheltered little pool we always went to, and Nonna was holding me firm and strong; and still, the sea took me.' Mimi looks down at her hands, palms up. The tiny shell is shining mother-of-pearl under the sun. 'All I remember of that moment was a tug, like arms reaching out for me and pulling. At first, I wasn't afraid – nothing bad could happen to me there, not when I was with my mamma and *nonna*, not there in our little pool – but then I couldn't breathe, water entered my mouth and lungs...'

'That must have been so frightening!' I remember the primal fear I felt when I was forced into swimming by my mother, and my stomach churns.

'It was. Nonna said that the undertow was so powerful, she had to use all her strength, and I was almost lost forever. They decided that I would never dive, because the sea wanted me, and we'd said no. And you can't say no to the sea, not without paying the price.'

'I'm sorry.' I feel almost reverent, that this quiet, proud girl would open up to me this way. I seem to have gained her trust quickly, just like she earned mine.

Sometimes human beings are like pieces of a jigsaw – they don't fit at all, or they fit perfectly without even trying.

'I sit on the rocks and watch Mamma and Nonna get ready to dive, and they look strong, you know, like they were meant to do this! They jump and become one with the sea, and I'm left there, hungry and thirsty and never satisfied. Yes, we prepare the byssus together, we work it together – but it's not the same. It can never be the same.'

I could never have guessed that behind Mimi's smile and confidence lies such frustration. Right now, with her flushed cheeks, almost trembling, she reminds me of Piroi – a volcano forever smoking, forever waiting to detonate but never quite there. Until one day, when it will blow up everything in its wake.

'Could you not defy them? Dive anyway?' I ask.

Her chest rises and falls quickly, as though the thought frightens her. 'If I did, they would know. They would feel it in their bones, smell the salt in my hair, off my skin; the island is so small, someone would see me.'

'Then tell them you need to do this. Tell them what you told me!'

The shell she holds in her hands makes a short, graceful arc into the waves, and disappears with tiny ripples and a thud too soft to be heard over the water. As if it was never there. 'I... Miss Mira, the truth is, I'm as afraid as my family are. Not long after my accident, my father's boat was lost, with all the men inside. Nonna said that the sea had wanted payment from us. But we don't know if the debt has been paid in full. My family's terror has become my own.'

I'd like to say that this is all superstitious nonsense. That what happened to her as a child was a freak accident, that the sea does not claim anyone, things just happen – and the loss of her father's boat was no restitution. The words are there, on the tip of my tongue: *Poppycock! You have no reason to be afraid!*

But they refuse to come out, because this is how Galatea islanders see the world, and they do so for a reason. Here, the sea rules every aspect of life; it's no wonder they worship it like a god, that they give it will and feelings and purpose. Who am I to subvert what they believe in; what consequences would this have for Mimi?

Also, behind my rational reasoning there's a vague unease.

What if it isn't nonsense?

This island is like a tiny world inside the bigger one. The Galatea women singing in the cove, the song itself and its eerie hum of whales and dolphins... It's easy, almost inevitable to believe that there's a web of hidden rules, a cause-and-effect system that goes beyond what I know. And so, I don't argue. I don't say that it's nonsense; I don't say that she *could* swim if she wanted to, that the barrier is in her mind, and in her family's mind.

Maybe that makes me complicit with the caging of Mimi, but we all know that fear is contagious. Still, even with great difficulties, what stops her from leaving? Fulvio?

'What about your fiancé? Would he come with you, if you left Galatea?' There's a heartbeat of silence as the pink on her cheeks deepens.

'Never. He wouldn't leave the island. Since his older sister passed away, he's all his parents have left. If he went, it would break their hearts. Also, he's happy here. He never thinks of the world outside. We've been paired since we were children. My place is with him.'

They've been *paired*? What a strange word to use. 'Are you... in love with him?'

'What is love?' is her answer.

I think of the intense joy, almost ecstasy I used to feel every time I was with *him* – the man who betrayed me. The passion I felt, how my feelings overcame all caution and ended up burning me alive. Yes, what is love? It's different for every person, for every relationship. And yet, I'd like to think that if I ever get engaged and someone asks me if I'm in love with my fiancé, there would be no hesitation in answering, *Yes, yes, with all my heart.*

'Fulvio is a kind, handsome, hard-working man who will provide for our family. Other girls envy me for being betrothed to him. Everything I know and believe in places me at his side.'

There's a slight edge to Mimi's voice. It's time to change the topic of conversation. 'Are you up for your English lesson?' I say, getting up and sweeping the sand off my dress.

'Of course!' she says, in English. I'm amazed at how easily it comes to her. And how once in a while she bursts into Russian sentences, thanks to Countess Alyova's teaching. Sometimes, as I lie in her bed at night, I wonder where she is now, and why she disappeared so suddenly.

We make our way back up the winding road, slowly in my case, with my muscles still trying to regain their strength, while Mimi moves like a doe. I rest my hand on my hat, so that the sudden breeze won't rip it off me and send it flying down to the sea.

'Do you know where Countess Alyova went, when she left here?'

Mimi freezes. She's too transparent for me not to notice that she's looking for a suitable answer. 'I don't know. Maybe your father knows, maybe she told him when she sold the house to him?' Her body feels rigid against mine. Mine was an innocent question – but after the way Mimi reacted, I do wonder about Countess Alyova's reasons even more. And whether Mimi knows things she doesn't want to share. Or can't.

'No, my father knows nothing... Oh, look!' I see that more boats have moored, and just beside the pier, on the beach, there's a certain hustle and bustle that's unusual for Galatea. 'What's happening? I've never seen so many boats arriving at the same time.'

'Did I not tell you? We'll have a little island celebration tomorrow night. To mark the end of the summer. There'll be stalls and music and the Fantasima...'

'What is that?'

'You'll have to wait and see!' she says with a smile – after our heavy conversation, she's brightened up, and it's lovely to see. I mirror her smile: I'm so curious now. I'm not sure what she's talking about, but – a celebration!

It's the old Mira who replies: 'Count me in. What shall we wear?'

❦ 7 ❦

GOODBYE SUMMER

MIRA

Half of the contents of my wardrobe are scattered around the room, but it was worth it. We found the perfect outfits, and I'm giddy with excitement. After long negotiations, I decided on my long plum-coloured dress, while Mimi is borrowing a short, light green silk one that makes her look a little like a mermaid. I plan to give it to her as a present − she'll protest, I know, but it's so perfect for her, she has to have it. I decided against wearing the diamond tiara my father gave me for my eighteenth birthday: I'll wait for the perfect occasion.

On the beach, rows of stalls have mushroomed everywhere; every inch of stony ground and up the path towards the hamlet is full of people. Boxes of ice keep ice cream cups cold, the scent of fried fish fills the air, and every man and boy seems to be holding a glass of wine. Women here don't appear to drink − I buck the trend, of course. Almost everyone is wearing traditional dress: women wear a silk handkerchief to cover their hair, white shirts and black skirts with aprons embroidered in bright colours, while men sport the knee-length black trousers and bright sash typical of local fishermen. The colour of the sash represents their island home: Galatea is red, Ericusa is green.

Mimi told me Giovanna's heart was set on her granddaughter wearing the traditional dress too, but she wanted to be *modern*. And modern she looks, turning heads under Fulvio's watchful gaze. We are overdressed – but who cares?

I'm here without a companion, but Mimi and Fulvio are with me and I don't feel alone, even if I'm not Fulvio's favourite person. The music and voices whirl around me. Lights dot the beach in a long row, where before there was only darkness. The houses up and down the island are lit up too, and Galatea itself seems wrapped in strings of twinkling lights. I've left the electric lights on at Villa Onda, to add to the festive atmosphere; and from down here, it looks a little like a star on a Christmas tree. And then, we're called to the beach – the Fantasima is there. It's like a dream, too strange and surreal to make sense of it. The shape of the Fantasima, a hollow pod in the shape of a woman, made with branches and hay, awaits on the sand.

'Mimi – what are those things tied to the... Fantasima?' I struggle a little to pronounce the word.

'*Petardi*,' she says.

I don't know the meaning of the word. 'What does that mean?'

She makes a gesture and a sound that mimic an explosion – firecrackers? 'Oh,' I manage, just as a different kind of music starts – a cacophony of drums and bells – and a line of dancing men and women dressed in traditional clothes, each carrying an unlit candle, make their way around the Fantasima.

A bonfire burns against the darkness and my heart starts beating hard. One of the female dancers breaks formation – she's thin and wiry, and twirls and whirls like a butterfly, her white dress and her hair flying around her. She enters the Fantasima pod and comes to a halt, her expression solemn. The dancers surround the bonfire and light their candles. One of them brings the fire to the Fantasima, and lights the girl's candle with it.

I can hear the sound of my own breath and heart even over the din of drums and bells – I find and hold Mimi's hand, and she squeezes it. Then everything falls silent as the girl stands inside the Fantasima, her candle dancing. In the deep, deep silence she lights the firecrackers one by one. As the first firecrackers go off, I want to shout to her to get out of there, to stop this madness, but in a liquid, almost unhurried movement, the girl jumps out: she's safe. The music starts again as the offering goes up in flames and the firecrackers explode into life. The Fantasima burns and the dancers whirl around, now with a sense of relief, all the tension gone – until the simulacrum collapses onto itself and falls into the water. Fire and light shine though the waves and then disappear, leaving only blackened twigs behind.

Summer is gone.

I take a deep breath and let go of Mimi's hand. I don't know where he came from, but all of a sudden Lupo appears at my shoulder. 'It gets me every year, you know? I've watched this since I was a little boy, and it never fails to move me.'

'It was... something, for sure! I thought that girl was going to catch alight.'

'Timing is everything. And being sure on your feet. Anyway, would you like some *zucchero filato*?'

I'm not sure what the words mean, but before I can reply he points to a candyfloss stand, with a dark-skinned, smiling man all dressed in white turning his steel cauldron with a pedal. 'I haven't had candyfloss since I was a child!' I say, as I take the gluey stick from the man. *It tastes of youthful dreams*, I think as I sink my lips into the sweet cloud, tingeing the sugar red with my lipstick.

Mimi is behind me holding some candyfloss too, with Fulvio's arm possessively around her waist – and then, after exchanging a few words with Lupo, they're gone. We stroll beyond the musicians and the stalls, and everyone seems to have disappeared. All of a sudden we're a hundred yards away from the party, far enough to feel alone, but close enough to still hear music. The moment I realise I'm alone with Lupo, I try to get back to the lights and the people and safety, but he takes me gently by the hand. 'Stay a moment, Mira.'

'I need to get back.' Suddenly Villa Onda, shining bright at the top of the island, is a refuge to run to, instead of a place of exile.

'Will you give me a moment to speak to you? Just a moment?'

Oh no. 'Lupo, please, don't—'

But he raises a hand – not in a commanding way, but a

pleading one. I stay silent, and a gust of wind seems to try and rip the dress from my legs. Waves break just behind us, drowning out every other sound. And then, the wind and waves grow calm again, and Lupo speaks.

'Since you've come to the island, I don't know why, but I can't get you out of my head. I know it's silly, and I'm usually more rational than this, but...'

Blood rushes to my head, and the rage that I usually keep buried deep down – if I didn't, it would burn me up – explodes inside me. I can't believe this man's audacity. I appreciate his support and friendship, and his help when Sally got hurt – but he has a wife and child. I lose all respect for him in a heartbeat. Are all men like this?

I take a step away from him, balancing perilously on the rocks, slippery with seaweed. 'Oh, I see. You think of me more than you think of Maria?'

Even in the dim light, I read confusion on his face. 'Maria... which one? There are about ten Marias on the island. Which one should I be thinking of?'

'It's not funny.' I try to walk away but he takes me by the arm, suddenly serious.

'Look, I made you uncomfortable, I'm sorry. I won't overstep the mark again, I promise you. But please don't play games – tell me what you meant. I deserve to know.'

'Me, playing games? The one playing games here is you! And I'm not going through that again, do you understand?'

'Through what again? Mira—'

'Go home to your wife and leave me alone!'

I jerk my arm away and take another step back. My foot slips on seaweed; I see the rock coming at me, anticipate the pain – but it never comes. For the second time, after he caught me on the pier, Lupo catches me before I fall.

'Be careful!' he says, and then: 'Wife?' It seems like he's spoken all three words at the same time.

'Maria. Not to mention your baby.' I'm panting and holding on to him, still unsteady, but I untangle myself, not caring if I fall face first. I can't have this man's hands on me for a second longer.

'I'm not married – oh!' He bursts into laughter, which makes me half angry, half bemused. 'You mean *Maria*? The one who just had a baby daughter? Mira, I helped her give birth. She had a difficult labour, so I kept an eye on her for a while.'

I was silenced.

'Where did this come from? I'm a doctor. I look after people. Maria is one of them. I don't understand how you could think—'

'Because you said... you were in my room the day I arrived, you—'

'Oh! I remember now,' he finished for me. 'When I was fixing the chandelier in your room, I said I was busy with Maria and the baby. I was talking about a patient, not a... a wife! And I can assure you little Assunta, her lovely baby daughter, is not mine! In fact, she's the spitting image of Antonio, minus the moustache, thankfully for her.'

I'm too astonished to speak, let alone laugh at his joke. I can't believe I made such a monumental mistake.

'Mira, listen.' Lupo takes me by the shoulders and fixes his eyes on mine. He's grown serious again, solemn. I sense that he's about to open his heart. 'I would never do something like that. If I had a wife, I would shower her with love. Believe me.'

Before I know it, my eyes fill with tears – tears of regret for the trusting girl I used to be and for the fearful woman I've become, ready to assume the worse, ready to believe betrayal is always around the corner. It shouldn't be this way. 'I do. I do believe you.'

He looks at me as though I'm a closed door, and he's searching for the key. 'You might believe me – an island so small doesn't leave much room for secrets – but you certainly have an exceptionally low opinion of me, to think I would have pursued you in such a predicament.'

'I...' That's all I manage to say. Words fail me – there's too much to tell, too much to explain.

'Wait. Come,' he says, and takes me by the hand, leading me away from the lit-up beach and into the silence and semi-darkness of the dunes. We sit on the sand – it's still warm from the day's sunshine, while the wind is blowing chilly on us. Mimi will be looking for me; I'll give her a fright, disappearing like this. I know I shouldn't be here. And yet, what has been in the dark for so long yearns to come to light – it feels almost obvious that I should speak to Lupo now, and yet it's so hard to put my shame and pain into words.

'Something happened to me,' I say, dragging the words out, one by one. The same way that ripping a weed you dig out its roots, ripping these words out of me unearths emotions I would rather forget.

'I guessed that. If you want to confide in me...'

The black sky above us, embroidered with millions of stars, turns into the bright, icy sky of the day I met *him*. The wind blowing through the thin fabric of my dress reminds me of how cold that day was, how frost had covered every garden and park in London.

'I fell in love. I mean, for real. For the first time. I was starved...'

'What do you mean, you were starved?'

I smile a bitter smile. 'It's difficult to explain. You'd need to meet my family to understand.'

'I see.' He speaks slowly, carefully. He senses how difficult it is for me to talk about this.

'It's the curse of the unloved, I suppose, to fall head over heels without a second thought. But no, you know what, Lupo? There were no alarm bells, not even for someone as naive as I was. He was one of us. Part of our social circle, where only the wealthy and respectable could belong. He was wealthy indeed, not that I cared; but he wasn't respectable.'

'Nobody warned you?'

'Nobody knew about us. And I wouldn't have listened anyway. I was too besotted to care about any advice I might have been given. I wouldn't have heeded any warning. For almost a year I lived to speak to him, to see him. It didn't matter any more that my mother never wanted me, or my father never cared for me, because *he* did. He cared. He loved me, like nobody did before. Isn't it pathetic?'

'No. Love is not pathetic,' he simply says. 'But why keep it a secret?'

'He was a lot older than me, and he wanted to start a political career. He said that being with a woman so young might attract criticism. But none of that would matter once he was established, that people would come round.'

Lupo snorts and shakes his head.

'Yes, I laugh at myself too. For believing it.'

'I wasn't laughing at you. It's that it sounds so ridiculous, this excuse he gave you.'

'I know. I could kick myself now. But at the time, I believed everything he said. None of it was true. It wasn't about becoming a politician, or my age. It was all because...' I swallow, bile rising in my throat.

No. I haven't forgiven.

'Well, he had a wife, in France. And a baby son. I know, I know I've been an idiot.' I cover my face with my hands, as the moment I discovered the truth comes flooding back to me, as painful as it had been back then. And I'm even more disappointed in myself, as I realise that the pain, the consternation, the betrayal, are still there, still raw.

'You haven't been an idiot. You were in love, and you believed him. You believed *in* him. Oh, if he was here in front of me, now...' I'm surprised at the anger in his voice. He's always so calm and mellow.

'He was desperate for nobody to know. But word got round, of course. London is big, but our social circle is close-knit. Everyone knows everything of everyone. I have no idea how he managed to keep a wife and son secret. Very skilful, I suppose.'

'Maybe he'd done it before,' Lupo says, his voice vibrating with contempt. Just the idea of not having been the only one makes me ill. But it's possible that I might not have been the first. And most likely not the last.

'My mother said I deserved it, because I'd been a fool. My father was furious – our family's good name, you know. My mother's friends act all modern and liberated, but it's just a facade.'

'No, you did not deserve this. Nobody would deserve this. And it wasn't you, tainting your family's good name! That man did it, not you!'

I hang my head. Every word he says is like a balm on my wounds.

'Mira, you're so young. A life is long, you will forget.'

I find it in myself to laugh. 'You sound like an old wise man.'

'I am a wise old man. I'm thirty-five.' I can imagine his smile in the gloom.

'I wish I could forget.'

'But you will! I promise you will.'

'What I told you, it's not the whole story, Lupo.'

He falls silent, and I brace myself to face the memories again.

'After a little while, I began feeling sick in the morning.' I hear him taking a breath. 'It was my maid at the time, Pat, who noticed the pattern. I knew nothing about pregnancies and babies, and my mother wasn't paying attention – but Pat had seen her own mother getting pregnant again and again; she knew the signs. I was horrified.'

The waves ebb and flow almost silently – or maybe it's me, not hearing them any more as I go deep inside myself and recall my heartbreak. I feel Lupo's hand brush mine, but I pull away. My skin burns, my nerves too tight to stand the contact. 'I tried to telephone him and tell him, even though I didn't want any more contact with him. I felt I owed it to him, that he needed to know. But he wouldn't take my calls. So, I wrote to him. He wrote back. He said... he said the baby wasn't his. He was sure of that, given my *reputation*.'

'Your what? But—'

'He was my first, and only. And I had no reputation to speak of. Until word got round that I was in a relationship with him, and that he was married. So now, I *did* have a certain reputation indeed.' A silent tear falls down my cheek, and I brush it away.

'The more you tell me, the more I want to kill the guy,' Lupo says quietly.

'I went to our house by the seaside,' I continue, trying to keep the tears out of my voice. 'I was planning to jump in the sea and end it all, but I just didn't have the courage to go through with it.

My parents took charge, and he – the baby's father – admitted that the child was his, agreed that he would compensate me, and that he would stay quiet, for his sake as well as mine. "How could you have been so stupid," my mother said. I didn't know how to answer that. How could I have been so stupid, indeed. Another girl wouldn't have mistaken some pleasure at the margins of a successful life for eternal love, an empty promise for a sacred bond. Would they?'

'Maybe not. But you were innocent. He was the one who failed you, not to mention his wife and son. He's the one to blame for all this, Mira. Not you.'

'I was innocent then, but not any more. He took that away from me.'

We are both silent as I ponder how true my statement is. And then, I find the strength to continue. 'It was given for granted that I would... see to the pregnancy. Sort it out. There would be no baby. It would all be fine, nobody would know. My chances of a good marriage would not be spoiled any further. Yes, everything would be fine, everything but me. Because I *wanted* that baby.' More tears spill down my cheeks. 'I refused to go along with the plan. I would not get rid of my baby.'

'I understand, of course. Where is he now? Or she?'

It seems to me that the stars change place, that the sea stops moving, suspended in an endless instant of grief. 'She's not here. She was born too soon.'

'Oh, Mira...'

Now, when his hand looks for mine, I don't resist. I let him take it, hold it tight. 'After that, I couldn't eat, I couldn't sleep, I couldn't get out of bed. Our doctor prescribed all those medications you saw, and after a little while, I couldn't do without them. I didn't *want* to go without them. They help me forget. I was already a... a failure in my parents' eyes. And now I was ill as well. So, end of story: I was shipped to Galatea... and here I am.'

'I'm so sorry. So sorry that you had to go through this.' He pulls me into his chest and cradles me as you would a child. I let myself soak in the tenderness. Lupo's embrace and the sound of the sea merge together, and I find peace... 'You'll find love again, Mira.'

'Love is an empty promise,' I say, my voice muffled in his chest.

'No, it isn't. I promise you.'

'You promise, but so did he.'

'Love is real. I know, because I felt it. I had it. I still feel it.' He takes a breath. 'I told you I'm not married. But I was. And in a way, I still am. Look, I still wear her ring.' He opens his shirt slightly and shows me a ring on a chain.

'You were married?'

'Yes. Her name was Fiorella. You've met her brother, Fulvio, Mimi's fiancé. She was my whole world. Like your daughter, she's not here any more. But what was between Fiorella and me, that was love. That's how I can assure you that love does exist.'

I'm left astounded. Mimi had mentioned that Fulvio's parents lost their eldest daughter. I'm so mortified. I feel a fool, a selfish fool, to have unburdened myself onto this grieving man. 'Lupo,' I murmur, but I don't know what else to say. I can only squeeze his hand harder, and cover it with my other hand. *I'm here for you*, I'm trying to tell him.

'I lost Fiorella, but before losing her, *she was here*. She was with me. We were here together, we loved each other. Love is true, and real, and I thank God every day for having found it.'

'Even if you lost it?' I whisper.

'But I didn't. She's still in my heart. She's in everything I do. I live every day the way I do because of her. I try to do the best I can because of her. I am who I am because of her. When she died, I wanted to go too. But what would have been the point? Tell me, Mira. What would have been the point of giving my life away?'

'If you couldn't bear the pain... but no, it would have been a waste.'

'Yes. And had I stayed home sipping laudanum?'

Oh. I thought we were talking about *him*, not me.

'I'm here tonight, am I not?'

'Then bring your heart here with the rest of you. Here, now.'

I shake my head. But then a part of me, the part that hasn't lost hope, responds. 'What do you suggest?' I say, and my voice sounds empty, much older than my years.

'Think of what good you can do in this world. Ask yourself why you get out of bed every day. Think of what your daughter could have done, had she lived, and do it in her stead.'

It was strange, intrusive, to go back to the din and the lights after our delicate, intimate conversation. I wanted to go home, and Lupo accompanied me up to the house, and away from the festivities.

'I don't want to leave you on your own.'

'Beatrice is here. I'll be fine,' I answer, even if I do feel a bit uneasy.

'See you tomorrow, then.' He gives me a soft kiss on the forehead – unexpected and tender – and I close my eyes and drink it in. Under Villa Onda's electric lights I watch Lupo disappear, and I shiver.

I know Beatrice is inside, but guarded by those strange statues, the house seems so big and full of shadows. I almost run through the hall and up the stairs to the safety of my room. Lupo's voice is in my ears, his calming presence still with me.

I'm tired in my body and in my mind, but it's too beautiful a night to sleep, and I'm too... awake. I lean on the windowsill looking out into the darkness, a sliver of moon hanging in the sky. A thin, wailing call comes from somewhere outside my window, somewhere close. I think I'm dreaming, but no: it's real. And yet, when I lean forward and the salty, warm wind caresses my face, the sound seems to drift further away, somewhere out to sea. I stand back, holding my breath – and then there it is again. Female voices rise and fall in a haunting song, one I've heard before. Of course! It's the same song Mimi, Giovanna and the Galatea women sang for me when I first arrived. Suddenly, nothing matters to me but finding out where they are. An irresistible force pushes me back towards the window. I sit on the sill and swing my legs over the window using a strength that I thought was gone. I jump and my feet land on rock, and it takes a moment to steady myself. I look up to the endless sky, to find the moon is now shaded by a lone cloud, but the stars shine like silver sand, reflected in the dark expanse of the sea.

I follow the sound and step over rocks to the edge of the cliff and, when there's nowhere left to go, I crouch, holding on to the crumbly stones and praying they will not give way under me, taking me down to the sea with them. Waves break on the rocks below, their white foamy edges ebbing and flowing with each thrust. The rocks are criss-crossed with white rivulets, like symbols in an ancient language. The women's voices rise higher, and make me want to push myself further and further, beyond the edge. Is there a way down? Either the sound is coming from the sea below, the women standing somewhere I cannot see, or from the inside of the cliff itself.

The sound is calling me. I can't climb down the rocky wall without falling to my death into the water below – the only way is to follow the path on the side, down to the small, secret beach through the garden, where Sally fell. I make my way there, almost running – and from the tip of the beach, where the sea meets the land, I can see a warm, golden glow coming from the inside of the cliff. My feet sink in the sand, but I'm almost there; I just have to make it through the water that has snaked onto the beach between us, me and the light and the song, barring the way. I stand, unsure – the song is calling, calling. I try the water with my foot and feel the current rushing in towards land, and then whooshing back trying to suck me out to sea, more powerful than I thought.

After all, the water will only come up to my calves – I think. I hope. I can't see very well in the feeble light of the moon and stars, even of the golden glow somewhere to my left. I step into the warm water gingerly, trying to stand strong against the current. It comes up to my calves, and then further – it's deeper than I thought, up to my knees, and then I sink further into the soft sand below until I'm up to my waist in saltwater. But I keep moving. Step after step I advance, guided by the song and the glow; I'm terrified now, but there's no going back. On the other side, black rocks jut out of the sand onto higher ground. I lift my body up, grimacing as my skin drags against the sharp edges. The water is tugging me down, and if I don't fight with all my strength, I will fall and be carried away. My shoes have sunk somewhere in the sand, and barefoot I feel stronger, steadier. Inch by inch I pull myself up, all my weight on my hands and arms; and then one knee and the other hit land. My dress is ripped, and the wind whips my bare legs.

I stagger towards the song, the sea on one side and the rocky wall on the other – until all of a sudden, it ceases. Silence enfolds me as I stop still, as if the song was what animated me. A young woman appears in front of me, as if out of thin air, her long dark hair blowing around her shoulders.

Mimi stretches her hand out to me.

'Come,' she says. 'We were waiting for you.'

The cove opens like a nest in the belly of the cliff. Giovanna and other women from the island, old and young, stand in a circle around a bonfire, some smiling at me, some serious. I know some of them, but now, in these strange surroundings, they look almost otherworldly. The flames dance red and orange with flashes of blue: they're burning driftwood. As surreal as the scene is, with this semicircle of silent women watching me, I'm not afraid.

Mimi leads me into the middle of the semicircle and I see threads of byssus, pieces of the woven fabric and whole artefacts sitting beside the fire in a basket – some untreated and still colourless, some shining like gold.

'Were you really waiting for me?' I ask Mimi.

Mimi doesn't answer; she simply smiles and looks to her grandmother. Giovanna takes a step forward.

'We come here to sing to the sea,' Giovanna says. 'The byssus women and our friends. The women of Galatea. We wanted you to be with us tonight, so we called to you.'

What does she mean by calling me? Was the song their way of summoning me? Because whatever it was, it was terribly powerful. I almost couldn't stop myself – I've walked barefoot on jagged rocks, I've stepped into powerful currents and risked being swept to sea, all to be here, my dress in tatters and my legs bare, drenched with seawater, my hands and feet cut and bleeding.

I long to ask how it is possible for them to sing in such a way – like whales or dolphins or some unknown sea creatures beckoning from the bottom of the sea. I have a million questions, but I can't quite speak. I can feel all their eyes on me, and all of a sudden, I'm overwhelmed.

Mimi takes me by the hand and the women begin to sing again, and I feel the vibrations in every muscle, every nerve, as it resonates through my body. And then the voices rise and the pitch gets higher, and it's as if my body is engulfed by a tidal wave; all my muscles relax at once, and I fall. I fall forever...

Mimi leaves the group to retrieve something from the basket – it's my bracelet. Still singing, she offers it to me once again. I give her my arm, and she ties it around my wrist. I know what this means: I'm one of them.

I'm a Galatea woman now.

❦ 8 ❧
THE GIFT

ANNIE

I jerked my eyes open and blinked in the bright sunlight. Immediately, my heart began to race – even before being fully conscious, I was already in the grip of panic.

It happened again.

In front of me was the face of someone I knew, someone from my own reality: I clung to it as if I'd been drowning, or floating away with the tide. 'Salvo!' My arms were around his neck and my face in his chest. I was shaking furiously, my eyes squeezed shut as hard as I could.

'Shhh... breathe. Breathe.'

'Where am I? Where are we?' There was something in my hand: a piece of fabric. The handkerchief I'd found in the cave.

'On the beach. See? You're safe. You're safe.' I allowed myself to open my eyes and look around me at the golden sand and the soft shoreline, the sea ebbing and flowing. The sun was warm on my skin. I sat up, my arms still entwined with Salvo's. 'What happened?' I asked, but I knew what had happened, and it scared me now even more than it did the first time.

'You tell me. We were talking, and all of a sudden you just... fainted, I suppose. Your eyes were closed but I could see they

were moving, and you were moving your lips as if you were talking. I carried you down the slope and into the sun.' Only now I
noticed that beneath his olive skin he was pale with fear, and his
hands were shaking.

'How long was I out for?'

'Just a few minutes, but believe me, it was long enough. I was
about to run up and get help. It couldn't have been heatstroke, or
sunstroke: I know the signs. Do you have any health problems?
Do you want me to take you to the doctor, or shall we go to the
hospital?'

'No, no. It's not my health. Oh, I'm so sorry I put you through
this. I'm so sorry I gave you a fright. Really, I'm fine.'

'Was it... emotion? Maybe the mood of the cave? Maybe you
were a little overwhelmed, and jetlagged, and it was all too much.
You need to hydrate and get some proper sleep.'

I doubted that water and sleep would make the visions go
away, but I agreed in order to avoid further explanation. 'Probably,
yes.' I rubbed my face with my hands. I desperately wanted to tell
him what I'd seen but he'd think I was crazy. Anybody sane would.

'I'm sorry, this barrage of questions...'

'No, no, it's not that.' I took the deepest breath I could and
leaned against the rockface.

'What is it, then? No, wait. It's none of my business, we barely
know each other – you don't have to confide in me. The right
question is, can I help in any way?'

I hesitated, and he sat beside me, his back to the rockface too,
looking out to the sea. 'Help with what? I don't need help. I just...
well, I guess I fainted. It happens.'

'It does, yes. But...' There was a moment of silence as he gathered his thoughts, his brow furrowed. The wind sighed among the
bushes growing on the dunes, like long-lost voices, and the sea
lapped the shore once, twice. And then he spoke with an intimacy
that belied the short time we'd known each other. 'You come here,
to Galatea of all places, from across the world. And you have this
mission, to find out about your dad's family, all alone. You fall
asleep on the floor, then you pass out up there... I don't know, I
can't quite put my finger on it, but it all seems a bit strange. And I

can't let you go through whatever you're going through without offering some he—'

'I've been seeing things!' I blurted out. What would he think of me now? I held my breath while the wind sighed among the bushes growing on the dunes.

'You... OK?'

'It's hard to explain. Impossible.' I sat up and tried to find the words.

'Try me.'

'When you found me sleeping on the floor, well, this will sound unbelievable, but... I opened the gramophone box, and I heard music.'

'The gramophone still works? I didn't hear anything.'

'That's the thing. I don't know if it works as such, because there was no record in it, the needle was up, but it played anyway. Like ghost music.' Oh, I didn't like that word. 'And I fell asleep and started dreaming. Except it wasn't a dream, it was a kind of vision. I was someone else. I saw life through her eyes.'

'Right.'

'You think I'm crazy.'

'Maybe. But interesting crazy. Tell me more.'

'I'm not sure that interesting crazy is better than boring crazy, but OK. I was Mira Goodman. I actually *was* her.' I looked up to the sky, then to the sea, and down to my hands – anywhere, as long as I could avoid Salvo's gaze. Could it be that the grief for my dad's death had taken such a toll on me, I'd lost my mind?

But when Salvo's eyes finally found mine, he looked serious and attentive.

He looked like he believed me.

And not just that.

He looked like he knew exactly what I was talking about.

Bella was waiting patiently for us at the top of the slope. We walked towards her slowly, following her into the rising heat of the morning.

'Are you saying they happen to Elvira? These... visions?'

'Yes. Here we call it the *dono*, the gift. They are premonitions; dreams that are more than dreams; knowing things that happened on the other side of the world and nobody ever told you. Elvira told me that in her time many women had it, and in her grand-mother's time, almost all of them. She told me of a woman she knew who saw her sister's death unfolding before her eyes, except her sister had emigrated to New York and she was in Galatea. When they phoned to tell her, she knew already, every single detail. It's like an open secret: everyone knows about it, but nobody puts it into words.'

'It's not just an Ayala thing, then?'

'No, it's a Galatea thing. But you need to ask Elvira, she knows more than me about this.'

'I will do that. And go through Mira's things properly. Salvo, maybe... maybe it's this island that's magical.'

'I think so, yes. I would have thought only islanders would have the *dono*, but apparently it works for tourists too.' He grinned. I was glad that he was making light of the whole thing – it helped lift the tension a little.

'I'm so relieved you believe me.'

'And I'm so relieved you didn't take ill or something. It was scary.'

'Salvo, the cave continued on. That's where the handkerchief was, inside that tunnel. If only I could go in and see—'

'Out of the question. Believe me, Annie. I told you, the sea comes in, and the whole place could come down. It's not some-thing to be done lightly. Certainly not without equipment.'

'But maybe it's another cave. As safe as the Mother's cave. Maybe it's a straightforward tunnel that keeps going to the other side of the island.'

'Maybe. Or maybe not. Can we run the risk? You're here on your own, I feel responsible for you. I won't let you go.'

'What? Are you telling me what to do?' I teased him.

'I'm saying I'd rather you left the island safe and well so you can spread the word about my beautiful Villa Onda!'

'Oh, I see, so you're just being nice to me as a marketing ploy. Good to know.'

'Having my first guest die would be very bad for business!' He laughed, and then his face turned serious again. 'Annie, if you *can* tell me, I'd love to know what you saw. Mira Goodman's story.'

'I will, I promise.' *But not yet. I didn't feel ready.* It was as if Mira's story had been entrusted to me like a precious secret. 'I want to know more. It might never come to me again, and I might never know what happened to my grandmother, and to Mimi.'

'Maybe we can make it happen. Maybe Elvira or my mother can help.'

We. I couldn't quite believe I had an ally in such a weird situation. It was so much easier to have someone to talk it through with. 'Salvo, you said maybe it's an island thing. Did it ever happen to you?'

'I'm a man. I don't get any of the gifts.' He laughed again. 'No diving or working the byssus; no gift; no vivid dreams or visions. Being a man is boring.'

I smiled. 'I couldn't have put it better myself.'

'Are you sure you're up to it?' Salvo's face was full of trepidation.

'Absolutely. I'm a million per cent sure.' *Not really. I'm so scared. But I'll do it anyway because I can't help it. These women's story has something to tell me, it's carrying me somewhere.*

We were in my room, cross-legged on the floor, the gramophone box between us. Through the window came the golden morning light and the song of the cicadas, and as always, the sound of the waves enveloped us.

'OK. What did you do, when it happened the first time? Did you just open the thing, and...' Salvo said, and went to touch the box: he hesitated, and his hands hovered over it without making contact.

'Yeah, I just opened it, and the music began to play. Like this.' I took hold of the lid and opened it carefully. I closed my eyes, and...

Nothing.

'Annie? Can you hear music?'

I opened one eye. 'No. Nothing. I'm going to try and concentrate.'

My eyes closed once again and I tried to think of Mira, until I felt utterly ridiculous. 'Are we really doing this? Am I really doing this?' I got up, frustrated. 'Come on, this is crazy. Simply crazy.'

Salvo stood too, and raised both his hands to soothe me. 'Have patience. Maybe it'll take some time, maybe you can't chase it.'

I sighed. 'I need to know about Mira. I promised my dad. I can't let him down.'

'You won't. I'll help you, it's a promise.'

'Why?'

'What do you mean, why?'

'Why will you help me? I'm a stranger. You've known me for like, two days, and you have enough on your hands with Villa Onda, and...' I said, making my way towards the room across the corridor.

'I don't need a reason. I just want to. I'm curious. You're intriguing.'

'Intriguing?' *Me? A plump, average-looking, boring American girl with zero life experience and no special qualities? Seriously?*

But then, why not? Why did I have to be so dismissive of myself – maybe a lifetime of putdowns, courtesy of my mother, had robbed me of confidence completely. All of a sudden, it struck me how similar Mira's mother – my great-grandmother – was to my own mother.

'*Sì, proprio tu*,' Salvo said and shrugged without looking at me. There was a touch of shyness in his expression, his body language. 'Don't make me say more. It's just fishing for compliments,' he teased me. 'Come then. Let's find Elvira and see what she has to say,' he said, and took my hand.

Elvira was in the kitchen, wearing an apron. Even while boiling jars and cutting piles of lemons she looked stylish in a khaki linen dress, small pendant earrings, her hair held back by tortoiseshell combs. Her big black eyes were rimmed with kohl, and the whole impression was that of an *ancient* face – Greek, Sumerian, Egyptian – an ancient Mediterranean face, one you would see in a mosaic or painted on an amphora.

When she saw us, she smiled and opened her arms – '*Annie, cara, siete andati a visitare l'isola?*'

It was frustrating not being able to communicate with Elvira directly, and it made me determined to practise Italian as much as I could. But those two words – *visitare* and *isola*, were clear enough. '*Sì, sì!*' I replied.

'*Vieni, cara. Mangia,*' she said, and pulled up a chair.

'She's going to offer you food. For a change.' Salvo smiled. 'You've never been fed properly until you've been fed by an Italian *nonna*.'

'*Grazie, grazie!*' I longed to be able to say more, but even before I could finish my *grazie*s, Elvira had placed a slice of thick, brown bread in front of me slathered in still-warm, fragrant lemon jam. A déjà vu: Mira had had this for breakfast the first day here, when she thought she couldn't eat.

Salvo and Elvira had a quick conversation I could not begin to understand. I was famished after all that climbing up and down cliffs and dunes, so I sank my teeth into the bread and savoured the sweet-sharp taste. Right at that moment, Elvira spoke to me. '*Dimmi, cara.*'

I looked at Salvo. 'I explained what happened to you, and she says ask her anything.'

'Did it ever happen to you, Elvira? Seeing the past?'

She shook her head, and I looked at Salvo while she explained. 'The gift has almost disappeared now. But even in her time, it was rare. She doesn't have it. She says the Ayala women in particular carried it, but others too. She's surprised that it happened to you.'

'I'm pretty surprised too. Can you ask her if she knows of any way I can, you know, bring it on? That I can cause it to happen?'

Salvo translated, and again she shook her head. Giovanna and Elvira seemed to melt into one in my mind, the two women sharing the same elongated eyes, the same black hair woven with grey, the same hands, strong and capable.

'However,' Salvo continued, 'she thinks it might be the bracelet. The bracelet belongs to Galatea.' He kept translating, waiting for Elvira to continue. 'And maybe that's why this is happening to you. Would you like to see her workshop? It's here at Villa Onda temporarily.'

'Oh, yes! I would love to!' I said enthusiastically, and my smile met Elvira's. She kept chatting as we walked down a corridor that ran parallel to the back of the house – room after room lay unused, furniture covered by the same spotless white sheets I'd seen in Mira's room. When it was finished, this place would be simply perfect – and Elvira and Salvo kept it so carefully, so lovingly.

'There was some damage to her old workshop, so she had to move up here. What we hope for is to open a small museum. One that shows the whole process, with photographs and vintage pieces donated by the island women, if they choose. But sadly, we're still far from making enough to get to that. I'm confident we will, though.'

The aroma of old things and long-closed spaces was giving way to the scent of lemon and spices, with a touch of... vinegar. *Yes, vinegar*, I thought, as my nose still worked hard to decipher the blend of smells. I followed Elvira into a room with open windows and the omnipresent song of the sea. Baskets of delicate byssus pieces, empty shells and linen embroidered with the golden thread lay everywhere. Some linen pieces were hanging from drift-wood on the walls, some were tidily folded. Dark bottles sat on a table in the corner – that was where the vinegar smell came from. Sun poured through the windows and made the byssus gleam. On the table were some mysterious wooden tools I didn't know the use of, and on the ground beside the window, flooded with natural light, was a wooden loom. It looked a bit like a string instrument, waiting to be played by expert hands. Inside the loom: a small linen piece Elvira was working on.

I brought my hands to my cheeks. 'Signora Elvira! *E' bellissimo!*' I managed to say in my limited Italian. 'Oh, look at this!' I rever-ently stroked the piece of embroidered linen with my fingers. *Imagine having such a skill.*

Elvira laid a hand on my arm and explained the process, accompanied by expansive gestures, almost acting it out. *Italians are so expressive*, I thought, and not for the first time since I arrived. Salvo was translating as she spoke. 'She dives herself, and handles the shellfish very, very carefully so it's not hurt. And then the thread is dried and spun and cured with her special mixture, and only then she can use it to make fabric or to embroider.'

'It sounds incredible. How I would love to do that,' I said – obviously being afraid of the water was a bit of an obstacle.

'She says she would love to teach you, but she can't. Only certain families are allowed to practise the skill.'

'So, who will be learning next?' I asked. What would it be like, I wondered, to dive deep, deep into the azure water, and hold my breath while my fingers worked the shellfish delicately? And then come up for air, and sit on the rocks with my skin covered in sea-salt, sunshine on my shoulders and a precious loot of byssus to alchemically transform into a thing of beauty. Whoever would learn all this was fortunate.

But sadness spread over Elvira's beautiful, dark face as she explained her predicament.

'She doesn't have a daughter to pass the knowledge on to. And the Ayala family has no descendants.'

'That is such a shame! Is it worth losing this precious skill because of an old tradition? Can she not teach someone else? Start a new family line, maybe?'

Salvo translated for me: Elvira was horrified, and was shaking her head emphatically. 'As you can probably guess, she says no. If she did it... Ah, *sì, capisco*,' he said towards Elvira. 'If she did it, the byssus would dry up, the shellfish would die. And it's already rare.'

I nodded, and thought of what the island girl, Mimi, had told Mira: that she wasn't allowed to dive because the sea wanted to take her. The islanders viewed the sea like a sort of creature – a god with its own will, its own demands. And Mira had hesitated to contradict her, because she worried about the consequences. It would have been rude, anyway, to belittle the tradition, as absurd as it seemed to me that such a wealth of knowledge would be lost.

'Can I watch you working, Signora Elvira?' I said, and Salvo translated for me.

'*Dovrai guadagnartelo*,' she said with a mischievous look on her face. I turned to Salvo for the translation.

'She said you'll have to earn it,' he explained with a smile.

'Oh. OK... but how?'

But Elvira smiled and said nothing.

We left Elvira in her sanctuary and she pointedly closed the door, in a soft but determined manner.

'Does she still dive?' I whispered to Salvo.

'Oh, yes.'

'Wow.' I looked at the closed door, and it seemed that should I open it, saltwater would come rushing out and flood us. Imagine diving into the sea, opening your eyes underwater and feeling the seabed for treasure. Handling it ever so carefully until your lungs were desperate for air, and you had to resurface, a tiny bundle of treasure in your hands. I could never do it.

Could I?

'What next?' Salvo said. He was looking at me for the next step, as if my quest was his too. By chance or by destiny – certainly not by design – I'd gained an ally.

As we stood in the gloomy corridor, I knew that beyond the wall was the dark side of the hill, and I wondered if the cave system was somewhere close to us, on the side or underneath our feet. Salvo wasn't to know, but I was determined to explore more; I had to see where that handkerchief had materialised from.

'Salvo, the handkerchief. It *must* have belonged to Mira – otherwise, why would I have had a vision by touching it?' I pondered for a second the fact that I was talking about having visions as if it was normal, and then recovered myself. These were the facts; this was happening. I might as well face it.

'But it can't have. I've been there many times, and I'm sure other people have too in the years between Mira's departure and now. Someone would have seen it. I would have seen it! I'm sure it wasn't there.' We were close, whispering like conspirators. I could feel the warmth of his body, his breath, as he spoke.

'It can't have materialised out of nothing.' I shivered. It was all getting a little too eerie for me. It seemed that not only was I somewhere else geographically, but somewhere *else* in a wider sense.

The two visions I'd had were like daydreams, powerful but soft, and in a way, innocuous. Objects that materialised out of nowhere were a lot more disturbing.

'This is giving me the creeps,' Salvo said cheerfully, and crossed his big arms in a way that was, I must admit, extremely attractive. In the middle of all that was happening, this man who looked like a Greek statue was being impossibly kind and thoughtful, and was standing remarkably close to me.

I swallowed. 'Me too.' As I spoke those words, I realised how spooked I was. I was torn between fear of the unknown, curiosity, and a strange sense of almost... possession. I had to know.

He took me by the shoulders. 'Look. Do you want to stop researching Mira Goodman's history? I won't take you to weird places any more. You can have a nice beach holiday, sunbathe, eat good food and have *aperitivi* on the terrace, OK? No more ghost-y vision-y stuff.'

I considered it. 'No. I owe it to my father to keep going. Also, I want to know more. For myself too. If all these strange things are happening, there must be a reason.'

'And what do you think the reason is?'

A silent communication passed between us. 'That she's trying to tell me what happened. Does it sound crazy?'

'I'd like to say that yes, it does, but right now...' He shook his head and lifted his arms in a gesture of confusion: it was such an Italian thing to do that I had to smile. 'So, what next?' he repeated.

'I'm going to go through Mira's things. And return her handkerchief.'

'I'll come with you. I don't want you to be on your own when it happens.'

'*If* it happens. And that is truly kind of you, but I'll be fine,' I said. I didn't want him to feel like he had to accompany me every step of the way.

Although I wanted him to.

'You don't want me, then?' There was a mischievous light in his eyes. He was teasing me again.

'Well, if you insist, you can come with me. I don't mind either way.'

My mother always said that flirting was demeaning. But I didn't feel demeaned, I felt... tingly.

'Well, if you *don't mind* either way...'

We ventured upstairs, my right hand in my jeans pocket, wrapped around the handkerchief. Once again, entering the room where Mira's things were kept made me want to whisper – as if she was still there, and we were somehow trespassing. The shutters were closed, and only a thin ray of sunshine seeped in. A soft, fresh shade enveloped the room and tiny particles of dust danced around the window. It felt like a sanctuary; at least, it did to me.

'I wonder if some of her clothes are still—' I began, and fell quiet when I opened the antique wardrobe and saw that it was full – hats and boxes on the top shelves, dresses and skirts and shirts hanging in the middle, and shoes on the bottom. Why, when she left the island, didn't she take these things with her? And nobody ever touched them, as if they were waiting there for her to return. I folded the handkerchief carefully and rested it on the top shelf, above the hanging clothes.

'I think your answer is yes,' Salvo said under his breath as I ran my fingers along the dresses, all hung in a row – silk, velvet, chiffon, a soft brown fur stole... I seemed to have inherited my penchant for impractical clothes from my grandmother. She must have been so sophisticated; the contents of her wardrobe spoke of wealth and beauty. The blue silk dress Mira wore when she arrived wasn't there, but my eye was caught by a dark shade of plum, almost purple. I slipped the hanger out to find it was a long dress with delicate frill sleeves, its skirt dotted with tiny purple diamantés.

'Oh, this is beautiful. Do you think it would look nice on me?' I asked Salvo shyly.

'I'll wait outside.'

'You don't need to. Just turn around.' I felt slightly unnerved at my own daring – was I really taking my clothes off with Salvo in the room? 'You can look now. Give me a hand?' I said, and turned to show him the unfastened back, holding the dress up on my chest.

He got to work – I think the zipper was a little worn – and all I could think about was the feel of his fingers on my skin. Once done, I turned back, and in doing so I realised that the dress was ripped on the side – a long, vertical cut that went all the way down from thigh to ankle, its edges frayed. And the hem, too, was irregular, as though it'd been slashed, and stained too. What had happened to Mira while she was wearing it?

'*Sei bellissima*,' Salvo said in a low voice. I was about to thank him, and to twirl like a little girl in a fancy dress – but I didn't make it in time, because once again his hands were on my skin, on my arms, trying to hold me up. My last, confused thought was, *So, this worked* – and then I fell into darkness.

GAVRIEL

MIRA

The coffee cup leaves a round brown mark on the newspaper on top of the mail pile. I'm trying to ignore its screaming headlines. *I don't have to pay attention to all that, tucked away here where nobody knows I'm a Jew*, I say to myself. But a part of me is afraid of the war spilling over to Galatea, and I know that I'm turning a blind eye to the news out of pure dread. If I fold the paper in four and hide the front page – no, if I scrunch it up – I can make it all go away, at least for now. Why am I still getting the papers, anyway? I thought I'd cancelled my subscription when Sally left. From under the ruined black-and-white sheets peeks a letter with a British stamp. It's from my parents.

Dear Mira,

We hope this finds you well. We've been worried about the dire situation in Europe, and your brother's circumstances...

Oh. I'm in Mussolini's domain, and they're worried for my brother?

...thankfully, it has been confirmed that his asthma prevents him from being called to active duty. We've considered sending someone to get you and bring you home, but Gavriel has dissuaded us. He maintains you're probably safer there.

Probably? So my brother has convinced my parents not to come and get me. I don't know whether to be grateful – I don't want to leave Galatea – or quite anxious that the possibility of me not being safe here is being brought up. Because this way, it makes it real. I scan the rest of the letter, and see that there is a note from my brother scribbled as an addendum. I wonder why he hasn't written a proper letter himself. Usually, he's formal about these matters.

I do hope that the wine there is as good as they say! Don't worry about writing to me again. I might not get your missives at all, with the way things are at the moment. I shall see you soon, anyway.

G.

Bizarre. Even for my family's standards. Although he did say 'I'll see you soon'. Does that mean he'll come and visit? If so, why did he not say it clearly? A generic comment about the local wine... It's strange. And was he asking me not to write? Why? It feels a little like rejection, and as for his promise to come here, I don't quite believe it.

'More coffee, Miss Mira?' Mimi offers. She has blue shadows under her eyes, probably mirroring mine. Neither of us has slept much, what with the Fantasima feast and then the gathering in the cave. Just thinking about that experience makes me feel warm, as though my heart is bathed in golden light. I was never part of a community before, but the Galatea women have embraced me as one of their own. Little girls, young women, mothers, silver-haired grandmothers were there together, entwined: all stages of a woman's life were represented, and we all belonged together. I must have felt so alone before that, because it seems to me that an icicle has been removed from my heart – an icicle I didn't know was there. Who knew that being a woman could feel so... sacred.

'*Grazie.*' I lift my cup for her to fill, and she smiles as the bracelet she gave me gleams in the morning light. Wearing byssus makes me a Galatea woman: I'm a stranger no more. Never mind the storm unfolding in the big world outside.

A moving figure in the garden catches my eye, and my mouth stretches in a smile that happens all by itself, born of pure joy.

'Miss Mira, Dottor Martorana is here.' Beatrice appears from behind me to tell me something I know already. She's quiet and reserved, like a little mouse, but works like a Trojan. It's useful in a house like this, with so much work required that I must do my share too – my mother would be horrified seeing me lifting buckets of rainwater and dusting intricate decorations. As for me, I'm just delighted I have my strength back, and proud that I can do more than sit on the ottoman, stunned with laudanum, as I did for a whole year in London.

'Yes, thank you!' I say, and I barely have time to grab another cup and lift it for Mimi to fill, before Lupo arrived.

'Mira. Mimi,' he greets us with a nod, and I'm touched to see that he's a little self-conscious. But no more than I am. I'm flushed scarlet, and I hope he thinks it's the warmth of the rising sun and not the easy joy that fills me in seeing him, and a strange sense of embarrassment, almost *shame*, after having bared my heart to him the night before. When we step out together, I can see from the corner of my eye that Mimi is smiling.

My arm is under Lupo's as we stroll down to the hamlet. His touch feels more meaningful now, less formal. And sure enough, people turn their heads: the English girl and the doctor, walking arm in arm? I'm sure tongues will start wagging.

As for me, I don't ask anything of him, or of myself; all I know is that I told this man my story, and let it come into the light for the first time. He knows, he understands, and he's hurting too, for his own reasons. The pain of yesterday and the joy of today join us together as we saunter down the winding road, the sky growing smaller and the sea bigger with every bend. 'It's a beautiful day,' he says, and it seems to me that he's not just talking about the golden light on the water, or the leaves trembling in the breeze.

'Yes.' I can see the beach now, with its usual bustle of fishing boats, women working the nets and children carrying pails. But something catches my eye and throws me back to the morning paper.

'Look, Lupo.'

Two young islanders, dressed in khaki, are preparing to board a boat that will take them to the mainland. 'That's Giovanni Longo, and that one, the shorter one, is Calogero Arena. I've known them since we were children.' Lupo's face hasn't changed expression, and yet his tanned skin seems a shade paler all of a sudden. 'I'll go and visit their families later.'

Why did I throw that paper away? No point in pretending it's not happening: even here on Galatea, where the world seems far away and of little consequence, we can feel the ripples. Ripples turning into waves. Suddenly I realise that I'm holding Lupo's arm a little tighter.

'It's all coming closer, isn't it?' he says. 'Some of the islands are being used as stepping stones, I would say, between Africa and Italy. Military bases all around. Galatea is away from the main routes, thankfully. And yet, there they are, two of our young men.'

'Stepping stones for what, exactly?'

Lupo shrugs. 'Who knows if they tell us the truth.'

'I don't *want* to know.'

'We can leave it to them, Mira. The people in charge.' He smiles a trusting smile. 'They do their part, and we do ours.'

I think that what he's saying is just another way to scrunch up the newspaper. And yet, what else is there to do? The winds of war blow so much stronger than us, with their mysterious intents. I tremble as I ask the question that is playing on my mind. 'Have you been conscripted?'

'There is no conscription on Galatea. Only volunteers go, otherwise women and children wouldn't survive alone on the island. We need to fish, tend the land, gather the water. There simply wouldn't be enough hands left to look after everyone.' On

Lupo's face I see the cares of his ancestors. His hands, I've noticed before, are strong and rough, not white and delicate like mine, or those of a city doctor. The hands of a man who doesn't only heal, but wields a spade and an oar. 'Places like Galatea and Ericusa,' he continues, as the Sicilian names roll off his tongue like a song, 'we're always a rainfall away from dying of thirst, if we don't have boats ready to go and replenish the water supply from the mainland. We can't survive on fishing alone; we can't survive on the land alone: we need both. Women must take care of the babies and the elderly as well. If they take the men away, the women, children and old people would have to leave Galatea or starve.'

'I understand. I mean, I understand in theory, but in practice, I'd be among the ones who'd starve. I couldn't do the work that Mimi and Giovanna do.'

'Yes, you could,' he says, seriously. 'If you needed to, you would work the land and haul the water and do all that needs to be done.'

'I'm not strong enough, silly!'

'Because you don't have to be. If you had to, you'd become strong enough. You *are* strong enough.'

It feels good, to be called strong. Of all the things I see myself as, strong is not one of them, and Lupo's words give me confidence. They distract me from the sad scene on the beach – until a voice brings me back to reality.

'*Buongiorno, dottore, buongiorno, Signorina Mira!*' Palmiro is coming up the beach path, barefoot as always, the bottom of his trousers wet with seawater. 'Two men arrived on the island,' he says, accompanying his words with plenty of gestures.

'You mean, left the island?' I say.

'No. *Stranieri.* They just arrived. They need—'

I feel Lupo tensing beside me. 'Do they need help, Palmiro? Is there anything I can do?' he says immediately.

'Not you, *dottore*. They need Signorina Mira. They're asking for her.'

Someone asking for me? Who could ever— *Stranieri*; foreigners. It can't be...

'I'd better go,' I say, somewhere between fretting and expectant. *Bad news from home?*

I would run, if the high-heeled shoes I'm wearing and the steep path going down to the beach could reach some kind of agreement. Click-click-click go my heels on the stones, and then, finally, through the olive trees I gain a sliver of a view onto the pier. The young soldiers' boat is bobbing away, and left behind are fishermen selling their catch, women in long skirts with their bags made of woven grass, a child helping his father unload the boat, another sitting on the bare wood swinging his legs over the shining sea.

And then I see him: a tall, bulky individual, sweaty and blinking in the sunlight, his jacket over his arm and a hand up to protect his eyes from the sun. He looks as incongruous as I must have when I first arrived, and unmistakably foreign.

'Do you know him, Mira?' Lupo asks.

'I don't think so, but I do think he's English... oh!' I shade my eyes with my hand to see better – my wide-brimmed hat is not enough to protect me from the blinding light. Could it be? A second figure is making his way into view – a young man, small and slender. He's wearing a fedora, impeccable linen trousers and a white shirt with its sleeves rolled up.

I know that man; I know the way he stands: relaxed, unconcerned, and somehow in control, as if he himself had chosen – no, *created* – his own circumstances and he's master of them. Immaculately dressed, spotless as he always seems to be, even after mad nights with his friends, drinking sessions or, in this case, a sea voyage and scorching heat.

Yes, it's him. There, like a peacock among pigeons, stands my brother.

I send Beatrice to prepare two rooms for my brother and his guest – Mimi and Giovanna are down at the market – and while his friend is refreshing himself and resting, Gavriel joins me for a glass of sweet wine under the gazebo. In spite of my protestations, Lupo took his leave, after a courteous but, I sensed, slightly cold greeting to my brother. I guessed that after I'd told him what had happened to me, he would be at least mistrustful of any member of my family. I probably should be mistrustful. But Gavriel is Gavriel, as always, and his smile is sunshine to me, even when it seems that the sun itself can't shine any brighter. 'You are here! I'm not dreaming!'

'Did you not get my letter?'

'No, nothing!'

'Not surprised. Outside this... haven' – he looks around – 'the world is in chaos. Not that I concern myself with that.'

I'm keen to forget that remark – I don't want to know about the world outside, nor its chaos. And I, too, prefer not to concern myself with it. 'Oh, I'm so happy you came! I can't believe you—'

'Kept my promise?' He smirks, and leans back on the chair.

'Well, yes!'

'You underestimate me as usual, sister. I said I would come, and I did.' *As if you're a man to keep your promises*, I think but don't say. 'Also, Mother and Father aren't exactly delighted with you being here on your own.'

'Mmmm. It's not as though Sally made a difference to my safety, Gavriel.'

'You know them. They don't make sense, much of the time.'

I look down. I don't want to remember how life was in London. I'm in the process of leaving it behind, like a snake shedding the skin she's outgrown. 'So... your friend. Julian. Is he here for a holiday? He's very welcome, of course!' I hasten to add, though it isn't completely true. I want Gavriel for myself, at least for a little while.

'A holiday, yes. But he won't stay for long. He's moving on soon. Keep travelling, you know. He's gone for a walk, now, by the way. He never rests.'

'Strange times to go travelling through Europe, especially after what you said... and I'm surprised he wanted to go for a walk, after all the heat and sun you must have endured travelling here.'

'I know! The shade and wine are wonderful, Mira. I thank you for your hospitality.' *Mmmm. Quick change of subject.* Gavriel's friends are of two breeds: kind souls under his thumb, or rare types that can stand up to him. I wonder which Julian is. 'He's quite adventurous, I think we can fairly say. Oh, there he is. Hello!'

Sure enough, Julian is standing in between the flapping sheets that shade us, with a smile so helpless and innocent, and bumbling words of thanks which make me immediately label him as the first type: a kind soul. 'Let me introduce you properly. Julian Kilby, this is my lovely sister.'

I didn't have time to look at my brother's guest properly on our way up from the beach – I was too excited to see Gavriel – and now here he is, this friend I've never heard of before. Sweat on his brow under his hat, rumpled clothes, the smell of sweat and alcohol seeping off his skin. I'm a little perplexed – Beatrice prepared a bath for him, and he *did* have a bag with him – in fact, he must have carried it around on his walk, because it was under his arm. Surely it contained a change of clothes as well?

'How do you do,' I say and offer my hand – his smile is endearing, his sweaty palm not so much.

'How very nice of you to have me.'

'It's a pleasure, of course.' I return the smile and yet, when I look into his eyes I see a blankness I did not expect. A kind of void. We study each other, and it's like gazing into a dark well. I can read nothing.

Ah, he must be tired, and not used to the heat, and here I am staring at him.

'Care for some wine?' I break the silence. I do think he probably had enough to drink during the journey, judging from the aroma, but I offer anyway.

'Many thanks, I would love some. You know, when I spotted this house and recommended it to Gavriel...' he begins, while I pour the sweet, fruity Galatean wine into his glass. *He* suggested buying this house? This man I didn't know existed? And he talked about it with Gavriel, not my father?

'I beg your pardon?'

'Mira, need a refill?' Gavriel jumps in. *Too* quickly.

'You suggested to our father that he should buy Villa Onda, Gavriel? I didn't know that. I thought he—'

'I brought you tea. A lot of tea. I thought you probably wouldn't be able to find proper English tea here.'

'Good grief, the tea abroad is woeful!' Julian rolls his eyes. I don't think tea is his drink of choice.

'Thank you. So, Julian, it was you who got word of Villa Onda being on sale, then—' But I can't finish the sentence, because Mimi is making her way across the terrace. She's like a doe, with her slender figure and lively step, and the strange pink hue in her black hair and eyes that more than ever seem enormous. I'm not looking at her with my own eyes, I realise, but with my brother's.

'Miss Mira, I'm back! Lunch will be—' She stops at once when she sees my guests. Knowing Gavriel as well as I do, my stomach churns.

'Mimi, this is my brother, Gavriel. This is Mimi. She helps with the house. She's a friend.'

She's *my friend*. And yet, what can I do if Gavriel throws her a glance like a cat looking at a bird? A glance that makes the bird long to be eaten.

'How do you do,' Gavriel says, and once again I am amazed at how much warmth he can inject into a word. You'd have to know him well, very well, to realise how quickly he assesses people and decides if they are of any use to him.

I love him; I'm just not sure if I always like him.

'Lunch is almost ready,' Mimi says, and her voice sounds a little smaller. She stares at Gavriel with wide, innocent eyes, as though she's seen something enchanting and absolutely perfect.

'Thank you.'

'Thank you, Mimi,' my brother echoes. 'And how lovely to have someone local to show us around. If you have time, of course?'

Mimi looks at me, and Gavriel's question remains unanswered.

We have lunch on the terrace, with Beatrice and Giovanna serving us and Mimi sitting with us, as she always does. Julian is drowning us in words without really saying anything of substance, and I notice that Gavriel is now trying to inch the bottle away from him.

'Your English is incredible, Mimi,' Gavriel says. 'And how quickly you learn!'

Mimi is pleased, but coy. 'Really? I think I sound strange.'

'No, you don't. The strange thing is that you *don't* sound foreign. You have our accent perfectly!'

'I parrot.' She laughs, and her hands go up to mimic a beak opening and closing – she's so childlike and so unknowingly seductive. I wish Lupo was here. I wish Fulvio would come and take her away. The joy I felt at my brother's arrival is slowly abating, the more I see him and Mimi together.

'*Tutto buono, signorina, sì?*' Giovanna asks, having spoiled us with a fragrant dish of meat and vegetables and bright spices.

Giovanna's face lit up initially, when she'd seen guests arrive – more people to cook for and look after, I suppose – but it has darkened now. And I know why. She brings a tray of dessert, and with it a warning. 'Mimi. Come, I need you.' Mimi follows her obediently. She seems to be the only person here who doesn't detect what's happening.

Oh, and Julian, who seems unaware of everything but himself, gives some excuse and wanders off to *explore*, he says, and disappears, tipsy and red in the face. This is the hottest part of the day, and I think it unwise for him to go for a walk, but he's gone before I can summon a warning.

'Well. It seems that everyone has dissolved into thin air,' Gavriel says, his words accompanied by another sip of wine. A whistle comes from above us – a lanner falcon is calling.

'I'll go and refresh myself too.' I leave him with an embrace, because he is my family, and he's here. He reciprocates it, and holds me a little tighter than he used to.

There's danger in the air, and I don't know where it's coming from – but I feel it, just as I feel the soft touch of my byssus bracelet on my wrist as I walk out of the gazebo and inside.

. . .

I don't know how it happened, but when I resurface from my afternoon rest, I find Gavriel and Mimi in the garden. She's barefoot and laughing, the hem of her dress wet and white with seawater and salt.

'Gavriel.' My voice resounds hard and strong through the garden, maybe harder than I intended it to be. The call of the lanner falcon echoes above us again — a sound of branches rearranging, as smaller birds stir and hide.

'Yes?' Huge, brown, innocent eyes with lashes long and thick — almost womanly. There's a flush in his golden complexion already.

'Mimi. I think Giovanna might be looking for you?' I bite my lip. My tone is that of her mistress, not of a friend, and I'm angry at myself. I'm angry at my brother, I'm suddenly angry at the world. I hear the call of the silver tray, as I think of how much a young girl deceived can suffer if she lets herself be prey. Mimi's eyes widen. I recall her lamenting her lack of freedom: am I now part of what keeps her bound?

She can't see I'm trying to protect her. I steel myself as she walks past me and inside the house, without a word. My brother is sitting on a low stone border, his legs extended in front of him, placid, unconcerned.

'*Sorella*,' he says theatrically. He recognises that I'm upset. And he's well aware of the reason why.

He pats the stone beside him, but I won't sit.

I stand in front of him and consider how anyone else would probably stand up too — but he remains in a seemingly subservient position. Because he knows he's not subservient, and never will be. 'Let her be.'

There's no need to specify who I'm talking about. His eyes become even wider, in a show of innocence that I don't believe in at all. 'Are you concerned?' he says, as if this idea is simply absurd.

'Of course I am! She's under my—'

'Or are you jealous?'

'Don't be silly. She's—'

'She's what?'

'She's my friend. Not just a servant. A friend.'

'You didn't speak to her as you'd speak to a friend.'

'I was not myself. When I saw you together...' There's no need to explain or excuse my behaviour. I take a breath. 'You must leave her alone. She's engaged, Gavriel. And yes, she is my friend.'

He's toying with me. There's no malice in his intention, just a refusal to take me seriously, or give up even an inch of his needs and desires. His eyes are mischievous. 'You're friends with a maid. Mother would have a fit.'

'Mother is not here.'

'And what about the good doctor? Is he a friend too?'

I bristle even more. 'He is, yes. Maybe more,' I add immediately – why hide it? I have nothing to be ashamed about. Not this time. I won't have shame taint what's not tainted, in the name of the past.

'Well, that's good. I'm happy for you, sister.' He gets up, his movements lazy and relaxed, and stretches himself. Only now do I notice that his trousers are rolled up, and he, too, is barefoot. I imagine him and Mimi together, stepping into shallow water while the sea laps them, and my dismay returns.

But Gavriel wraps his arm around my waist, and I can't bring myself to shake him off. We contemplate the view – the lushness of the garden, the black rock beyond and the glimmering sea. My fingers touch a late-blossoming lilac flower, and before I know it, I'm leaning into him. I'm the queen of contradictions, I suppose.

'Imagine finding love so far away,' he says. Something in his voice is so familiar, so intimate and Gavriel-like, that I melt a little more. 'Imagine,' he repeats, and this time he sounds forlorn. Not like my brother at all.

'I don't know if I've found love. Don't be so hasty. And please—'

'Yes, yes, don't worry. I won't cause *her* any trouble.'

There's no need to specify whom he's referring to. Can I believe him? I don't have time to consider this, because all of a sudden, in the distance, I see a figure standing quite perilously on a sea-rock – it's Julian. 'Gavriel – I'm not sure your friend is safe,' I say, and it occurs to me that I mean more than what I'm saying. The man gives me goosebumps. Is this sense of alarm instinct, or just paranoia?

'Oh, he'll be fine. Thick skin, and used to alcohol.'

'Mmmm. How do you know each other?'

He shrugs. 'He's a Cambridge boy too. We've known each other for a while. He has some business here, and—'

'Some business on Galatea?' I'm astonished. Gavriel is usually a better liar. This sounds practically impossible.

'Well, he's a journalist, and he works in the Foreign Office as well, and he's here to feel the pulse of the situation, you know, with Mussolini and the Allies and all that.' He waves his hand as though it's of secondary importance.

'He wants to feel the pulse of the situation, and he comes here? All that's happened on the island because of the war is two men leaving for the front and fewer provisions coming from the mainland. We don't even have a local *fascio* – you know, the fascist party division. Nobody is wearing a black shirt. Why on earth would he come here?'

'It's too hot for questions, o inquisitive sister of mine.' He's poised to move, but I won't let him off the hook, not yet.

'Gavriel, there's something he said that was quite surprising. He's the one who spotted this house? Not Father.'

He frees himself and takes a step towards the house – he grabs my hand and pulls me forward. 'Mira, what does it matter?'

I stay put. His tone – the underlying tension rare, almost unseen in someone as cool as my brother – alarms me once again. '*Why* is Julian here? Why are *you* here, Gavriel?'

To see you, I expect him to protest – but he remains silent, and this time, when he pulls me, I follow.

Shadows are gathering around Villa Onda. Lupo is here, thankfully. Maybe he can help me figure out if this disquiet I feel is my imagination or has its roots in reality. But I don't have time to speak to him in private, as everybody gathers in the dining room for dinner – a chilly breeze is blowing, and I asked Giovanna to serve our meal inside.

'Where's Julian?' I enquire.

Gavriel shrugs. 'Around. There's no need to wait for him. He'll do his own thing.'

'Sure. Well, it's your chance to get to know Lupo a little better.'

'It will be my pleasure.' Maybe his pleasure, but Lupo's not so much; his lips are set in a tight thin line.

And there's Mimi, of course, gazing at my brother when she thinks nobody is watching. Her demeanour is serious, almost solemn. As though she's suddenly older than her years.

I take in our motley group and a thought burns my mind at once: *There is more here than meets the eye.*

'Excuse me for one moment, please,' I say on impulse, and make my way upstairs, tiptoeing as if I weren't in my own home. Up the stairs and to the left, towards the corridor parallel to mine – towards Julian's room.

I step in as silently as I can, though every click of my heels on the tiles seems to echo all around the house. Julian seems to have slept on the covers, because the bed is crumpled but not unmade. Dirty clothes are scattered on the floor – at least it looks like he changed and the bag he arrived with, a shapeless tapestry thing that's unusual for a man to carry, is on the floor too, open. I kneel beside it.

I shouldn't be doing this. I should not be rummaging in my guest's luggage.

But I do it anyway.

With trembling hands, I take out the contents one by one – a pewter flask, a pair of scratched, battered glasses, a leather pouch sealed with a button. The buttonhole is narrow, so I have to try a few times until it finally yanks open and some scrunched-up papers fall out. In the same moment, I hear my name being called from downstairs, and I jump out of my skin. My hands are now shaking so much I can barely hold the pouch, but I steady them. I need to put everything away, but first… I catch a glimpse of some neatly folded papers underneath the scrunched-up ones.

Passports.

Plural.

With different names, but always the same photograph: Julian's.

'Mira!' It's my brother's voice this time, and once again I jump. I jam everything into the pouch and struggle again with the buttonhole, and finally I'm up and out of the room. I endeavour to keep a straight face and a steady smile as I join everyone at the table – but both Gavriel and Lupo study me. I think they guess there's something on my mind.

As for Julian, he joins us just as I walk in – our eyes meet, and he's not the flushed, drunk, blabbering jovial character he presented himself to be, but a sharp, cold and very much sober man. And his eyes pierce me, as if he knows what I've just done.

Julian.

If that is even his name.

❧ 10 ☙

A TENDER KISS

ANNIE

I opened my eyes into darkness, fearing that I'd gone blind. And then the world around me took shape again, and I was Annie once more. I looked for Salvo's eyes, and I anchored myself in them, using them like a beacon to return to this reality. *My reality.* But as soon as I recovered myself, I ached that the vision was over.

'I'm in the middle of her story! I must go back there, Salvo! I want to know! I need to know.' He held me close to him and I trembled – for the shock of the experience... and something else.

I was longing for Salvo, longing so hard and so intensely that I almost panicked. The attraction I felt for him was like gravity – irresistible. The power of the vision and this unexpected passion overwhelmed me, and I lost myself. No: I found myself again.

It'd been so long since I could be just a girl, without responsibilities, without worrying constantly for my father and trying to please my mother – did that ever even happen? Was I ever allowed to be just a young girl – did I ever allow *myself*?

Any man that came into my life since then had been blurred, not quite in focus – always secondary to all that I had going on in my family. And now that I'd cut the rope with my old life, I could pick up where I'd left off as a teenager – I could be the girl I was meant to be. All the desire and love and cravings I'd kept locked in my heart and my body came pouring out.

'Salvo...'

His lips were on mine, and neither of us could let go. And yet, he pushed me away, gently. 'You're vulnerable now, I don't want to...' he whispered.

I couldn't speak. I just nestled into him until I didn't know where I ended and he began.

It was the strangest feeling, to be with someone I'd known for such a short time, and yet it felt like I'd known him forever. His attempt to protect me might have been wise and generous, but it didn't work, because we fell into each other again. We kissed for what could have been a few seconds or a lifetime: and then it was all too much, too soon. I forced myself to pull away. Salvo let me go but kept his arms around me, as if to say, *Take your time, I'm here.*

We stayed like that for a while, in peace, as my body and mind relaxed after the surge of emotion. He was comfortable, I thought. He smelled of soap and lemon and the sea, and I nestled against him as if I'd been doing it my whole life.

'Her brother came to the island,' I said dreamily.

'Mira's?'

'Yes. I think he's no good. She thinks he's no good. But she loves him.'

'Mmmm. You know, I wish you'd fill me in. When – if you feel ready, I'd love to know what happens when you go there. In the past.' It was beyond words, something that I'd never thought I could experience. Something I never thought could happen in real life.

'Well,' I said, my voice muffled in his chest. 'Mira was so sweet. And unloved. Yes, she was unloved. She was sent here because of a scandal.' I was more comfortable in sharing my visions now, but at the same time, it felt a little like giving a friend's confidences away. 'And now her brother has arrived from London. She thinks he's bringing trouble with him.'

'Oh?' He waited, but I didn't elaborate. 'And?'

'And what shall we do now?' I laughed and freed myself.

'Oh, I see. I guess this piece of the story will have to do for me.' He smiled. 'Well, as for us, do you know what's happening in the village today?' he said with mock excitement.

'What?' I whispered, playing his game.

'Market day!'

'Is it?'

'Oh, yes. People come from all over the nineteen square kilometres of the island just to buy *fichi d'india* from my cousin.'

I laughed. 'Sounds amazing. Can I have some? Though I don't know what they are.'

'You can. And I'll throw in some freshly squeezed orange juice, from oranges that were on the trees just this morning. Let's go,' he said, and the taste of him was still on my lips.

The market was a cute little collection of stalls in the square outside the church, full of colours and scents and voices speaking in the local dialect. Men and women with dark skin and surprising blue and green eyes, bright against their complexions, bought and sold and wandered around, carrying grocery bags and produce boxes. In one corner was Ciro, the old fisherman, selling fish and seafood – some were still alive in boxes of water and ice, and I preferred not to look. The rainbow colour of another stand caught my eye – it sold beautiful scarves, painted with flowers and leaves.

'Local women used to wear them on their heads. It's part of the traditional costume,' Salvo explained. Of course! I remembered seeing them in my vision: what a surreal thought. 'Would you like one? *Te ne compriamo una, Rosalia!* We'll buy one*, he called towards the owner of the stall, a middle-aged woman dressed in modern clothes, but modelling one of the headscarves. It looked lovely on her dark hair: old-fashioned, but also timeless.

'*Che colore, signorina?*' Which colour... yellow like the broom that grew all around; dark blue like the sea; light blue from the sky; the austere black with red flowers; or the red itself, the symbol of Galatea.

'You choose,' I said to Salvo.

'Definitely light blue, the colour of your eyes,' he said. I was satisfied with the choice. Rosalia worked on my ponytail until it was a loose bun, and she covered it with the handkerchief, securing it with hairpins she kept in the pocket of her apron.

'*Bellissima*,' she said, and I revelled in the moment of joy and admiration. She noticed my bracelet shining, and she said something else, too quick for me to understand.

'She said you're a real island woman,' Salvo translated.

This made me smile even more.

Salvo took me to his cousin's fabled *fichi d'india* stall. They turned out to be juicy, sweet green fruits encased in thorny pods: cacti outside, sweet flesh inside. I couldn't help but notice two things about Salvo's cousin: first, that his fingers were so hard and calloused that he peeled and chopped the cactus in front of us without feeling the thorns, and second, that he kept smirking and looking from me to Salvo and back again. I suppose this was a small community, and if you saw a local man stepping out with a foreign girl...

We stood with a cup of cut *fichi d'india* and a spoon; the cups were made of ceramic and the spoons were steel, and once we'd finished, they were to be placed in a box beside the stall. He'd wash them all at the end of the market day, Salvo explained. 'This is so much more beautiful than those plastic ones that taste chemical on your lips and end up in landfill,' I said, holding up my cup, which had a little picture of a hen and a chip on the side.

'Agreed. Galatea has no landfill – rubbish has to be burnt, which is why we produce so little of it. We take great care.'

'I'll keep it in mind. Thank you for my scarf, I love it,' I said, tapping my silk-covered bun lightly.

'And I love how it looks on you,' he said, so earnest, his words as sincere as a child's. His compliments didn't make me squirm, but simply smile. 'Everyone is about to go for lunch and a siesta. Would you like to?'

'Would I like lunch, or a siesta?'

'Both, or either. I have to leave you — tons of work to do at Villa Onda.'

'I see. Well, I've just had a snack. So, I would say siesta.' In fact, now that I thought about it, I was sleepy. It was so hot, and the day had been so eventful — it would be nice to let myself lie between fresh sheets, and slip away for a bit.

It would be even nicer if Salvo were with me.

We danced an awkward dance at the bottom of the stairs, both of us tempted to go upstairs together, both of us aware that it was too soon.

'I'll tuck you in,' he said, and I thought: *Is this the corniest line?* But Salvo looked deadly serious, and he did just as he'd said: he tucked me in, brushed my hair away from my face and kissed my forehead with infinite tenderness. 'Rest up,' he said. 'And no more Mira visions, *va bene?*'

'*Va bene,*' I said, and closed my eyes as he touched my lips with his, ever so gently, and left the room.

I was grateful he didn't push for more.

All the warmth and sweetness and simmering desire made me want to stretch like a cat and feel my body unravel, the burden of loneliness laid down at last. I curled into myself, and wondered if this could be happiness — an elusive feeling I hadn't experienced since I was a little girl. For the first time in years, I was hopeful, and I looked forward to what would happen next, what surprises and discoveries awaited me.

Sleep came slowly — but when I closed my eyes, Mira returned to me. In a dream or a vision, who knows? All I knew was that once again, Annie was gone, and I was looking through my grand-mother's eyes.

❧ 11 ❧

INNOCENCE AND SEDUCTION

MIRA

'So, will you show me around, Mimi?' Gavriel asks over breakfast once again, and I quiver inside.

He looks at her as though he wants to eat her, and she looks back at him wide-eyed. Mimi's hunger for life beyond the island and my brother's disregard for anyone who's not himself: the perfect recipe for disaster.

'We will, of course,' I answer, but Gavriel keeps his eyes fixed on Mimi's. My coffee cup clangs on the plate, and for the first time in a long time I long for my medication. 'Is Julian not coming down?'

My brother's guest has been in a drunk stupor since he arrived, a strange mixture of charm and vacuity, as if his mind is somewhere else entirely. And yet, the way he looked at me after I'd discovered his fake papers – it was as if he *knew* what I'd done, and he didn't look tipsy at all.

'Oh, you know him by now. He's very independent. Don't get me wrong, he's grateful for your hospitality.' *No, actually. I don't know him at all, and maybe neither do you.* Does my brother know that Julian carries several passports with him, with several fake identities? What would I find if I looked through my brother's luggage?

'I'm sure.'

'Lupo? Will he be around?'

'Not today. He's working.' Is that relief I see on his face? I suppose I should not be surprised. Despite Gavriel's attempts to charm him, Lupo is impervious.

'Let's go!' Mimi calls cheerfully but hastily, and I realise why: Giovanna has appeared at the door, and she's about to call her. But Mimi is gone, the sun behind her, a halo of light that makes her look like a painting. I wonder where Fulvio is; even though he's been hostile to me from the time I arrived, I hope we bump into him. Or I might make a 'chance' encounter happen.

We spend the morning sightseeing, from the village to the marina to our gardens, and wherever we go my smartly dressed, handsome brother draws people's looks, as though the laird of the land has come to visit. He smiles and nods and waves as if he loves them all – and makes a point of stopping and looking at the fishermen working, as though what they do is of the utmost interest to him. They're flattered.

'I heard there's a cave system within the island. That the place is half hollow. Is it not?' he asks as we walk along the shore. It's a perfect day: not too warm, not cold, a soft breeze blowing in from the sea and the golden light of the Galatea autumn enveloping us. And yet: the way Mimi turns her head to look at Gavriel, the way he brushes her hip with his hand – how can I enjoy the beauty with this thorn in my side? At every turn, I hope to see Fulvio.

'Mira? I asked you about the caves?' I hesitate – I'm not sure I want to tell him about the caves, in case he somehow finds himself where the Galatea women gather. As far as I know, they don't talk about the cave at all, to shield it from strangers – so I don't know what to say. I translate the question for Mimi, who answers in English – she's come on leaps and bounds in her knowledge of English, in a way that is almost miraculous.

'Oh, yes. I can show you.'

'Giovanna will have our lunch ready, won't she?' I intervene.

'Well, we can—' Mimi begins, but Gavriel interrupts her.

'Let's not keep Giovanna waiting and delay her afternoon. I

say, why don't we eat and rest in the hottest part of the day, and we can regroup later?'

'Good idea. Maybe Lupo can come with us,' I offer. I hope so. More than ever, I need an ally to counteract this *fascination* Mimi is falling prey to. 'Or even Fulvio? He might want to meet your new friend.' Have I succeeded in sounding clean-handed?

Mimi's face falls, and all of a sudden I hate myself. No, these petty expedients won't do. I must speak to her clearly and honestly.

I take her by the arm as we walk back up the hill, and squeeze her – *I'm your friend, I'll always be on your side*, I'm trying to tell her. She smiles, but I can sense that she's uneasy.

Giovanna does have lunch ready for us, but greets us with a scowl. I've never seen her so cold, so quiet. She sends Beatrice to serve us, and then, as soon as we're finished, she calls Mimi to the kitchen.

'Please, Mimi, would you tell your lovely grandmother that her food is spectacular. In England we couldn't even dream of such a lunch.'

How naive. If Gavriel thinks he can charm Giovanna, he can think again. Mimi obeys, and Giovanna nods in silence. No smile ripples her lips. Gavriel is undeterred.

'Can you please ask her, if Mira agrees of course, to let you stay with us for a little longer? It would be such a shame if you missed out on a drink with us, before we retire for a rest.'

'*Vieni, Mimi.*' *Come, Mimi*, Giovanna says before Mimi can open her mouth. A flash of annoyance passes over my brother's face, so quick and subtle you'd have to know him well to notice it. And Mimi?

It's her expression that kills me.

She looks resentful, like I've never seen her before. Her lips are pursed and her eyes cold. Now I'm sure: this was our Eden, and Gavriel has come to offer Mimi the apple.

The heat has risen, and the whole island is in that little hollow between morning and afternoon – some sleeping, some resting in the shade, before the second part of the working day begins. Except, of course, that when we're all supposed to be sheltering from the heat in our rooms I'm unable to relax, so I take a book and some lemonade onto the terrace. I can't say I'm surprised when I see Mimi's slight figure making her way through the garden, followed by my brother. Mimi is barefoot and smiling; my brother's shirt is open.

I knew it would happen.

I long to see Lupo; and I must find Fulvio.

Finally, Lupo is here. I run down to meet him, feeling the first rush of pure, untainted joy since my brother arrived. Slightly crumpled after a day's work on the land, he's wearing rolled-up trousers and a loose shirt, and his hands have soil in their grooves. I'm about to throw my arms around his neck, when he takes me by the waist and studies my face.

'You seem troubled,' he says, and pulls me close.

The scent of the rhododendron bushes behind us is sweet and heady, and the cicadas sing a chorus around us. Autumn on Galatea is as warm as July in England, though the sky is a deeper blue now, and a cooler breeze blows across the island.

'I'm happy now, at this moment,' I answer, and it's certainly true. Lupo feels strong and safe, and any worries seem almost muted, like an out-of-focus photograph.

'So am I. But what I mean is, you don't seem happy about your brother being here. I know you said that your family are hard to handle, but—'

'It's complicated.'

'Sibling relationships are complicated.'

'Some more than others. He promised to come and see me, and he did – but I have this feeling he's not here simply to visit his sister. Maybe it's all in my head, I don't know. But that friend of his is so strange.'

'I saw him coming up – it had to be him. We were never introduced, but I'm fairly sure there aren't any other dishevelled, tipsy Englishmen on the island at the moment. It was pretty strange, now that I think about it. He was on a ledge beside the beach, inching sideways and trying not to fall. Where he was going, there are only cliffs. And a couple of caves. And then a boat appeared out of nowhere, and he started talking to the fishermen inside.'

'He doesn't speak Italian. And I doubt the fishermen speak English.'

'Well, they were communicating somehow. Now that I think about it, I'm not sure they were fishermen at all. The boat was tiny, and they had no nets with them... but they were dressed like our fishermen, red bands and all.' He's referring to the red bands the fishermen wear in the traditional costume.

'Did you know them?'

'It was too far to see their faces, but I didn't recognise them. Obviously, if they wore the red band they must be from here... Look, I'm sure your brother's friend is just a quiet kind of person with a penchant for drink, and—'

'He's not quiet. Actually, he rambles on and on and on. Almost like... like he wants to distract us.'

'You're writing a novel here, Mira.'

I pull away from Lupo and look him in the eye. 'Maybe. But I found something in Julian's room. Papers – as in, documents. With different names.'

Lupo's eyes widen, and he says nothing.

'How can you explain that?'

'I can't. But if your brother's friend is doing something illegal, well, you need to speak to him. He might get everyone into trouble. Yes, Galatea is tucked away, but it doesn't mean there are no checks, no police. And if Julian has stolen papers, or forged ones...'

I rub my face with my hands. 'My main worry right now is for Mimi. Gavriel is interested in her. *Extremely interested.* And when my brother has his sights on someone, he uses all his charm, and Mimi has no idea.'

Lupo frowns. 'He does know that Mimi is engaged.'

'That kind of thing is simply not an issue for him. He doesn't see the world that way.'

Lupo's expression is as hard and cold as Giovanna's was. It

seems that people in Galatea are not as easily charmed by my brother as most. 'Mimi is a grown woman. I'm sure she'll see through it. She has a good head on her shoulders.'

'She does, and she's no fool, I know that. But she's been confiding in me about... I know I shouldn't share a friend's confidences, but I care for her too much. Please promise this will stay between us.'

'Of course.'

'She told me she feels caged, that her engagement is weighing on her heart. That she'd like to see the world, and dive for byssus like the women of her family. She's not allowed, did you know that?'

'I did, yes. And I guessed she resented it. But I had no idea she resented her engagement. And I'm sure Fulvio doesn't either. Fulvio and I are close. He would have told me.'

'He didn't guess, even after Mimi put off the wedding twice?'

'He just thought she wanted to work for a bit longer, set some money aside. He wasn't happy about it, and I know he's been quite reserved with you, but he has no idea of the extent of her unhappiness. He has no idea she feels the way she told you, I'm sure of that.'

'What do you think we should do?'

'My opinion hasn't changed. As I said, Mimi is a grown woman, she'll make the decision for herself. If she's so unhappy, if she doesn't want to lock herself into marriage, then she should not be forced, by a betrothal or in any other way. Fulvio would be devastated, but he'd be even more devastated if he ended up married to a woman who never wanted to marry him in the first place.'

Funny, I ponder. Mimi told me that Fulvio used the same words – *grown woman* – as if that should immediately mean you're independent and allowed to make your own decisions. It seems to me that even the best, kindest and cleverest among men, like Lupo, can't fully grasp the web of obligations and expectations women are tied to, grown or not, whatever social classes they belong to. Grown woman does *not* mean free woman. A woman is almost never free.

'Lupo, you don't understand. That's not how it's going to unfold. My brother will make promises he won't keep, and she'll be left behind with a broken engagement and her reputation in tatters. He'll leave, and he won't take her with him. That, I can guarantee.'

'You're making a novel again! You're taking scattered threads and making a whole tapestry. Oh, there they are,' he whispers.

Mimi and Gavriel are passing through the archway from the beach to the garden, Mimi's hair tangled with salty wind, my brother with his shoes in one hand. Both are smiling: Mimi with joy, Gavriel with supreme confidence.

'Did you have a good time? Where have you been?' I try to keep the unease out of my voice and my expression, but I know that Mimi can sense it. She looks at me as if she's surprised and confused – as though my apprehension makes no sense to her. There's something in her eyes, something I've only seen once before – when she challenged Giovanna. Strength, and defiance. But not the serene, deep power I saw in her when she was singing with the Galatea women: this is a combative kind of strength, a me-against-the-world stance.

'We did indeed. We've been exploring the caves. How very fascinating. And how excellent to see you, doctor.'

I translate for Lupo, but there's no need, because the gesture of offering his hand is universally understood. Lupo's eyes are inquisitive, while Gavriel looks mellow, inoffensive; like someone who could not hurt a fly, even if he tried.

'Fulvio will worry, knowing you're climbing in and out of those caves,' I say to Mimi, in English.

She doesn't reply, and there is a moment of silence, immediately filled by my brother's charm. 'Mimi's English is incredible. She has a good teacher, and she's certainly a good pupil. You look so similar, and she imitates your accent so well. You could be mistaken for one another,' he says.

Mimi smiles at me, a silent question in her arched lips – *Are you proud of me?* – but her face empties as she acknowledges my disapproval.

'I saw your friend – Julian, isn't it? Walking along the cliff,' Lupo says in Italian, and I translate.

'Well, I'm not surprised. He likes talking to the locals wherever he goes. He meets people scandalously easy. Well, I'll go and refresh a little. Mimi and I are going to—'

'Mimi is needed here, Gavriel.'

'Mimi?' Gavriel gazes at her.

What did I say about choices, before? Mimi has no choice. She's my friend, but she's still my maid and my companion. 'I'll see you later,' she says softly.

A strange metaphor for something that happens on a sun-baked Mediterranean island, but it's like ice breaking, a single, long crack opening in a frozen lake and shattering the whole surface. Something has broken between Mimi and me, and I don't know if it can ever be repaired.

'Well, I'll take my leave then,' my brother says, and he seems amused. As though it's all a big game. They both leave, going their separate ways, and I'm left shaking and wondering what I should do. Should I do anything at all?

Lupo is right. It's Mimi having to make the decision, and I hope with all my heart and soul that she sees my brother for who he is. Because I know, as true as the sun shining above us, that he will not change for Mimi, or anyone else.

Days pass with long lunches, white nights, alcohol-drenched afternoons on the beach where my brother drinks wine and suns himself. And almost always, Mimi is with him. Does Fulvio know? I don't think so, not yet. But surely soon.

Nothing physical has happened between Gavriel and Mimi, I can tell – but we all know, we all see, that it's a betrayal of the heart, and that it won't be long before Fulvio and his family will get wind of it. Mimi looks like someone who's walking the line between heaven and hell – lost in the novelty, lost in my brother's eyes, and knowing that the time of reckoning will come.

Giovanna walks around with thunder clouds over her head. Nothing of what's happening has escaped her, of course, and one hot evening, while Gavriel is drinking limoncello on the terrace with Mimi sitting there, hanging off his every word, Giovanna takes my arm without paying heed to convention. She does so as if I were her own granddaughter.

'Miss Goodman, I am so very worried,' she says, and she doesn't need to tell me what about – but I ask anyway, to gauge how much she knows.

'What's wrong, Giovanna?'

'You know very well what's wrong,' she says, and I wince a little at being addressed so familiarly. 'She is *engaged*. What she's doing is wrong. It will destroy her, and us. Help her.'

'I'm trying, believe me! There's only so much we can do.'

'She has obligations! To Fulvio, to us. To herself. If her father were here he would lock her up in the house, and marry her off straight away!'

'Is that right, Giovanna? To hold someone against her will and force her to marry?' I'm almost shaking with anger. Yes, Giovanna and I agree that Mimi is making a mistake, but we certainly disagree on the solution.

'I always thought my granddaughter was an honourable woman.' I can't accept Giovanna speaking ill of Mimi. Her life had been set up for her since she was a child – of course she agreed to marry Fulvio, what else could she have done? Was there ever an alternative?

'Maybe she doesn't *want* that particular place that you and her family chose for her, have you thought of that?'

'Miss Goodman. We both know that if any of that is going on, your brother is not the answer. He's no good. I can see it in his eyes.' My stomach churns as I see she's tearing up. A loyal sister would defend her brother, but in good faith, I can't.

'I'll speak to her. And to Gavriel. I'll do my best.'

'Thank you, Miss Goodman,' she says, and holds my hands in hers. 'Please, don't let my granddaughter's life be destroyed.'

'But you can't ignore that she wants more. She wants to see the world.' For a second, Giovanna looks like a seabird – fixed, cold eyes. She loves Mimi, I know that. But she will never set her free: I know that too.

'*This* is her world.'

I'm lying in my bed when a strange noise captures my attention. Something is tapping against the window. I switch on my bedside lamp and pull the curtains aside: tiny drops of water are covering the glass. At first I wonder how the splashing of the waves could reach up here, and then I realise: the noise that seemed so strange to me is one I've grown up with, in faraway England. It's simply rain. How long has it been since I last saw rain? Another fan of raindrops splashes against the window, making a louder, whipping sound. I cup my hands around my eyes to see better; the rain is stronger now, falling hard and noisy on the volcanic ground. I open the window and a gust of wet wind engulfs me. Blades of lightning cut the sky and the sound of waves crashing on the shore, harder and harder, resounds both outside and below me. I wonder if the caves are now flooded, or will be soon.

My eye is caught by something moving against the outline of the lit-up sky – someone is wandering in the wind and rain, making their way across the hard black rocks. But who? I strain my eyes to see, and then, on impulse, I switch the lamp off – I don't want to be seen by whoever is there. Intermittent lightning illuminates the sky, and against its yellow-blue, ghostly glimmer, I can see make out two figures, a man and a woman. I can't see their faces, only their outlines: a long-haired woman and— No, I can't see anything more.

A terrible thought hits me.

I take hold of the first candle I can find and light it quickly – I don't want to switch the electric lights on and attract attention to myself. By the light of the trembling flame, I almost run to Mimi's room, stop in front of her door, take a breath. Quietly, very quietly, I open the door.

Her bed is unmade, a bundle of light blankets and pillows. And in the middle of that nest lies Mimi, asleep. Her dark hair is strewn around her, the shadow of her lashes on her cheek, resting on her hand. Her side rises and falls very, very slightly, with every breath.

The woman outside wasn't her.

When I return to my room, the call is irresistible: I pour myself a spoonful of oblivion for the first time in weeks, and try to blot out Lupo's reproachful face hovering in my mind.

ANNIE

I returned to this world with a jolt, my consciousness so full of images and words and sensations from long ago, from Mira's and Mimi's world, that I didn't quite know who or where I was. But as my brain cleared, a thought hit me with immense clarity: Salvo was busy, he'd said, and the sun was still a decent way from setting. It was the perfect time to sneak into the caves and go just where Salvo said I shouldn't go. Because I *had* to.

I slipped on my trainers and made my way to the terrace – I didn't dare go out through the main door. Half of me was here and now, tiptoeing like a thief towards a forbidden place, and half was back in time, with Mira, in her world. Every step I took on the stone, every inch of the balcony I leaned on, they had stepped on and touched. The way their story was evolving, the way this cast of characters were playing their parts towards a conclusion I didn't know, made me feel sure that there was a reason for those visions. There was something I needed to discover.

I was so surprised about the latest developments. After all her struggles, my grandmother seemed very much in love with Lupo – was *he* my grandfather? While her friend, Mimi, seemed in high water with Gavriel, my great-uncle. There was undeniably a cruel streak running in my family – something that my father somehow avoided. But then, he'd been raised away from them. As I passed a gilt-framed mirror in the hall, I saw my reflection: but the freckled, ash-blonde American girl had morphed into a dark-haired forties beauty, wearing a silk dress and dark plum lipstick. A gasp escaped my lips and I jumped backwards, knocking over some knick-knacks from a dresser behind me.

So much for stealth.

'Hey,' Salvo called, hearing the noise and appearing from somewhere behind me. He wore the tattered t-shirt and shorts he had on the day I arrived, and he was splattered with paint. A tuft of hair on his forehead was completely white. 'Are you OK?'

'I'm so sorry,' I said, and straightened the statuettes in disarray.

'What happened?'

I looked into the mirror, and instead of my reflection, I saw Mira. Like saying Bloody Mary three times, but make it forties glamour. 'I lost my balance.'

'You lost your balance? All by yourself?'

'Clumsy. Anyway, you have...' I touched my hair, and then my face.

'Yeah, I know. I'm kind of covered in paint. I'm trying to do as much as I can myself, but I think it'll take me *years* before everything is done. Did you sleep?'

'A little bit.' My chance of slipping out was gone. I was sure that if I told him I was just going for a walk, he would read the truth on my face.

'Would you mind coming to see Elvira a moment? She'd like to speak to you. Also, I could do with a drink,' he said, and turned towards the kitchen. I couldn't bring myself to say no and disappoint Elvira. Besides, to be honest, I was a bit shaky after what I saw in the mirror: maybe it was better to face one spooky thing per day.

'Me too, yes.' *A strong one.*

'Ugh. I think I have half the crumbing roof down my throat.'

'Salvo, are there no grants available? To restore this place?'

'The grant was swallowed up by structural work. But onwards

and upwards! We'll make it, even if I have to get Elvira up on the roof herself. I'm joking,' he added, seeing my shocked face. 'But you know what the worst part of this job is?'

'What?'

'The rows of monsters staring at me, ten centimetres from my face. Honestly. At one point, I thought one was going to reach over and lick my face.'

'You've inhaled too much paint, Salvo!'

'Says the woman who has visions.'

'Ha.'

I followed him into the kitchen, where Elvira was working her magic. Her hands were blessed, whether she was making byssus or food to nourish the people around her.

'*Eccoti! Ho una cosa per te*,' Elvira said, opening her arms. She was flawless as always, with subtle make-up and her hair pinned back in a tidy bun. She wore a linen dress with a silk scarf knotted around her hips, a style as uncommon as it was elegant. The scarf and the hoop earrings made her look exotic, as though she came from an ancient civilisation. She turned around, took something from the counter behind her, and handed it to me. It was a kind of utensil, made of – bone? Tied around it, a soft red ribbon.

'She says she has something for you,' Salvo translated unnecessarily.

'*Grazie.* What is it?'

A look passed between Elvira and Salvo, and Salvo smiled. 'I'll tell you in the garden, yes?'

'Oh, OK. *Grazie*, Elvira, *grazie!*' I said with a half-bow and felt slightly ridiculous – people don't bow in Italy, it was just to make up for the lack of words.

'*E ora vediamo di che stoffa sei fatta*,' Elvira called after me as we were already on the doorstep, Salvo holding a pitcher of lemonade and two glasses.

'What did that mean?'

'That now she'll see what you're made of.'

'What? Oh, can we sit here?' I asked. The bench under the rhododendron tree, where Mira and Lupo had spoken in my latest dream. I could almost see them.

'Sure. Ah, I needed this,' Lupo said, after downing a glass of sugary lemonade in long, greedy sips. He extended his legs in front of him, and once again I noticed how handsome he was. His southern looks were such that he could have been cast in a period drama set in Renaissance Italy. He looked like a young heir of the Medici family. 'This thing that Elvira gave you. It's a comb.'

'It doesn't look like— oh! Yes, I saw it in her workshop. She uses it to comb the byssus. But why—'

'Remember she said you'd have to earn the right to see her working? That is how you'll earn it.'

'By combing byssus? I thought I wasn't allowed.'

'You're not. I'll explain tomorrow. When we have plenty of time before it gets dark.'

'Doing *what* in darkness?'

'You'll see tomorrow.'

I didn't know whether to feel apprehensive, expectant or slightly annoyed that I had to wait so long to know what this was all about. I studied the comb – it had no teeth, and with its triangular shape it looked more like a guitar pick. I began untying the scarlet ribbon, but Salvo stopped me. I looked at him questioningly. 'Better leave it,' he said.

'Why? Oh, let me guess. I'll know tomorrow.'

'Yep. Drink up, it's good for you.'

'Yes, Mom.' I smiled.

'So, are you ready to tell me about Mira?'

'Tomorrow,' I quipped, and he laughed. 'No, really. I am ready. I kind of feel the need to share all this with someone – and not just anyone, you know.' Was I blushing? I hastened to continue. 'Well, when she arrived here she was traumatised by a bad relationship, but she met this doctor guy called Lupo, who's pretty awesome. But now Mira's brother – my great-uncle – has turned up on the island and he's the *opposite* of awesome. He's got his eye on Mira's best friend and is trying to mess up her life. I can't believe I'm telling you all this as if I'm relaying the plot of a book or something. It's crazy.'

'Do you see it all unfolding as if it were a film?'

'No. I see through Mira's eyes, I speak through her mouth... I feel and sense everything around her. It's like I *am* her.'

'And that man, Lupo – do you think he might be your grandfather?'

'I'm not sure. You know...' I took a sip of my lemonade. 'Every time I come back to this time, to my own life, I worry that I can never return to Mira. That I'll never know what happens next.'

'I can imagine. And to think that we know... we know that somehow, Mira will be taken prisoner and sent to a concentration camp, and there she'll give birth to your father and die.'

'Poor Mira.'

'They were terrible times, I suppose. Anyway, Annie. This will cheer you up. I'm about to pop *that* question,' he said with a mischievous look in his eyes.

'You what? Oh, Salvo, I didn't know you cared!' I said, laying my hand on my chest dramatically. 'What question?'

'My mamma is back. She called while you were asleep, and she'd like you over for dinner. Prepare yourself: eating at Mamma's is no mean feat.'

'What do you mean?' I laughed.

'Her celebratory dinners are like the food Olympics. Also, she's invited a few relatives. So that means about twenty people between uncles, aunts, cousins and assorted relations.'

'Oh my goodness. No pressure, then.'

'Trial by fire! No, I'm joking. They're all very friendly, they'll love you. They never met Tanya, you know. They're looking forward to meeting my girlfriend. Especially Mamma.'

'They're looking forward to meeting...'

'My girlfriend? Sorry, maybe I shouldn't have said that? Of course you're not... we're not... I mean, we've just been spending so much time with each other... Sorry.' It was sweet, seeing such a tall, strong, broad-shouldered man blushing and stammering. Then again, I'd blushed too. Again. In fact, my cheeks were on fire.

'Don't say sorry. I like what you said.' I did. I really, really did.

This fast and sudden romance in my life, like a bolt from the blue, had come at the right time, just as I was shedding my fear and eternal lack of confidence. Was Salvo here to stay? Or would it be a summer romance that I would recall one day? Who knew? I just wanted to live in the here and now, and embrace life as I hadn't done in my teenage years, in the shadow of my parents.

'You do?'

'Yeah. And I'll do my best to impress your mamma.'

'She'll love you. It's impossible not to. *La mia ragazza*,' he said, and placed a kiss on my lips. I could have drowned in those lips... and I did.

I stood on a rock in my swimsuit – a one-piece, of course, because bikinis were just too much for my insecurity. Salvo was beside me, in swimming trunks, holding the byssus comb with its silk ribbon tied around it.

The sun wasn't high in the sky yet, but high enough to have warmed the water. Back in New York, the sea would have been chilly – but here, it was still balmy. The rocks we stood on were low and not as jagged as most others on the shoreline, so the waves broke on them gently, lapping at them more than trying to devour them. I could see the bottom, clear and mainly sandy – and then, the sand ended and the darkness began.

Salvo and I looked at each other. There was a smile on his face, and his eyebrows were raised, as if he was saying, *You know by now what Elvira is asking you to do, don't you?*

I did. 'You're going to throw that in, and I have to retrieve it. If I do, she'll let me see her work.'

'Yep.'

'So much for not wanting your first guest to come to any harm,' I said drily.

Salvo laughed. 'You won't. I'll be there beside you. It'll be easy. She just wants to see if the sea likes you.' He shrugged.

I rolled my eyes and sat on the rocks. 'That's something Mimi's grandmother would have said. In fact, they have a lot in common, Elvira and Giovanna.'

'You don't have to do it. We can always have a nice paddle and then go to my mamma's for the enormous lunch she will have prepared for us. Give the comb back to Elvira...'

'No way.'

Salvo smiled. Of course, he had predicted my reaction. Keeping his eyes on me, he threw the comb into the water – the red silk ribbon made a beautiful arc in the air, and fell with a gentle plop.

My stomach churned. My disastrous swimming lessons, my refusal to go boating came back to me in a scary flashback. I couldn't do this. There was no way I could do this.

I dived.

I opened my eyes underwater and decided I would not panic. I simply would not. Red, red, red. My eyes scanned for red. It was all I had to do. I swam like I'd never swum before, certainly not back in New York, with my mother terrorising me into hating the water. Salvo was beside me, which was comforting, but I paid no attention to him. I needed to do this on my own.

Stones and seaweed and puffs of sand lifting as I searched made the water murky – but I would find it. Red, red, red, my eyes scanned for red.

I was running out of air. My lungs began to squeeze and my fingers tingled. I needed to breathe and kicked my legs back to the surface. As I broke the surface, the sun kissed my face and I closed my eyes as a memory made its way into my mind and made me tremble: the freak current that had almost carried Mimi away when she was a little girl.

She wants to see if the sea likes you.

What if the sea did not?

Salvo emerged beside me. 'You all right?'

I didn't answer but frowned, took a deep, deep breath, and down I went again.

Red, red, red. I would find the comb, and give it to Elvira, and she would let me sit there and watch her making miracles with the golden, sacred thread.

Suddenly I spotted a flash of scarlet inside a cloud of murky sand. Swimming towards it, the water began to tug at me, pulling me away. I would not let it. I gathered all my strength; I was not a fit person by any means, but I had to make it, I had to. I would not let the current sweep me away as it had done to Mimi.

But the sea is a mighty adversary. It pulled and pulled. My fingers touched the scarlet ribbon floating in the water. I almost had it.

And then I didn't.

I was sucked away, dragged backwards, and the flash of red disappeared into the dim, sandy waters. I pulled myself to the surface and took a long spluttery breath as a wave of frustration took me as violently as the current had. Salvo came out of the water easily, smoothly, and stood in front of me – he was smiling. Smiling? He was smiling at my failure?

I lifted my empty hands. 'I didn't make it.'

'Who said you only had one chance?'

'Annie! Annie, *benvenuta!*'

A small woman with jet-black hair streaked with grey, golden hoops at her ears, waddled quickly towards me, like a friendly hen. At first glance, there was little resemblance between tall, athletic Salvo and this tiny lady; but looking more closely I could see that their eyes had the same almond cut, and that they shared the same bright yet slightly bashful quality.

'Thank you for having me,' I said, and smoothed down the traditional Galatean handkerchief over my still-wet hair. I was still smarting after my failure to retrieve the comb from the seabed, but I'd mostly recovered myself. Would I try again?

'*E' un piacere*, Annie,' Salvo's mother said. She pronounced my name the Italian way, with a strong double *n* in the middle, which made it sound sweeter, like a term of endearment. 'Rosaria,' she added, pointing at herself and bending slightly forward in greeting.

'Rosaria,' I repeated with a smile. She was giving me such a warm welcome, I was moved. She chatted quickly at Salvo, but her eyes were fixed warmly on mine.

'She says she didn't have much time to prepare,' Salvo

explained. 'So she kept it simple. She hopes you won't mind.' I could gauge from Salvo's expression that this was far from true.

'Of course not!' I said, following her to the terrace where a set table – *several* tables joined together to make a single big one – waited for us. The plates and glasses were all different from one another and the tablecloths were faded, but this just added to the rustic loveliness of the set-up. My mother wouldn't have thought so. But then, I wasn't my mother.

I could see how much care Rosaria had put into preparing everything beautifully, with small vases of yellow, fuchsia and blue wildflowers lined up in the centre and embroidered napkins neatly folded beside every plate.

'This is beautiful!' I said. 'It looks perfect, I can't thank you enough.'

'*Il cibo*, Annie! *Non ho avuto abbastanza tempo.*'

'She says didn't have time to prepare *enough* food.'

'*Perche' ridi, disgraziato?*' She looked over to Salvo, who was leaning against a wall, his arms folded, smirking. Rosaria pretended to raise her hands to him, and Salvo laughed and held her. The whole exchange was so Italian, it made me smile.

'She's asking me why I'm laughing. The answer is, because I'm sure she's cooked for an army!'

'*Ma che dici!*' Rosaria said, and laid a hand on his face. '*Il mio ragazzo parla inglese, vedi che bravo!*' This I could understand: *My boy speaks English and is very clever.* Italian mammas... I wished I had one, to be honest.

'And here comes the family,' Salvo said.

I was suddenly overwhelmed by a wave of Salvo's relatives – old ladies, young men and women, a few children, so many that I had no idea how we'd fit at the table – and each of them kissed me and shook my hand warmly. I recognised some of them, having seen them around by the harbour or at the market. Was Salvo related to the whole island? Probably. One of the children, a dark-haired and dark-skinned girl in a little white dress, handed me a posy with a shy smile. She was so cute I could have squeezed her. I'd never met a family so welcoming and warm – my cheeks were sore from smiling.

No wonder Salvo had decided to return to the island, where he belonged.

And me? Where did I belong?

I thought of my big, silent family home, expensively furnished in tones of blue and grey and dark wood, with everything matching and bought new – in the distance, the Atlantic Ocean and its cold waters. How different all this was, with the light of the sun warming body and heart, and all these people sitting around a makeshift table with mismatched, colourful crockery, packed so tight their shoulders and elbows touched – revelling in each other's contact and company.

And I was among them. I couldn't believe it.

'Salvo, *aiutami*!' Rosaria was calling for Salvo to give her a hand, and I followed them into the kitchen: now I knew why Salvo was smirking when his mother had mentioned not preparing enough food. The table and counters in the kitchen were overflowing with dishes: from fried seafood to moon-shaped filled dough pockets; spaghetti with fragrant tomato sauce and thin fish slices in lemon juice; brightly coloured couscous and cakes covered in a sugary, pastel-coloured paste. Not to mention the bottles of wine and jugs of lemonade brought by the guests; it was a feast.

'I wonder if it'll be enough,' I whispered to Salvo, and he winked at me.

'Told you,' he said in a conspiratorial way that made me feel special.

The meal was endless. We sat for hours all squeezed around the table, chatting and laughing, while the children played in the grounds. Bella, surrounded by running kids, was seraphic as ever and accepted sugary treats with great dignity, as though it was her birthright. In spite of my protests, I'd been given the place of honour at the head of the table, and from there I had the perfect view towards the shining sea. It was a dream.

Even if my Italian was woeful, I discovered that with a mixture of hand gestures and smiles we all understood each other pretty well. After a lot of food and just as much chatting, the afternoon began to cool, and the sky slowly turned pink and lilac. The family, after long goodbyes and hugs and kisses on both cheeks, began to leave, and Salvo and I were left alone with Rosaria.

'Now I'd like to learn Italian even more,' I told Rosaria, with Salvo translating for me. 'So I can speak to you.' She was so small that even I had to look down to meet her gaze – the more I observed her, the more in my mind she resembled a little black hen, vivacious and cooing over everyone. *Imagine growing up with such an affectionate mom, wearing that proud expression every time she looks at you.*

'She says she's happy you came to Galatea, she's happy for— *Mamma!*' Salvo protested, sounding a lot like a teenager. 'She says she's happy for me' – I laughed, half delighted and half embarrassed – 'and that she hopes you'll stay a long time.'

'I'm happy I came too,' was all I could say, and not just because my Italian was so basic, but also because I didn't have an answer to the question implied in her words, about how long would I stay. I had no idea.

Rosaria smiled and came a little closer to me. '*Se son rose, fioriranno,*' she whispered in my ear. I didn't know what that meant, but I had a feeling she'd spoken so that Salvo would not hear.

On the way back, Salvo held my hand.

'I'm proud of you.'

'What have I done?' I smiled.

'You're a fighter. You're... like Bella.'

'I'm like a donkey? Why, thank you!'

Salvo's words came out mixed with laughter. 'No, no, what I mean is you're your own person: strong, resilient and kind. I've never met anyone like you.'

I was silent. His hand was warm and strong, wrapped around mine. And then he stopped and pulled me to him. We kissed in the gathering darkness, the scent of night all around us.

'Stubborn,' I said, as soon as I could breathe.

'*Scusa?*'

'Donkeys are stubborn,' I whispered. His breath and mine were mixing, and our lips kept meeting even as we spoke, in little butterfly kisses.

'I said strong and resilient, silly. Not stubborn.'

'Mmmm.' I hid my face in his chest.

'What?'

'I didn't do it. I didn't retrieve the comb. I failed, and now I won't be allowed to see how byssus is worked.'

'It was a silly thing to make you do, a silly challenge that means nothing! They have all these weird things around the byssus, like a religion or something. Ignore Elvira, OK?' He fished into his pocket and took out the comb, wrapped in its scarlet ribbon like a chrysalis. I was surprised — I thought he'd left it there.

I took it gently from him, and slipped it into my own pocket.

'Of course. It was silly,' I said, and then he silenced me with another kiss, and another, and another.

Salvo had a meeting at the town hall, so he left me at Villa Onda. I relished the chance to be alone for a while and process all that had happened. *Se son rose, fioriranno*, Rosaria had said. I looked for the translation in my pocket dictionary. It was a proverb, an Italian saying: 'If they're roses, they will bloom.' The song Mira and Mimi sang, 'When our garden blooms again', came into my mind. *Yes: we'll wait and see if what we're planting now will wither, or bloom.*

I made a decision: I would record everything I saw through Mira's eyes, so that I would not forget a thing. I sat on my bed and opened the notebook I'd brought with me to keep travel notes, when I heard Elvira calling my name from the corridor, and her footsteps approaching.

'*Telefono!* Annie, *è per te!*'

That was easy enough for me to understand. A phone call for me? I hadn't given anyone Villa Onda's number — in fact, I hadn't even told anyone my exact destination, so much so that I was sure my mobile was going to explode with messages as soon as I returned to wifi land.

'*Grazie*, Elvira,' I called, and followed her downstairs barefoot and in my pyjamas. I took the vintage-looking eighties telephone from Elvira and thought I would see a hint of disdain or disappointment in her eyes since I'd failed her challenge. But no: her eyes were warm as ever, her expression motherly. I thought of the comb sitting upstairs on my bedside table.

'*Pronto?* Hello?'

'It's me. Mom.'

I felt my stomach tighten, a knee-jerk reaction to her voice. The contrast between the day I'd just had, with its warmth and laughter, and my mother's voice, was stark. I knew – I just *knew*, that if I gave her even the smallest chance, she would burst my bubble of happiness. 'How did you find me?'

'I didn't think you were hiding, Anna.' *It's Annie.*

'Of course not. I meant... Oh, never mind.'

'I called every single accommodation in the islands around Sicily. Thankfully, there weren't many. It was still a huge waste of my time, though.'

'Then why did you do it?' I said wearily. When you live with someone who drains you day in and day out, you almost don't notice. It's only when you live *without* it for a while that you realise how much it was depleting you.

'It's my duty to see you don't end up on a wild goose chase and make a mess of things.'

'I'm not on a wild goose chase, and I won't make a mess of things.' Why was I rising to the bait? Was that a note of insecurity slithering into my voice? Why, every time my mother was around, physically or mentally, did I revert to my childhood self?

'Don't expect me to come and sort—'

Right at that moment, Salvo walked in. 'Oh, hello, the meeting didn't...' he began, but his voice trailed away as he saw me on the phone. Mouthing *Sorry*, he backed out of the hall and left me to it.

Obviously, his words didn't escape my mother.

'Oh. I see someone has got in there already?'

'In *where?*'

'To your father's money.'

That made no sense. Salvo had no idea about my inheritance. I didn't know whether to laugh or cry. Laugh, because my mother's efforts to sabotage me were bordering on the ridiculous; or cry, because her view of the world was so completely, impossibly dismal. 'Get off this, Mom.' Oh, I was so tired all of a sudden. A sigh. 'Tell me how you are.'

'How do you think I am? You upped and left just after your father died.'

'I'm here *for him*, Mom. I explained that to you.'

'Yeah. For your father, and for some sleazy Italian guy who—'

'He's not *some Italian guy*. He's a friend,' I said, involuntarily echoing Mira's words about Mimi. I couldn't believe I was letting myself get involved in this conversation. I just wanted to put that damn phone down and go back to the joy of the island.

'Right. You've been away for two weeks, not even that, and there's a *friend* already. You found someone else to drag down.'

It took me a moment to truly grasp what she'd just said. Clearly, implying that Salvo was after my money hadn't worked, so she was trying another tactic. But why, with what aim? Why on earth did she work so hard to hurt me? 'What are you talking about!'

'Like you dragged down your father and I.'

She sounded satisfied. As though she'd finally found the right opening, the little rip in my heart that she could tear through. But this time, it wouldn't work. I wouldn't let her get to me.

'That is nonsense, Mom, how would I have dragged you down? I don't even know what you mean.'

'You know very well what I mean. All the issues. The problems. You were never happy. Hiding away in the house while everyone else was out making something of themselves.'

Furious, the beginning of tears crept into my voice. 'Did you call me for this, Mom? To tell me I'm useless?'

'No, I called to see how you were because I know you couldn't possibly exist on your own resources. Money is not enough, you know? It takes brains and strength to survive out there. And you don't have either. Listen, I won't hold this against you.' *Hold what against me, exactly?* 'I wanted to tell you that if you choose to come home, my door is always open. And I think you *should* come home. I don't see another option. But whatever you do, please *please* don't involve that guy, whoever he is, into your mess. I don't know him, but I know you, and it's not fair on him to—'

I put the phone down.

Hot tears streamed down my face. I hurried back to my room – I was ashamed of my tears, ashamed of how easily I was brought down once again, even after all the progress I'd made, even so far away from my old life. But Salvo must have heard me putting the phone down, because he emerged from the sky-blue parlour just as I was on the first step of the staircase.

'I'm so sorry I interrupted you there, Annie. Oh... bad news from home?' he said, seeing my face. I dried a tear with the ball of my hand, flustered.

I am bad news, I wanted to say.

'You're crying – what's wrong? Is there anything I can do?' He stepped towards me, his arms extended and ready to hold me.

'No, no. Thank you, but... no.'

'I'll pour us a glass of wine, you can tell me what happened, and—'

'*Buonanotte*, Salvo.' If I tried to say anything more, I would have burst into tears again.

A few hours later my pen lay idle on the open notebook, while I looked out into the darkness. Tonight, even the cicadas' song seemed hushed, and the meal around Rosaria's table, surrounded by people talking and laughing and eating and enjoying each other's company, seemed long past. A knock at the door found me so listless, it took me a few seconds to get up.

'Salvo.' I looked down. I couldn't meet his eyes. Suddenly, I realised that I was holding the comb in my hand, dangling from its red ribbon.

'*Cara*... I'm sorry to come knocking at your door so late, but I was worried.'

'I think we've moved too fast,' I blurted out. Just like that. I didn't want him to come in, to sit with me and kiss me. It would all go to my head, and I wouldn't be able to stop. And the poor guy would end up involved in my mess, in my real life that I didn't know how to sort out.

The expression on his face killed me. 'What? What are you talking about?'

'I'll only *shove* all my problems on you, and it's not fair.'

'What are you talking about? Annie, I don't understand. Everything was going great. What happened?'

'Nothing happened. Only, I can't lay all this on you.'

He laughed, without any joy. 'Lay what on me? Wait. You got that call, and— Who was on the phone? A boyfriend you didn't tell me about?'

I shook my head. 'No, no, of course not. It's not that. It was my mother. Nothing happened. Look. I came to this island and just landed myself on you. With all my issues. And the crazy stuff about my grandmother and these dreams I'm having. It's all madness, I'm probably going crazy. I've only known you for two weeks – and your mom is so nice, I can't disappoint her, disappoint you. I can't possibly deal with all this.'

'You'd never disappoint me, I'm sure of that. I've only just met you but it's like I've known you forever. And it's not easy... it's not easy to let someone come close to me, as I've done with you. And I think you've been dealing with everything pretty well!' I snorted. Salvo gave me one long look. 'What did your mother say to you, Annie? Why are you pushing me away?'

'Because I'll only drag you down,' I said, and closed the door on his stunned face.

I cried for a long time, the kind of sobbing you can only indulge in when you're alone, and the child inside you is doing the crying for both the little girl you were and the woman you've become. I must have cried myself to sleep, because before I knew it, Mira took me again, and leaving my life behind was a relief.

MIRA

Days have gone by so fast and so slow at the same time. It is like seeing someone falling: in a moment they're on the ground, and yet the descent also feels like it lasts forever, watching them losing their balance and taking a downward trajectory, irresistibly drawn by gravity towards disaster.

'I must tell Fulvio,' Lupo says to me. 'He's like a brother to me. I must.'

'I cannot believe that this is happening, and he doesn't know,' I whisper, horrified at the idea of Lupo talking to him. I recall his huge frame, his hands like shovels. Yes, Fulvio must know and put an end to Mimi's fall, but how will he do that?

Can we still salvage something? Has my brother already done too much damage? Will the engagement be broken, will he upset her, will he... *hurt* her? I don't dare asking Lupo. The ways of this island are mysterious to me, and frightfully ancient. But after all, hurting a woman who chooses to leave never goes out of fashion.

'I'll tell him. And make sure Mimi is safe,' Lupo says, and his words – the reference to Mimi's safety – don't reassure me at all.

I know that a part of Mimi yearns for freedom. Maybe she's in the process of destroying everything on purpose, so that once she's finished, the choice will be made: freedom will be thrust upon her, and she'll have nothing else to do but take it.

In the meantime, my brother is deaf to my pleas, and I'm powerless. I see their infatuation taking place in front of my eyes, and it almost looks like she's taken too much of my medication; it's as though she's under the influence of something, not quite herself. Is this what I looked like when I was so in love with—

No. This is not love. This is a fire that burns everything in its wake.

And then, the day of reckoning comes. It doesn't start with Lupo or Fulvio, but Mimi herself. She comes to my room late at night, the place where we chatted and laughed and danced to 'When our garden blooms again'. The Decca is now silent, and we're both standing barefoot, her in a new dress I gave her, and me in my nightgown, shaky with anxiety.

'*Io lo amo*,' she says simply, before I can open my mouth. *I love him.*

'What? You barely know him! You don't know him at all!'

'And do you know Lupo?'

I let myself fall onto my bed. My hands tingle and a film of cold sweat covers my forehead.

It's too late to stop Gavriel – I know that much is true.

'I know you don't approve. And I know what you think of Gavriel. I'm not stupid, Miss Mira.'

I shake my head slowly. 'I never thought you were.' My voice is hoarse.

'This is not about Gavriel manipulating me,' she says forcefully.

'And Fulvio? What's his role is all this?'

'If you think I'm being deceitful towards Fulvio, yes, I am! And I hate myself for it.' She sits beside me. She's calmer than me, collected, though her eyes shine with tears when she mentions Fulvio's name.

The realisation is deep, sudden and leaves me astonished, wide-eyed: this is not a woman thrown about by fate, a puppet in her own life. This is a strong woman who's made a decision. I feel she's gathering her thoughts, and I wait.

'I never took notice of anyone but Fulvio – not other boys from the island or from the other islands, on market days or at festivals. *Nobody* ever turned my head. But Gavriel is different. I've never met anyone like him. He's in control of everything around him. He could tell anyone what to think and what to do and they would think it, they would do it. It's the way he looks at me – not like a child to be protected or a girl to be preserved from the world, but like a woman.'

'These are just words, Mimi. The fact remains, my brother will chew you up and spit you out.' I sound cruel, but there is no other way to put it. This is how it will be.

'You don't know what you're talking about. I've never been so happy. I count the hours, the minutes to when we're alone next. Time with him flies so fast, I can never have enough,' she says, and the calm woman once again morphs into a girl in love. 'Nobody is supposed to be this happy, I don't think,' she continues. 'Life is being content with what you have, doing your duty by your family. Anything else, anything more, anything *different*, is just selfishness.' The ancestral resignation of generations of women living on a hard, heartless land. I look outside, beyond the window: the cold, barren volcanic ground shines black under the light of the moon. One of the many faces of Galatea: the merciless one.

'That's not true. You can look for happiness, you deserve happiness. But I promise you, the only happiness that matters to my brother is his own.'

'You don't know him the way I do.'

'Of course I do!' I throw my arms up. 'I've known him for almost twenty years, you've known him *three weeks*!'

'That's not... it's the way I know him. With me, he shows his vulnerable side, the way he's been sidelined by his family.'

'Sidelined by his family? Oh my God, Mimi. You're falling for his lies. It's all lies.'

'He's good and kind. Gentle, funny, loving, and so intelligent!'

'Manipulative.'

'I understand you're afraid for me, afraid that I'll destroy my life and break Fulvio's heart – and I'm afraid of that too. But you shouldn't say such things about your brother. I feel free, Mira! As if I've been allowed to swim, at last! How could such a feeling be wrong?'

'Mimi. Let's say that you're right, that my brother is as good as you think, that he loves you and he won't betray you or leave you. Then what about Fulvio? You said you hate yourself for deceiving him. What good does that do to him, hating yourself? You can hate yourself all you like, but it will be no consolation to him when he finds out.'

'I don't want this love to be a *secret*. I don't want to deceive Fulvio, or my family, or his family. I want to walk out with Gavriel freely, as it should be.'

'Then do it,' I said. 'It's a mistake. But like Lupo said, you're a grown woman.'

'I'd like to. But Gavriel won't allow it. He wants to protect me.'

I've heard that line before. I remember that man's words as if it was yesterday: *Mira, we must keep this secret. I don't want to frighten the horses.*

The horses, it turned out, was his wife.

Of course Gavriel would twist this as concern for Mimi. I cover my face with my hands in frustration. 'He said that?'

'Yes. He wants to *protect* me,' she repeats, and I feel ill. The last vestiges of respect I had for my brother fall from me, like a blindfold.

'Mimi. What happened to me in London, what broke me... he, too, wanted to keep it all a secret. Except I didn't know why.'

'You can't compare, Miss Mira! That man was married, Gavriel is not!'

'Then *why* the secrecy? Why does he not take matters into his own hands, like a man, and speak to Fulvio?' Her certainty falters for a moment, so I insist. 'He needs to fight for you, Mimi. Not let you do all the fighting.'

'No. It's not him having to speak to my fiancé and my family. It's me.'

'Mimi.'

She gets up, her face now serene. The frown is gone, replaced by a look of resignation; her fate has been sealed, and I feel cold.

'I don't want to spend another day doing something behind Fulvio's back. I will tell him tonight.'

I can't stop it. No one can. Mimi and Fulvio are not meant to be. And I will not abandon her to face the consequences of her choice alone. 'Mimi, listen. If you're feeling trapped, if you want to end things with Fulvio, I understand. You have my support. But my brother will give you nothing. That's what he does, he moves on from girl to girl and leaves only debris behind.'

'I'm not like the other girls he's had. He *loves* me.'

And now, suddenly, she looks innocent again. I sigh and look down, then rub my face with my hands.

'I'll go with you if you want. And Lupo too.'

She stares at me, and then recognition lights up her face. 'You can't mean... Fulvio won't hurt me.'

'I know. Of course.' I don't know. 'Just for support. I'll wait outside with Lupo.'

I despair, thinking how many women, in how many different eras and places in the world, must have said the same thing. Only to find they were wrong.

. . .

I'm woken in the middle of the night by my door opening, and Mimi's familiar step coming towards my bed. I switch the lamp on, alarmed, and what I see is her tear-stained face, calm and solemn. She climbs into the bed beside me and holds my hand. Her fingers are icy. I tuck her in under the blanket – I notice, then, that she's shaking all over. 'I told him,' she whispers. She seems almost numb. Shocked to the point of not really being there – her body is lying beside me, but her mind is far, far away.

'You spoke to Fulvio?' I murmur in the silence of the night. 'Oh, I wish you'd waited for me, and for Lupo – Fulvio will need him, now!'

'He's going to war,' she replies simply.

I pull myself up and lean my head on my hand. 'Fulvio's enlisting?'

A small nod, then she doesn't speak again. I hold her in my arms – her tears are on my nightgown, now – and let her curl up against me. I stroke her hair slowly, to try and calm her shaking, and begin to count the hours until dawn: until I can speak to Gavriel, and make sure he will not abandon her. I don't believe that he will stand by her, and I pray and pray to be proved wrong.

A strange calm has come to Villa Onda and all of us. Gavriel and Mimi are often together, but not as often as Mimi would like. And there doesn't seem to be much joy between them. They give each other long looks, something passing between them that I do not understand. I didn't think Gavriel would stay for so long, but he and Julian don't show any signs of leaving. When Gavriel leaves the island, will he take Mimi with him? He disappears often, Julian almost constantly. But it's as if they're waiting for something.

Fulvio has gone. He's joined a group of five other men who enlisted with him. We didn't speak before he left, and he didn't speak to Gavriel either. I think of Fulvio often, more than I thought I would: a man whose life has been dismantled in the space of a few days.

Mimi and I are on our way to the emporium under a deep and dark blue autumn sky. Every Wednesday provisions should arrive from the mainland – things like sugar and flour, anything the islanders can't produce or make – but the war has put a spanner in the works, and now deliveries come once a month, if at all. Nobody checks our ration cards, but they are the only evidence we have of the storm that ravages Europe; such a tiny price for us to pay, compared to what's happening outside. But eight island men have enlisted, and their fate is not known.

'We could have had the goods delivered, Mimi. You didn't need to do this,' I say in a small voice, as we walk side by side, our gaze straight ahead. People nod towards me but most ignore Mimi, making a big show of looking the other way. The island has turned on her, and it kills me. When she left Fulvio, Mimi was prepared to be shunned by some. But since he enlisted, she's almost an outcast – even if it was his choice to go to war, even if she never wanted him to go and risk his life somewhere far away. Fulvio's parents had already been devastated by Fiorella's death; the fear of losing another child was too much. They'd called for Lupo and explained that they might have been able to get over Mimi breaking the engagement, but Fulvio going to war had dissolved any possibility of reconciliation.

Now Lupo can't hide the shadow in his eyes every time he mentions Mimi. He blames her too, in a way. It's almost imperceptible, and it doesn't reflect in the way he speaks to her or treats her – but I can sense it. It's inevitable, I suppose: Fulvio and Lupo grew up together, and they're brothers-in-law, though the woman they have in common is no longer with us.

'It's my island. It's my home. I'll go to the shop if I want to,' Mimi says, and the pain behind the defiance is plain to see. For the hundredth time I ask myself: *Where is my brother?* He and Julian vanished together again after breakfast. What business this is, nobody knows, except Gavriel, Julian and the men coming to see them, dressed like Galatea fishermen. Black market, Lupo says through gritted teeth – a man who lives and dies on the right side of the law – profiteering on war scarcity. He doesn't give them away because Gavriel is my brother, but their relationship is strained, almost to the point of breaking. Gavriel treats Lupo as if they're old friends, but there's a patronising edge to his tone. A sense of superiority that doesn't escape Lupo; but he's too confident, too controlled to rise to the bait. Oh, Lupo is a thousand times the man my brother will ever be.

To me, Lupo's theory has a fundamental fault: Gavriel is wealthy, not someone who needs to earn scraps on the black market. And so the question remains, along with: *Why is he not leaving with Mimi, after having promised so much? Why does he not take her away, somewhere she's not been forsaken by her own community?*

'Miss Mira,' Mimi calls me, and points down to the beach. From where we stand, on the winding road that goes down to the village, we see a commotion; it's a blue-grey bundle, but I can't tell what it is.

'What's happening?' I stand on my tiptoes. And then I see it: the bundle is a dolphin; it came to die on our beach.

I'm not sure why, but this seems like a bad omen. But that's just superstition, of course, and I shake myself out of it. But not Mimi: when I glimpse her face, I see that she's pale, almost grey, and her eyes are enormous. She seems terrified. 'Mimi?'

But she doesn't answer: she just gazes as me, as though she's lost in a dream, and walks on. When we get to the square, not one person greets us or even looks us in the eye. This is even worse than usual. Yes, it's been bad, but not this bad.

Silence falls around us as we walk, and then I hear a word hissed towards us from somewhere. A word I don't know, but I can guess it's not a compliment.

'What does that mean?' I ask Mimi.

'*Slut,*' she whispers. 'They called me a slut.' She says it matter of factly, but I can see she's broken inside. I'm ready to pounce on whoever said that, but Mimi lays a hand on my arm that says let it be.

'*Buongiorno,*' I call to Diletta, the shop owner, as we enter the emporium; no reply. There are two women in there, and both I know, having helped one of them with fees for her daughter's boarding school, and the other to pay for medical treatment for her husband. Still, nobody speaks.

'A bottle of wine, please. Red,' I ask. It's not even what I came out for; I can't remember what we need, and I can't face looking for the list in my purse under everybody's gaze. My tone is clipped, but doesn't quite reflect the rage I feel right now. I have no words to convey how deeply I resent the way Mimi is being treated. I wonder if she doesn't react because she thinks she *deserves* it. Her beloved island people, her extended family, hate her. In their eyes, she's responsible for a young, capable man, someone's son or grandson and a potential husband for an island girl, leaving the island and risking his life for someone else's war. And yet, here she is – in the village, shopping, instead of hiding away in shame.

'Red wine, please?' I repeat, my eyebrows high, because Diletta shows no sign of moving. She's crossed her arms in front of her body.

I'm about to give her a piece of my mind when a strangled sob comes from behind me – it's Mimi. She can't take it any more, and runs outside. The hanging bells at the entrance jingle and clash, and cover a shout – but it's not Mimi shouting. Somebody is screaming *at* Mimi. I run after her, and what I see chills me to the bone. Fulvio's mother, her hair in disarray, blood on her fingers, is screaming. '*E' colpa tua! L'hai ucciso tu! Tu l'hai ucciso!*'

It's all your fault.

You killed him.

And I know, of course, that she's not only talking about Fulvio's enlisting, that something terrible has happened, something that can never, never be made better again. And Mimi knows it too. I realise it at once as I look at her face. Now I know why Fulvio's mother has blood on her hands: it comes from the scratches on Mimi's cheeks.

I stand in front of Mimi like an angry wolf protecting her pup – anyone who tries to hurt her will have to go through me first – and the image of the dolphin who came to die on our shore burns in my mind.

I will never forget this moment; it's etched into my memory

forever. Fulvio's mother keeps screaming, and she would have thrown herself onto me if it wasn't for Lupo materialising from somewhere behind her, rushing to hold her waist. I hear someone shouting furiously at her to go away, to leave us alone, and I think it must be me. Another man is now trying to stop Fulvio's mother from attacking Mimi again – he looks like Fulvio's double, it must be his father. They hold up the distraught woman between them. I'm panting with rage, but my heart is broken for the poor woman, crazed with pain.

'You killed him. You're nothing but a whore! Sleeping with that foreigner... You were like a daughter to me. A daughter. And you left Fulvio, you killed him!' The tidal wave of her grief and wrath hits Mimi over and over again, and I'm sure it hurts more than the scratches on her face. 'He loved you. He loved you like a wife, like a sister. And you betrayed him. Whore!'

Every time she uses that word, Mimi flinches as though she's being whipped. Lupo is doing his best to drag the woman home, Fulvio's father is silent and stony faced, and Mimi's hand is on her cheek, blood trickling between her fingers. She's in shock.

'Where's Giovanna?' I cry out to Lupo.

'She's in Ericusa today. Take Mimi to Villa Onda,' Lupo says, and I just want to hold him in my arms – he, too, lost someone he cared for deeply, and I need to be with him.

And then, of all people, Gavriel saunters towards us. Drunk.

'My good lady! What is this shouting! You truly are hurting my ears!' he says, and he's unsteady on his feet. Julian is even worse for wear.

'Here you are, bastard foreigner,' Fulvio's mother spits out. 'Are you happy now, Miracolo Ayala? Look at him! This is the man you left my son for. This is the man you killed my son for! Are you *happy*?'

'There is no need for slurs,' Gavriel mumbles, while Julian sits beside me with a sound that's somewhere between a snort and a sigh. He reeks of alcohol and he's sweaty and red, and I wish I could just kick him in the side.

Suddenly, when she hears my brother's words and sees his demeanour, Fulvio's mother is calm. Her expression turns from frantic to pure, focused hatred. In the sudden silence, her words sound ominous.

'*This* is your punishment, Miracolo. It will not bring my son back. But at least now I know that you'll never be happy.'

I lead Mimi into the blue parlour – she leans on me, as I used to lean on her – and I help her sit on the ottoman. We've lost Gavriel along the way – good riddance. I'm furious with him. While helping to take Fulvio's mother home, Lupo turned around to say, 'I'll be up soon.' I'm waiting for him anxiously, because Mimi is in shock and needs a doctor – and because I'm truly afraid for her safety.

'Fulvio has not been killed,' Mimi repeats under her breath again and again, trying to believe it, trying to believe it has all been a mistake. 'Fulvio is not dead, he never went to war, I never left him.

'He's not dead. I did not kill him,' she's murmuring again and again, grabbing my hands as I try to help her lie down. Steps resound into the hall, coming towards the parlour, and I'm afraid – but it's Lupo who comes in, eyes red but calm, as befits his role. His hands are steady as he reaches for the medicine on the silver tray. Mimi is sitting up, rigid, my hands in hers, as if she's hanging on to me to stop herself from drowning. I pour the laudanum between her lips and she takes it meekly, without any protest.

Finally, mercifully, the medicine takes hold, and she softens slowly, falling back on the ottoman pillows and closing her eyes. I pour some liquor on a handkerchief and gently clean the scratches on her face – she doesn't stir.

'I'll look after you, Mimi,' I say, and kiss her forehead.

'Gavriel,' she whispers, and I know for sure he will not answer her call.

'How can it be? He's gone such a short time... he *was* gone such a short time.' Lupo and I are whispering, sitting at the bottom of the stairs. Lupo has carried an unconscious Mimi to my room.

'We don't know how it happened. They just brought the telegram early this morning. I was down at the harbour when the boat arrived.'

'Who brought it?'

'Two soldiers in uniform. There was a man with them – he looked like a civilian.'

'He *looked* like a civilian?'

'Yes. But he didn't act like one. I can't explain, but there was something about him... the way he walked, the way he moved. Like an officer. He drew my attention. And then, when they asked for Fulvio's house, I went with them. I knew they'd need me.'

'I'm so sorry, Lupo. I know he was like a brother to you.'

'First Fiorella, then this... that poor family,' Lupo says. I lean my head on his shoulder and entwine my fingers with his.

'I'm so sorry,' I repeat. We hold each other in silence for a short while, and then Lupo speaks.

'Mira, that man. The one I told you about, the civilian. He enquired after your brother,' Lupo says.

'What? Why?' *Oh God.* The fake papers in Julian's room. The disappearances. The black market. Of course. Everything is coming to a head. My heart is beating harder and harder, faster and faster.

'He took me aside and asked if I knew an Englishman who'd just arrived on the island. He showed me a picture of him, and I recognised your brother's friend, so I said yes. He asked me if there was someone else with him, and I told him about your brother. I said that they were staying here at Villa Onda.'

My stomach churns. 'Oh my God.'

'I... I had to. Mira, I can't hide whatever they're doing. I've never broken the law.'

'It's not just about that. Lupo, I don't think I ever told you, but we are Jewish, my brother and I – our family. I don't know much of what's going on out there now, but it wasn't looking good when I left for Sicily. We don't... well, we don't talk about it.'

'You are Jews?'

'Yes.'

'Mira. You should have told me.'

'Why?' I swallow. Could he be... I didn't even ask myself what his political ideas are. We've been so removed from everything, out here.

'Because I wouldn't have told them about Gavriel living here at Villa Onda! You have no idea of what's happening out there? Jews are being rounded up and taken away, so many have disappeared already. Nobody knows where they're taking them—'

'Where's Mimi?'

It's my brother, stepping into the blue parlour silent as a cat, slightly more sober and surprisingly put together. Of course: handsome outside, rotten inside. I'm surprised at the intensity of my rage – years and years of anger towards this selfish little man I used to adore.

'She's sleeping.' What should I say? *Please leave? Please go to her and comfort her?* I'd like the first; Mimi would choose the second. Lupo is looking down, his fingers flexing. The way he masters his emotions is astonishing to me.

Gavriel chooses to try and pacify us. But he miscalculates his words, and they fall between us, heavy, senseless. 'I'm sorry for what happened. But it's not my responsibility. Nor is it Mimi's.'

I have to breathe in deeply, or I will slap him across the face.

Lupo stands, and the same rage I feel is painted all over his face – I've never seen him like this. So much for mastering his emotions – it seems to me that he's burning up. 'You took Mimi from him. And for what? To have a bit of fun before you go back?' My brother doesn't know that much Italian, but *this* he understands.

'Lupo...' He needs to lower his voice, as hard as it is, because Mimi will hear him, and I don't want her any more upset than she already is.

Gavriel's charm has fallen off, like a snake shedding its skin. 'People make their own decisions. They make their own happiness. Or misery.' He speaks Italian for Lupo's sake, faltering, but clear enough.

'But you certainly helped their misery, Gavriel! There are two families destroyed, do you understand? Fulvio's parents have already lost a daughter. And Mimi's family are now pariahs on the island.' I'm trying not to shout, and my words come out like a hiss.

His face is blank. How often have I seen his face so devoid of feelings? Every time he thought I wasn't looking at him, every time he wasn't charming me. Gavriel is a man who can hide what he feels and what he knows so very well, and I wonder what else he's hiding from me now.

'It's not my responsibility,' he repeats.

'Gavriel. Someone is looking for you. Today, when they brought the news of Fulvio's death. A man – an officer, I suspect – asked after you, and your friend.'

When you hear the expression 'all blood drained from his face', you'd never think it would be so literal. His skin is suddenly white as the dead. 'What exactly did he say? *Cosa ha detto?*' he asks Lupo.

'If there was an Englishman on the island. I said yes. I said your name, and that you were staying here.'

Gavriel's expression morphs into panic, and then the usual confidence takes the place of fear: except there is something off about it, something not quite right. Like someone who's used to wearing a mask, but inadvertently puts on the mask upside down. 'Well. I'd better go find Julian. And then, Mira, you'll come with us.'

I laugh. 'I what? Come with you where?'

'Away from here. And fast. Lupo, would you be so kind as to find us a boat? And refrain from telling anyone where we are, or anything else about us?'

'I'm not going anywhere. I've done nothing wrong.' I translate for Lupo, and Gavriel's proposition – command, more like – doesn't go down well, unsurprisingly.

'You're not taking Mira with you, Gavriel. And you're not going anywhere either. You're staying here to await whatever comes to you.'

'Oh, sure, of course. Although I warn you that Mira will be held responsible, just like Julian and me. Is that what you want?'

I quickly translate for Lupo, and our answers, in both

languages, overlap. 'Held responsible for what? Gavriel, *what have you done?*'

'I've done what every single person on this earth should do. Take responsibility. Fight. Can you not see what's happening in the world, Mira? There's a battle going on, a battle between right and wrong! And I want to be on the right side!'

And the pieces of the jigsaw fall together in my mind. Julian finding this house, right here on this island away from everything, but in between Africa and Italy. The fishermen, or not-fishermen, and their comings and goings between islands. And before then, Gavriel's trip to Russia. I'd been so blind. So blind to him, so blind to the bigger world around me. How can I not have seen? How can I not have realised that the literary types, the political refugees that gathered in my house, did more than just talking?

'Oh, Gavriel. I don't even know who you are.'

'I'm someone who had the courage to take sides.'

'I want you to tell me everything. Everything that I need to know. I want you to explain all this.'

'I pass information on. That is all. A simple yet deadly business. I don't work for England, obviously, and I don't work for Mussolini or Hitler. I work for communism. Because it's the only way this world will change. When the war is finished, a new order will come. A just world. This is what I'm risking my life for.'

'You've betrayed our country!' I cry out. I sense Lupo's impatience, but I'm too overwhelmed to translate.

'Like I said, I've done the right thing. I have taken sides, and so has Julian, and so has Countess Alyova.'

'Countess Alyova?'

'Oh, yes.'

'Who else worked with you? Our parents?'

'No, of course not. Professor Ferretti – he prepared you, he made it so that you could settle here.'

My jaw falls open. I've been a pawn all along. What else do I not know? How long has he been preparing this?

'That was why you sent me that cryptic note with our parents' letter. You knew it would be read, and didn't want our names to be linked!'

Lupo is looking thoroughly confused, and I quickly translate everything for him. His face mirrors my shock, while Gavriel looks on with a hard gaze.

My brother is trying to save the world, but me: I'm just trying to save the ones I love. And so, I only ask about what truly, truly matters to me.

'What about Mimi?'

'I shall take her with us, and marry her, of course.'

From somewhere behind me comes a soft scent of flowers and saltwater. Mimi is here, she's heard Gavriel's grand declaration, and she throws herself in his arms. I meet my brother's eyes over her shoulder, and I see something I did not expect – a flash of pain, of fear. Maybe, a passing flash of love.

✿ 13 ✿

SCARLET THREAD

ANNIE

I woke up exhausted and upset, after an almost sleepless night. I'd
gone from seeing through Mira's eyes to being lost in my own
nightmares, and they too felt real. There was something I needed
to do: and I needed to do it for myself, nobody else. I climbed out
of the window in my room, and in the pink-orange-lilac light of
dawn, I walked to the beach. My skin came up in goosebumps as
my feet touched the cool water, before the sun had risen to warm
the sea – but it wasn't cold, it would never be cold, not until
winter came. I closed my eyes and hurled the comb towards the
blue. Its scarlet ribbon, like a comet's tail, landed with a soft plop
in the water. And I dived in after it.

At first, I could barely see – it was darker and sandier than I
thought – so I came up for air. Then down and up again many,
many times, my determination stronger than the physical strain I
wasn't used to. Stones and sand, gnarly, shell-crusted rocks and
seaweed, seaweed everywhere, floating around me. The shapes of
whirling sand turned into images, my brain tricking me into
seeing fish, human figures dancing underwater. There was no sign
of the comb, no scarlet to be seen. Maybe I was in the wrong
place, maybe I'd misjudged the throw.

The reels and swirls of sand were all around me, creating figures I didn't want to see. Up for air, down again, up for air, down again. The water wasn't very deep – perhaps it would have been easy for Salvo, or anyone with a modicum of swimming ability, but I hadn't swum in a long time, and I'd always been afraid. Gasping for breath as I broke the surface again, I decided I would try only once more. Why, oh why did I decide to try and prove to myself I could do this, when I clearly could not? My body was cramping and my eyes were stinging from the salt.

Once more. I would only try once more. I took a deep breath and willed my body to go under, to scan the whirls of sand and feel the rocky ground, and everything in between. And then, something caught my eye – a flow of sand and silt that took shape for a heartbeat, only to dissolve as quickly as it'd appeared. It had looked to me like the figure of a woman, a slender girl lying sideways, a hand extended and white fingers pointing to a tiny mound on the sea floor. A trick of the eye, of course, but I still buried my hand into the sand. My fingers curled around something. The comb! Now I could see the scarlet ribbon, floating like red seaweed. I pulled it away, but the ribbon was stuck and wouldn't budge. I pulled and pulled, and I was about to run out of air. If I swam to the surface I was sure I would never find it again. Suddenly, I felt something wrap itself around my hand and pull upwards. The force made the comb came loose, and I swam towards the sky. I looked at my hand, my fingers curled around the comb and what was left of the ribbon. Something, someone, had helped me. I was sure. But who? I was all alone in the water. I accepted it as yet another gift from Galatea.

'*Grazie*,' I said towards the water.

I was still in my swimming costume, dripping water on the tiles, when I made my way back to Villa Onda. Elvira was in the kitchen already, and Salvo was sitting at the table in front of a cup of espresso. They both stared at me when I came in, hair soaking and flattened on my head, barefoot, my hands scratched where I'd felt amongst the jagged rocks. I took Elvira's hand gently and turned it palm-up. And in her open palm, I laid the comb with the remains of the scarlet ribbon, now frayed and hard with salt.

. . .

Changed and dry, after an espresso and a brioche and Salvo's compliments – *You are amazing, do you know that?* – that made me grin from ear to ear, I sat in Elvira's workshop, and immediately I felt like I'd travelled back in time. Her gestures were slow, sacred, carefully measured. As she worked, she sang ancient songs that repeated the same lines again and again: ritualistic, hypnotic. She took the small brown bundle of byssus, barely big enough to fill her hand, and combed it with the tool I'd retrieved from the sea as gently as you'd comb a baby's hair. Slowly, the bundle began to produce a single thread that she worked with her fingers, rolling it with immense care so it wouldn't break. It was so delicate, gossamer-thin, and yet strong enough to be rolled around a spindle. She then moved to her loom, and the precious yarn was used to embroider a linen towel, each millimetre of fabric requiring so much work, so much thought, so much effort. The way Elvira sang and spun and weaved felt ancient, and yet timeless. Her skilled, strong hands could have been those of a woman a hundred years ago, a thousand years ago: she could have been one of the ancestral women living on the island when they worshipped the Mother, the statuette I'd seen in the cave. She sang and worked for what felt like hours until she sat back and rested her hands on her lap. She turned towards me with a smile full of warmth, full of secrets revealed, and I felt part of an unbroken chain. The chain of sisterhood, of motherhood, of womanhood.

I smiled back, a smile that came from the depths of my soul. The smile of someone who's just come home.

I needed to be alone as I stepped upstairs in the ripe, sun-drenched morning, and I called Mira to me. Because now I knew that I didn't need to wait. I could call Mira and be the protagonist, the main character of what happened next.

I opened the Decca and sat on the floor beside the window. Slowly, deliberately, I closed my eyes.

❧ 14 ❧

THE CAMBRIDGE BOYS

MIRA

Night has fallen, and my brother is worried. I can see it. And yet, he tries to pretend everything is fine, that he has everything under control. I've refused to go anywhere, to leave my home, to leave Lupo. Mimi is pale and silent. Oh, for the joyful girl she once was to come back. What have we done? Because although I know it's Gavriel who made this mess, it's me who brought Gavriel here in the first place.

'You know the officer will come for you, don't you, Gavriel?' Lupo says, and when I translate for him, my brother loses his customary composure.

'Will you tell your gallant knight to please be quiet?' he snaps. But Mimi is hurt by his tone – she frowns and looks down and trembles – and he retracts. 'I'm sorry,' he offers, but he doesn't look it in the slightest. Beads of sweat crown his forehead.

'Gavriel has done nothing wrong,' Mimi says. 'They're just coming to check everything is in order, that is all. This is what they do, all over the country. It's normal. What is strange is that they've left Galatea out up to now.' She seems to want to convince herself. She's certainly not convincing me.

'We just have to pray they don't realise we're Jews, Gavriel. If so, we will be in trouble.'

'Nothing that a little bribe can't help, sister. But look at that moon!' he exclaims, almost frantic. 'Why don't you dress up, Mimi? We'll make a celebration out of the full moon. Maybe my sister can lend you something to wear?'

Mimi looks at me. She's worn out, I can see it – with grief for Fulvio, and with fear. She doesn't *believe* Gavriel's innocence.

The stash of papers I found in Julian's room keeps coming back to me – where is he?

'Of course,' I reply, over the alarm pounding in my mind, unceasing and unbound. The huge, white moon rising over the sea doesn't seem to be something to celebrate right now – it seems to me that it's compounding our fear with its paleness, its indifference. I remember a half-joking warning I read in a book somewhere – don't sleep under the moonlight, it will make you mad. Maybe I've spent the night with my head in a pool of moonlight.

It's then that we hear it – the chanting coming from the cave, the song of the sea. Lupo and Gavriel seem none the wiser, but Mimi and I look at each other. The women have gathered, and they're singing. *Without us.* Consternation fills Mimi's face, and I desperately want to take her into my arms.

'Would you like that, Mimi? To dress up for the full moon?' Gavriel says in an enthusiastic tone that makes me think of something completely out of place, like snow in July. Mimi simply nods, and her smile, I know, conceals her sorrow.

I need music. I cross the room to lower the needle on the Decca, and I'm sure – quite sure – that Gavriel and Mimi exchange a look behind my back. What does Mimi know that I don't? This is like a theatre play where the parts have been already written and are impossible to stray from. What is my part? To ground us if I can, before we all float out at sea.

'Let's go, Mimi. Let's get dressed and make merry, my sweet,' I say, and lay my diamond tiara on my head. What better occasion to wear it, than when everything is falling apart?

· · ·

Mimi and I are in my room, and she's wearing the blue-green silk dress that makes her look like a mermaid. I've given her a thin, intricate silver chain with a diamond in the middle to wear around her head, and I've brushed and curled her hair. The song of the island women continues beyond the dark rocks, echoing from inside the island. Tonight, somehow, it's stronger than ever. I know she must be thinking of her mother and grandmother, there without her. I wonder if Fulvio's mother is there, if she found the strength to sing, even after her loss. If she's there, Mimi could not have been: the community is broken. My bracelet glimmers in the moonlight, and its light speaks of loss. And yet, Mimi and I are together.

'Look, Mimi. The byssus still shines, doesn't it? You and I are still together, we're still sisters, aren't we?'

'Yes. Sisters,' she says, and smiles a sad smile, while her eyes go to the window and to the women beyond, singing without her.

'Then take it. Wear it, tonight. To remember our bond.' I fasten it around her wrist.

'Miss Mira...' I'm sure she's about to say that she should have listened to me, and I'm ready to tell her it's not too late, that I won't abandon her, that she doesn't have to do anything she doesn't want to. 'I don't regret anything about Gavriel. I love him,' she says instead.

Even if Fulvio is dead?

I'd like to throw these words at her like stones. But I can't.

'What do you know, Mimi? About what Gavriel and Julian are doing here? I found fake papers in Julian's room. The fascists are looking for them, and it's just a matter of time until they come here.'

'Gavriel is trying to do good, he's trying to see beyond this war, to stop all wars. And there is a way. If the whole world was pacified, at last. Countess Alyova told me about this before. She tried to do the same as Gavriel, and they came for her too. The whole of Russia is on their side, though. They *will* win in the end. When I started receiving Gavriel's letters—'

'Gavriel has been *writing* to you? Before I came to the island?'

I let myself fall on the bed. I can't believe it. She knew Gavriel before she knew me. She's part of this strange game – is she a pawn like me, or one of the players?

But I don't have time to process what Mimi is telling me, even while the words *Russian spies* are forming in my mind, and everything is falling into place: Professor Ferretti giving us Italian lessons, Julian finding this house, Gavriel convincing my parents to send me here as... what? A decoy? A smokescreen? Countess Alyova's disappearance is a piece in this jigsaw too. But the web of thoughts connecting in my mind shatters as deep, commanding voices explode outside the house. They've come for Gavriel and Julian: but have they also come for those who sheltered them?

'Stay here, Mimi,' I order her, but she follows me as we run downstairs. Two men in fascist uniforms and a civilian with a black band around his arm stand in the hall outside the parlour, the door having been kicked open. Julian is with them, soaked, hunched over with a bloodied face.

Lupo stands, eyes wide, frozen. The officer is perfectly courteous. 'And here you are, Dottor Martorana. You didn't tell us this morning that you *knew* Gavriel Goodman.'

'He has nothing to do with all this!' I cry out, and Lupo raises a hand to silence me.

'I don't. I've spoken to him once or twice. But he's no friend of mine, and I know nothing about whatever he's been up to,' he says, sounding calm and dignified, even if his eyes betray his fear. 'And neither do my friends, Signorina Mira and Signorina Mimi. We ask only to be left out of whatever mess this gentleman is in.' Gavriel glances at Lupo, and there's no anger or hatred in his expression – he's endeavouring to look bemused, as though this is all a big misunderstanding.

And yet, Julian has blood dripping from his face.

'You're coming with us,' the officer says, and the two men in uniform grab my brother. I see now that they have pistols, and my thoughts blend into a fog of panic. Gavriel doesn't resist, except for a few polite words, as if this is a disagreement between gentlemen.

'I'm sure we can come to an understanding. This is, of course, a mistake,' he says coolly, though the beads of sweat on his brow give him away.

Lupo takes a step towards him, ready to stop him if he should try to flee. 'This is no mistake, Signor Goodman. You've brought trouble to your sister's door. Leave her be and never return.' My brother's Italian might be basic, but I know he understands the gist of this.

Lupo trusts the law. He's a man who's always been honest and upstanding, and might struggle to grasp that the law is not always just, and not always discerning.

'Which one is the sister?' the man with the black band asks.

I'm about to take a step forward when Gavriel speaks up: 'Mira, tell them you have nothing to do with me, apart from an *unfortunate* bond of blood!' He smirks. But he's not talking to me. He's talking to Mimi.

And Mimi takes a step forward.

'I'm his sister! I'm Mira Goodman!' I cry out. I can't let them do this. I can't let them orchestrate whatever plan they've decided on.

'Enough games!' the officer shouts, and hits my brother with the pistol – Gavriel folds in two, and when he takes his hands away from his face, they're as bloody as Julian's.

'I have papers. My papers. I am Mira Goodman!' I stride out, towards the stairs – I need to get my documents, and then they'll stop this nonsense.

'She's lying,' Mimi says, in a calm, quiet voice that makes everyone fall silent. She turns around for a second, searching under her dress, and when she turns back to us, she has something in her hand.

My papers.

'Mira Goodman, come with us,' the officer says just as calmly.

'No! No! Can you not see? Her name is Miracolo Ayala, she's from here, she's from the island! Anyone can tell you that. I am Mira Goodman. Ask her!'

And Mimi replies in perfect, unaccented English, and then she smiles at me, as if to say, *This has all been decided: you shall be saved.*

Of course. Dressing up for the full moon, so that Mimi would look the part of the upper-class, wealthy English woman. Mimi stealing my papers. When Gavriel realised it was all going to fall on him like a house of cards, he and Mimi had agreed the swap... so that I would be spared.

The officer nods towards Mimi, and one of the men takes hold of her. I can't bear to see them manhandling her – I hurl myself at them, I shout and scream to leave her alone. The officer grabs me by the shoulders and shoves me against the wall. I hit my head and a numb, nauseous sort of pain makes throbs through my body. After that, it's all a blur: shouts and calls, and the short, sharp crack of something exploding, followed by a metallic smell. Lupo gasps and falls.

I throw myself on my knees, blind and deaf to anything but Lupo, my Lupo, lying there with his eyes closed and his body limp, while blood colours his shirt red. Maybe I'm screaming, maybe I'm crying – I don't know, because everything melts into one as panic floods my body. All I can see is Gavriel and Mimi, calm and quiet as they are led away, until they become an imperceptible dot bouncing amongst the waves.

Nobody could have seen this coming, none of us.

There's silence outside, and silence inside me. I can't move, I can't cry for help. Nobody would hear me anyway. Lupo's eyes are closed, and the red flower is in bloom on his chest. On the ground beside him lies the silver and diamond tiara I'd given to Mimi – she must have taken it off.

I stumble out and let myself fall on the rocks. My love is dead, my friend and my brother are lost; and the sea is calling me.

The night is so still, and the moon is a hunting moon, a grieving moon as I stand on the rocks and follow the little lights of the petrol lamps dancing on their way to the horizon, bobbing up and down with the boats that are taking Mimi and my brother away. A low, never-ending call is in my heart: *Lupo, Lupo, Lupo*. But he's lying dead on Villa Onda's floor, and I'll never, ever hear his voice again, never feel his arms around me again.

The air is almost still now, and nothing stirs – everything is finished, everything is gone. I let myself fall on my knees and wonder if joining Lupo on the other side would be easier than facing what will come now.

Suddenly, the lights out to sea sway and then expand. They flicker more than they should – the water is on fire. Flames spread over the waves, and they're so fierce I think there's going to be an explosion – but they die down almost as quickly as they came. Nobody is swimming back; nobody is ever coming back.

Still – something happened out there! It's enough to give me hope. I squint and strain to see if maybe, by some miracle, the boats came into some difficulty and are now turning around...

But as I look out to sea, something changes behind me: all of a sudden, the house is illuminated. I turn around and see that one by one, the lights in every room are being switched on – but there's nobody there, no Giovanna, no Beatrice.

I'm about to run in when a stranger appears by my side, long dark hair loose over her shoulders, large black eyes, fisherman's clothes, bare feet.

With my mind's eye, I see once again the scene from my bedroom window: two people on the black rocks, in the storm. It wasn't Mimi then, it isn't Mimi now, of course. It's the woman who disappeared: Countess Alyova.

৩৫৩

PROPHECY FULFILLED

MIMI

Nobody will ever know what happened that night, on the dark sea.

The boat bobs slowly, slowly on the waves. The light of the petrol lamp is swaying as we go, following the smaller light on the boat ahead of us. Every second is an hour, every minute an eternity, until we'll sail into the right place – the spot where the currents from the rocks meet those from the shore, and weave themselves with the currents from the open sea.

Gavriel has done the right thing in sending me with these men, and with him. Mira couldn't see it, but I could. Because she would be helpless out here now, and all I have to do is wait for the perfect moment.

Gavriel won't meet my eyes. I know he's ashamed, but he shouldn't be. He wanted to save his sister.

When we were in the cave and he made all those promises, I knew he wasn't being truthful. He and Mira both believed I was under his spell, but I knew. That night in the cave, my first time, I knew he never loved me. He doesn't know how. But his lack of love for me has saved Mira's life, and for this I'm grateful. And now my love for him will save his life.

The men, the ones who followed in Gavriel and Julian's wake and brought their filthy, senseless war to our island, they aren't watching me either. Maybe they're ashamed – they should be. Or maybe, more likely, they're sure that there's nowhere for us to go.

I caress the water with my fingers. I can feel the movement and direction of the currents. I know where we are. I've been with my father, Nonna and Fulvio, even if I was never allowed to dive.

The men on the boat might think all there is to this voyage is to sail straight towards the mainland, but I know the geography of water. I can read watermarks as well as I can read landmarks. I shift towards Gavriel – a movement so small nobody is aware of it – and I feel for the fabric of his shirt on my bare skin. I slip my arm under his and I whisper in his ear; my heartbeat runs faster and my muscles tense as the moment comes near – until it's time. 'Don't be afraid. I'll take you back,' I whisper in Gavriel's ear, and yank him towards me as I roll backwards, dragging him into the sea with me.

❀

The sand is dry and prickly under my feet, full of little jagged stones. The water beyond me, instead, looks like pure happiness. Nonna is standing strong and upright on the sea-rock beside me, her black-grey hair blowing

*in the wind, ready to dive. She straightens the bag she carries across her
body when she goes underwater to gather the shells. 'Why can I not come
with you?'*

'Because the sea will take you.'

'Is that a bad thing?'

*Nonna lets go of the bag and looks at me as if she's seeing me for the first
time. She comes to sit beside me on the sand. 'Yes, it is a bad thing. Because
you'd be gone from us, Mimi.'*

That doesn't sound good. 'I don't want to go away from you.'

*'And we don't want to lose you, Mimi. That is why you can't dive.'
Nonna's feet, brown and gnarled and powerful, dangle over the rocks.
Mine are small and white and soft.*

*'But I want to dive,' I whisper, and I know with all my body and soul
that it is true.*

*Nonna is not looking at me any more; she's searching the waves, and
her face is combative, as though she's challenging them. As though she's
ready to fight for me. And I feel the change inside me: now, I'm afraid too.
The waves don't look as heavenly as they did before. Nonna's fear has
ebbed inside me.*

*I lean my head on her shoulder; she smells like saltwater. I feel her
words vibrate from her body into mine. 'The sea will have her last word,
Mimi. She always does.'*

⚜

Nonna's words come back to me as the dark waters close over my
head for a long moment, and then open again for me to breathe.
I'm steady, my body instinctively navigating the currents and the
weight of the water, but Gavriel isn't. He's terrified, flapping and
waving his arms, yanking me under. I hold him closer to stop him
from flailing, and I feel my strength, the suppleness of my own
body, my instinct taking over. I don't need to think, my body
knows what to do. All I have to do is keep Gavriel steady, help
him calm down. The water is alive and whirling around me
according to its hidden geometry, and I know how to swim with it
to stay afloat.

I'll make it back.

I'll take Gavriel back.

I'll leave the men who took us to the mercy of the sea herself.

I'll protect this little life inside me with everything I have. It's early yet, but I'm sure she's there: the moment she was conceived, that night on the shoreline, I knew.

The men on the boat are standing and shouting, their weight unbalancing the boat so it's not difficult to pull on the side and tip them in. Petrol spilled from the lamp sparks up in a flame, a tiny lick that flickers, wondering what to do next, then engulfs the boat in a sudden blast. Blazing petrol spreads across the surface of the water faster than I ever imagined it would. Heat envelops me and burns the air around me. It throws me backwards, and I'm blind and deaf to everything but the sound of my own gasping and spitting and coughing.

Suddenly I'm alone in the dark water. Gavriel is gone.

Saltwater mixes with tears as I dive in and out, screaming his name every time there's air in my lungs. I'm losing all sense of direction. If I don't swim back to shore now, I won't know where the shore is any more. It's so dark, now that all the petrol has burnt away.

Nonna. Nonna, help me...

All of a sudden, a light appears in the distance. I wonder if it's a mirage. I think of the small lighthouse on Ericusa, but no, it couldn't be, we couldn't possibly have sailed so far. Am I drowning, and this is the light that leads me away? Was Nonna right all along when she said that the sea would have the last word, that she would take me away?

The glimmer grows brighter and bigger – parts of it flicker on and off, making it even more conspicuous against the night, or maybe it's not the light that's changing but my sight, blinded by tears and water. Suddenly I realise what it is: Villa Onda, illuminated by the electric lights Countess Alyova had installed, showing me the way home. I wonder if the countess knows, I wonder if she's there. I start to swim towards the shore. I'm almost safe now – the road ahead is open, I know where I am and where I'm going.

A voice calls me from the opposite direction, from the open

sea – a voice I can't help but heed. I turn and see them coming towards me – the other boat, with Julian and one of the men who came for us, the only survivor. But it's not them who make me stop, it's not them calling me: there's a third man on the boat.

Gavriel is alive, and I can't leave him alone.

They seem surprised when they see me treading water without making any effort to escape, and then lift myself on the boat. There's silence as I sit beside Gavriel and cover his hand with mine.

And so it is not the sea that takes me in the end, but I am taken anyway. And who knows, now, what will happen to this baby, Gavriel's baby. If he'll ever be able to return to the island, if I will ever be able to return. *Please, please*, I beg the sea, who has known me since before I was born – *take me back to Galatea.*

❧ 15 ☙

ON THE SHORELINE

ANNIE

I awoke with tears in my eyes, maybe Mira's, maybe my own. As truths and lies layered and unravelled in my grandmother's life, my heart swelled with emotion, and suddenly nothing mattered any more but love. Not fear, not my mother's poisoned words. I knew that Mira's story was coming to the point of no return, I could feel it, and all of them – Mira, Mimi, Lupo, Gavriel – were dancing with death.

The moon shone outside my window and drenched Mira's dress, abandoned on a chair, in white and silver rays. I slipped it on, and went outside in my bare feet.

Salvo opened his eyes under my kisses, and pulled me to him – 'Not here,' I whispered.

We walked in the shallow water, somewhere between the sea and the land, under the light of a pure, tender full moon. The sea was so calm that its waves were more like caresses made by the long fingers of moonshine. I watched the ripples that my slow gait created on the surface of the water, step after step. The breeze was soft on my shoulders, my arms, my hips, but strong enough to make my skin vibrate, covered only by Mira's silk dress. I held the hem with one hand and tried to keep my hair off my face with the other, as the breeze danced in it. For a flashing moment, I wondered if I looked clumsy, or ungraceful – and immediately, my insecurity threatened to suffocate me. The stiff, rigid, twenty-going-on-forty persona I'd built didn't need to feel insecure, because she was never out of her comfort zone: but that person wasn't the image I wanted to see reflected in the mirror any more, the image I wanted to see in Salvo's eyes. That night, I wanted to be free. And I wanted to embrace my desire instead of denying it.

Salvo was gazing at me with a look I'd never seen in the eyes of a man, and instead of blushing or lowering my eyes, I decided that the Annie who'd been struggling inside me, trying to set herself free, would finally be allowed to flourish. The Annie full of reserve, modesty and fear that had marked the days of my life until then would not fight the woman I was to become, not any more. The hem of my dress fell to the water's edge and as I stood in front of Salvo, an unspoken question reached out to him from my whole body. He wrapped his arms around me, and his lips on mine were as sweet as the *fichi d'india* that grew juicy and abundant on the island. A simple kiss, gentle and chaste, was enough to ignite my body. He carried me out of the water, just like he'd done when I first arrived, and when I leaned my head against his chest and felt his heart beating wildly, I knew that it wasn't from the physical exertion: his heart was beating for me. He laid me down on the dry sand. I wondered if the first time I made love, it would be right here, where the sea met the land. Once again, the sea would be my companion in one of the most important moments of my life.

Salvo began kissing me, and I responded so hungrily that I surprised myself. And as he'd been doing since we met, Salvo looked out for me. 'Are you sure you don't want to wait a little longer? We can go at your own pace. I can wait.'

A tiny twinge of pain accompanied those words. Was he protecting me, or maybe he wasn't convinced of how he felt? I lifted my head to look for his gaze again, but I saw no doubt in his eyes, only desire and respect. I read the promise that he would wait for me, if I asked him to.

'I'm sure. If I listen to all my doubts and fears, I'll be robbed of this moment. Only you can stop me from burning.'

Salvo smiled as he began to undo the buttons on his shirt. 'Annie, I can't put out that fire inside you,' he murmured. 'I can only make it burn harder.'

I opened my eyes in the moonlight, naked but covered by Mira's dress and Salvo's shirt, and warmed by his body. The scent of the night was incredibly sweet and potent – but the sweetest scent for me was that of Salvo's skin. I was sleepy and boneless and the happiest I'd ever been, and it was with a mixture of regret for being dragged away from my enchanted moment, and desire to know more, that Mira stole me away once again.

MIRA

I don't know whether I want to bless Countess Alyova for being there, or strangle her for being one of them – like my brother, like Julian, messing with things bigger than them and bringing disaster on all of us. But I can't decide now, and I let her follow me as I run back to the house, to my Lupo. I can't believe my eyes when I see that the floor where Lupo lay is now an empty space, the electric lights shining on the wood.

'Mira,' a feeble voice calls me from somewhere on the other side of the room.

It's Lupo.

I fall on my knees beside him, hold his face in my hands, put my forehead to his. 'You're alive.'

'It's just a graze,' he says, and lifts his hand slowly from his bloodied chest. Only then do I see that his doctor's bag is open on the ground beside him. 'I tried to see to it myself, but I can't—'

'But you weren't breathing any more!'

'I passed out, I think it was shock,' Lupo says, and his other hand comes to my face.

It's drenched in blood. I gasp.

'I know you're frightened. But I promise you, it's not as bad as it looks. Please, Mira. Do as I say. I don't have much energy and I might pass out again.'

I compose myself. Lupo needs me. 'Yes. Yes, I'm here. Tell me.'

'Who is that?' he asks suddenly, as Countess Alyova lingers on the doorstep.

'I'll show you to safety. Please, trust me.'

Her presence here is surreal, but on the other hand everything is, right now. My love is lying on the floor in a pool of blood, and his reassurance that it's not as bad as it looks doesn't quite convince me. I turn my head away – it's Lupo who needs my attention now. She stands in silence while Lupo guides me: I must remove the bullet, disinfect the wound, wrap it in gauze. I don't know how I get it done with my hands shaking as they do, and with Lupo biting his lip until it bleeds, and still crying out in pain.

When I'm finished, I hold Lupo's hands, and he clings to me with the little strength he has left. And then he goes limp – but it's a good sign, I realise, as I see that his features have distended.

'Now come with me,' Countess Alyova says, with a sense of authority that infuriates me.

'Look. Thank you for springing out of nowhere and trying to help, but why should we trust you?'

'My friend Mira, you will pardon me if I use a cliché here, but when it comes to trust, I don't think you have a choice.'

'She's right,' Lupo says, and Countess Alyova reaches us and takes Lupo's left arm, while I take hold of the right.

'I can't believe you've been on the island all this time,' Lupo rasps, weak with blood loss and pain.

'I didn't have a choice either,' she says, and we're on our way out, into the dark.

Lupo leans on me heavily as we make our way out of Villa Onda from the window in my room, but then becomes stronger as we advance, as the shock ebbs away and determination sets in. I keep whispering encouraging words to him – 'We'll be fine, we'll be fine, we'll survive this. We'll survive.'

Oh, Mimi, Mimi. Will you survive?

Everything is silent and dark, clouds covering the moon and stars, our footing hard to find, had we not walked that way a thousand times, towards the beach. But it's not to the beach that we follow the Countess Alyova, but to the thin, ledger-like shelf that snakes along the cliff, lapped by the waves of the sea. This is uncharted territory. I feel Lupo weaken against me, and I hold him to me. In front of us, Countess Alyova's long dress flaps and dances in the wind, almost an extension of sea foam. It would be so easy – a moment's mistake – to step too close to the crumbling border and fall.

But we don't. One moment we are flattened against the rock wall, the next we are inside an opening in the cliff, the mouth of a cave I've never seen before.

It's pitch black in here, and it's as if this is the womb of the island, dark and warm.

'Better to have no light, in case someone sees us from the sea,' Countess Alyova tells us in heavily accented Italian – I realise then how loud the sound of the sea is, because I can barely hear her. Lupo and I exchange a glance, and he gives me a little nod. Unspoken words pass between us: will those men come back, will they still be targeting us? Shall we be helped by the islanders, or given away? Round and round in my mind goes Mimi's sacrifice, and how it should have been me on that boat. Too many questions scramble for my attention, while as we stand in the dark, the sea screaming behind us, our first and only worry has to be survival. And so, we follow the countess on and on, and end up crawling through a low tunnel – thankfully not for long, because Lupo is moaning and panting in pain.

Finally, we reach a space that is high and wide enough to sit up – I help him catch his breath, and while I am doing that, all of a sudden, the place is illuminated. I can't believe my eyes: the countess sits on her heels in front of a petrol lamp, surrounded by stores of food and water, a makeshift bed, piles of books and folded clothes arranged into boxes, and shelves made with drift-wood. She even has a little display of framed photographs and a ball gown, forest green, hanging up on driftwood and displayed like all that remains of a time long gone.

The first question that comes out of my lips is: 'Did Mimi know? That you were here all along?'

'She doesn't know what I came to Galatea for, or why I had to hide. She agreed to help me because she cares for me, that is all. She has no fault in—'

'And still she's the one who's been taken away, and you're here, safe,' I can't help saying. The image of Mimi boarding that boat without protesting, without fighting for her life, because she knew she was saving mine, will haunt me forever. I fight back tears as I know that there won't be one night for the rest of my life that I don't dream of her in that mermaid dress.

'I hate myself for that, Mira,' Countess Alyova says – and her hard, weathered face betrays her pain. 'Her fate is not sealed. She will come back. I'll go and check the entrance,' she says, and leaves us curled up against the wall in the light of the lamp.

I grab one of the bottles of water stored in a corner, and give some to Lupo. 'How are you feeling? Are you in pain?'

'Not too bad. You might not believe me, but it's just a graze.'

'Thank goodness.' And just like that, panic rises inside me and I can't breathe. I lay my hand on my chest and kneel, trying to get oxygen in, trying to recover some semblance of order in my thoughts.

'Mira? Mira...' Lupo knows better than trying to comfort me with words that would just fall into the chaos of my mind and get lost in it; instead, he pulls himself to me, and we curl up against the wall. I cover my face with my hands; I would lose myself if it weren't for the countess coming back. I don't want to show weakness in front of her. I am grateful for her help, but I can't forgive the part she's played in my brother's machinations, and how they have finally resulted in Mimi's arrest. Mimi, the only innocent amongst us.

'Dawn is breaking. Get some sleep now. I'll keep watch.'

'I don't think so,' I whisper to Lupo. 'I'll keep watch, you sleep.'

'There's something I need to tell you, Mira. You were out of the room for some reason, and Mimi was in bed, after Fulvio's news arrived. She told me she was late. That her cycle was late. I'm sorry to have to be so forward.'

'She's pregnant?'

'I don't know for sure. She skipped a cycle, that's all we know. It could have been stress—'

'What shall we do?'

'Wait for the end of the war. Until it's safe for you to go home to London.'

'Oh. I see.'

'You have to choose, though.'

'Choose what?'

'Shall we get married there, or on the way?'

My last thought before slipping into unconsciousness is for Mimi.

☙❧

DORSET, SEPTEMBER 1946

It wasn't difficult to explain my brother's arrest: he'd been taken because he was Jewish. There was no need to explain what he'd been doing, the web he'd woven with his Cambridge friends, and how even buying Villa Onda had been part of it. My parents were heartbroken enough. They employed Eli Singer, the investigator who'd made it his mission to trace people drowned in the maelstrom of the concentration camps. He came back empty-handed: there were no news of Gavriel Goodman, nobody knew what had happened to him. It was as though he'd dissolved into thin air, like so many others. However, he had information about a Mira Goodman, who'd passed away in Bergen-Belsen, probably from the typhoid fever that had swept the camp in waves. All he could find out about her was the name – no belongings, no photographs. What a terrible coincidence, my parents said, that this unknown woman shared my name.

Before he left our house I had a moment alone with Singer, and I asked him the question that had been tormenting me: the

Mira Goodman they had found, did she have a baby with her? Was she pregnant when she died?

But Singer didn't have an answer for me. Like he'd said, all he could discover was her name and her death. Mimi had told me that the sea was meant to take her, that Giovanna and her whole family were convinced that this would happen. And they were right: in the end, the sea had taken her away, though not in the way they'd predicted.

The night that Singer unknowingly told me about the destiny Mimi had encountered, I played 'When our garden blooms again'. I wondered where my old Decca would be – still in Villa Onda, my father having left the house and all it contained to the island of Galatea? Or maybe someone had taken it away and my records resounded in a stranger's house somewhere on the island. I lit some candles and sang along a little, as Lupo and I danced slowly. I leaned my head on his shoulder and let the tears flow. I closed my eyes and recalled her face, her smile, her lovely laughter – and I asked myself once again, as I would every day for the rest of my life: was she expecting? And if so, what had happened to her baby?

It was just my imagination, of course – when I looked for Lupo's gaze, he was oblivious – but in the distance, over the grey sea of my home, I thought I heard the Galatea sea-song, and Mimi's sweet voice joining the others to tell me, *I've gone home, I've gone home.*

A sense of peace filled me, and at that moment I knew that Mimi's spirit had gone to rest in Galatea.

17
LEGACY

ANNIE

I came back to the surface with a sigh, a breath that emptied my body and mind and heart of all the memories, now that the story had been told. 'It's not Mira Goodman,' I blurted out, breath and words mixed, as my eyes searched for Salvo's, as they always seemed to do when I came back to myself. 'The girl I saw when I arrived, the girl in the blue dress. The girl who appeared in the mirror. It was never Mira Goodman. It was Mimi, wearing her mermaid dress.'

'What?'

'*My grandmother.* She's not Mira Goodman, but Mimi. Mimi Ayala. Oh, Lupo.' I'd felt the wave of her grief, and it'd been almost unbearable. 'And Countess Alyova, she was there! She was there all along.'

'You're losing me. One thing at a time.'

The story came out of me like a flowing river, and I almost tripped over my words as I tried to convey to Salvo all that had happened: Gavriel's deceit, Mimi sacrificing herself for Mira... and for Gavriel too. 'That note, *Tak Me to Galatea.*' It was Mimi who wrote it. She was pregnant with my father. And she had the bracelet – Mira had given it to her before she was taken away.'

'You're an Ayala, then. Annie, you know what that means?'

'That I'm related to Elvira, somehow.'

'That you can learn to work the byssus. The line is not broken.'

'The line is not broken,' I repeated, thinking aloud. 'I suppose that means I'll have to learn to swim a lot better than I do,' I said, and my very soul smiled. 'Come with me.' I took his hand.

'Where?'

'You'll see.'

I convinced him to grab a torch, despite his protests. He suspected what I was about to do, but he knew there would be no stopping me. Down to the beach, along the cliff wall, into the caves. I ignored his warnings about it not being safe – I knew that, but I needed to see.

I needed to see where they'd hid, where they'd slept and ate and kept safe, where they looked out to sea and waited, waited. Beyond the Mother's statuette, we folded ourselves in two and crawled on, until we reached the little stone-carved room I'd seen in my vision. Salvo was gazing upwards, and I could see he was worried – but I was sure, for some strange reason, that the island would not bury us there. She would not let me die in those caves, while I was about to go full circle.

'Look, this is where they went! This is where they hid!' I exclaimed, feverish with the discoveries, with the vividness of it all. There were bundles of clothes, a rusty petrol lamp, even some hardened, mouldy bread. And something shining: something untouched by time. The silver tiara and its diamond.

'What is that?'

'It's Villa Onda. This is how Villa Onda will be yours and Elvira's, and it will never be torn down.'

Was it possible? Who knows. But I can swear that right then, I heard them whisper, Mira and Mimi: *Welcome home.*

EPILOGUE

I often take little Mimi to the cove. We sit huddled together and watch the waves, or I let her take a few wobbly steps towards the sea. She will, one day, dive just like I do, and work the byssus just like I do. The workshop I've made over and expanded in Villa Onda will be hers, and our line will remain unbroken.

Because Villa Onda now belongs to us: to Salvo, and me, and our daughter. The diamond tiara and my father's money together have saved the villa and the grounds, kept them intact and restored them to beauty. Salvo and I take care of it with Elvira's help, and we welcome guests into our fold, to share the bounty of our island.

At every full moon, the Galatea women come and join us, and we sing the song of the sea. At those moments, as I hold little Mimi by the hand and see her tiny feet caressed by the waves that ebb and flow, and I hear her tiny, silvery voice joining us, I know that my family history, with all its twists and turns, was always meant to take me here. I'm not a girl any more, I'm not a lost soul. I'm a woman, an island woman, with a baby in her arms, roots in the ground and wings to fly. And still I hear them whisper, when I dive for byssus or when I sing or when I sit on the rocks, my feet in the warm water: *Welcome home, Annie Ayala.*

A LETTER FROM DANIELA

Dear Readers,

Thank you for picking up my latest story! If you'd like to hear about what I'm writing next, then please follow me on Instagram and at the link below to be notified of new releases.

www.bookouture.com/daniela-sacerdoti

This novel was long in the making, and like most books of mine its elements have brewed in my mind for years before being shaped into a story. The ideas of fabric born of the sea and long-lost civilisations of the Mediterranean, layered with the recurrent theme of different destinies during the upheaval of the Second World War, and led by the story of a contemporary girl looking for her place in the world, are the building bricks of *The Italian Island*. I feel that we can all relate to the search for home and family, young and old – a search that maybe never stops, because the ultimate home is inside ourselves. For me, *The Italian Island* follows the theme I began with *Watch Over Me*, now ten years ago – and all my protagonists, Eilidh, Inary, Margherita, Izzy, Anna, Cora, Grace, Callie and Luce join Mira and Mimi in telling their story. From Glen Avich to Seal Island, from Montevino to Bosconero, I have now reached the sunny, mysterious Galatea, an island off the coast of Sicily.

It's been a privilege to take you all on this journey with me, especially in the last two years, with all that has happened around us. I hope *The Italian Island* finds you safe, having weathered the storm of these strange years, and once again thank you for being part of my world and the other half of my writing process. I feel that books belong to the reader as much as they belong to the writer, because creating a world and its characters is a joint process between us. No two readers will perceive the same story or see the same characters.

I would love to know what you think of *The Italian Island*, so please leave a review, and I'll treasure your thoughts. True, I have a mixed relationship with social media, but whenever I surface from my writing I'm so happy to hear from friends all over the world.

Sending you a big, big hug and a heartfelt well done for surviving these two tough, tough years!

Yours ever,

Daniela Sacerdoti

www.danielasacerdoti.com

ACKNOWLEDGEMENTS

My heartfelt thanks go to Jessie Botterill, to whom this book is dedicated, and everyone at Bookouture, a safe, respectful, creatively free home for its writers.

To my readers: I've thought of you all a lot during these crazy times and wished you safe and happy!

To my tribe and to everyone who made this writer's life easier while writing in lockdown: Francesca, Irene, Simona, Lucia, Graziella, Cinzia and her forever-inspiring music, and the beautiful, kind, talented Cristina Caboni. And as always, Ivana Fornera and Edoardo Sacerdoti, who know every side of me and still love me. Last but not least, to Giovanna, for gifting me the character of Elvira. I hope I have done her justice. A heartfelt thank you to Claire Glatzen, who has proof-reading superpowers.

If you've read my other books, you'll know the three people who are always mentioned last, and who are first in my heart: Ross, Sorley and Luca, thank you for keeping love, kindness and grace while stuck at home 24/7 with a writer on deadline. I'm so proud of you three for navigating the 2020 and 2021 storms. I love you more than ever.

May this book find a more peaceful year for all of us!

Made in the USA
Monee, IL
17 February 2022